**POP
HERESIARCHS**

POP
HERESIARCHS

Steve Beard

LEDATAPE ORG
MMXXV

Produced by

The LedaTape Organisation

on behalf of the author

May 2025

ACKNOWLEDGEMENT

Thanks to Simon Strong for

midwifing the book

BOOK PRODUCTION
WAR ECONOMY STANDARD

This book is produced in complete
conformity with the authorized
economy standards

for
Victoria

CONTENTS

INDEX OF CONCEPTS

PREFACE

When I was a relatively young man back in the long decade of the 1990s (a period which, for me, lasts from 1987 to 1997), I worked as a contributing editor for a London-based style magazine. I was a regular face on the lunches and launches circuit in Bloomsbury and Soho. Occasionally, I flew to San Francisco or Tokyo. My responsibilities as a journalist were vague and my interests general. I was, as my girlfriend of the time put it, a "penniless writer". I found myself covering a wide range of subjects, from architecture to literature, cinema to stand-up, politics to pop music. I didn't have to specialise so long as the topic under review was fashionable.

Many items came my way which were decidedly unfashionable. I did my best to ignore them. My cubbyhole in the office overflowed with unsolicited records, books and tapes from corporate PR firms. I either sold them at the second-hand markets in Camden or threw them away. More intriguing were the literary offerings from the ragged fringe of the magazine's readership. There were confessional manuscripts, conspiracy-theory print-outs, pornographic zines and comics, occult film outlines and poison-pen letters. Some of these texts were astounding. But when I brought them to the attention of my editor, I was told covering them in the magazine would be "inappropriate".

When moving house from London to Hove, I discovered many of these source documents hidden at the bottom of a filing cabinet. Getting them out and reading them again, I was struck by how many of them seemed to come from an intellectual underclass which was processing Continental theory (as it used to be called) through Anglo-American rock and pop music. Foucault, Baudrillard, Benjamin, Kristeva, Virilio, Deleuze and Guattari and others were being mobilised by post-grad drop-outs to think through fixations on Thee Headcoats, New Order, Gang of Four, Psychic TV, Crass, the Pet Shop Boys and other post-punk bands. A dialectical synthesis of thought and feeling was struggling to emerge here, one which had already been staked out in the rock weeklies by the likes of Simon Reynolds and Ian Penman. "Pop theory" is what it came to be called by the time Mark Fisher got hold of it on his "K-Punk" blog in the early 2000s.

I wondered. How far back in time could the pop theory moment be projected before it became untenable as a concept? Both theory and rock music had their origins in the new social movements of the 1960s. But they had operated in separate milieus – one bound to the seminar room and the other to the nightclub. Could they be brought together in some imaginary way? It would take a dose of Borgesian inspiration to do it. I began to dream of hypothetical encounters.

An architecture student seeing Jimi Hendrix play guitar at Regent Street Polytechnic in 1966, a copy of Virilio's "bunker archaeology" issue of the *Architecture Principe* review in his hand. An ex-roadie for John Lennon's super-group The Dirty Mac stumbling across a copy of Barthes' *Mythologies* in a head shop in Ladbroke Grove. Jim Morrison exiled from the Doors in Paris, drinking alone at a cafe, listening in on the Vincennes students talking about the Deleuze lecture they'd just attended.

Hendrix, Lennon, Morrison… 1960s pop stars who like Sam Cooke, Brian Jones, Janis Joplin, Graham Bond, Mama Cass and Bob Marley all suffered untimely and very often violent deaths. And who were joined in their cult of counter-cultural martyrdom by later rock rebels such as Marc Bolan, Sid Vicious, Ian Curtis, King Tubby, Kurt Cobain, Tupac Shakur and Wendy O Williams. There was something about the paroxysmal rock star death – whether by gunshot, by hanging, by drug overdose – which wedded itself to the idea of sacrifice, in the Bataillean sense. The archetypal rock star death belonged to a kind of voluntary shamanism, the performer dismantling themselves in order to live forever in the hearts and minds of their fans as a weird recombinant being. So, here, I thought was a way of linking dead pop icons not just to theory but to religion, to notions of pagan worship and sacred murder.

In a way, the link had already been made in 1968 by Nik Cohn. His prophetic account of the "Golden Age of Rock" in *Awopbopaloobop Alopbamboom* listed out the pop scenes – "Highschool", "The Twist", "Spectorsound", "Merseybeat", "Mod" – as if they were so many fanatical religious sects to be included in an appendix of his father's famous scholarly work *The Pursuit of the Millennium: Revolutionary Millenarians and Mystical Anarchists of the Middle Ages*. It was no wonder, to my mind, that so many conspiracy theories and occult legends had attached themselves to the altars of dead rock stars. The real Paul McCartney died in a car crash in 1966, Jimi Hendrix was secretly killed by the Illuminati, Jimmy Page had encrypted Satanic messages in Led Zep recordings, Jim

Morrison faked his own death. These were the fevered dreams of pop heresiarchs, the gnostic gospels of rock fans who couldn't stop thinking about the strange deaths of their idols, the apocryphal tales of holier-than-thou record collectors.

Are these stories meant to be believed? Or are they vernacular renditions of Fisher's much more highbrow pop theory? That's to say, are they cultural products which think through obsessions with rock music using references drawn from folklore rather than theory? Not the Frankfurt School, but the CIA's MK-Ultra project. Not Deleuze and Guattari, but Crowley and his various occult mediums. Not Virilio's *Speed and Politics* in Compendium Books but Toffler's *Future Shock* in W H Smith's. It's an intriguing thought. Vulgar conspiracy theory – just like donnish Continental theory – offers new ways of treating subject-matter plagued by the curse of being either over-familiar or impossibly obscure. Both types of theory expand the space of narrative possibility by introducing modes of fiction to considerations of fact which are felt to be inadequate to their personal – or even world-historical – significance. Either because there are gaps in the archive, an over-abundance of conventional wisdom or a haunting of the past by a delayed future. The result is a flourishing of hybrid literary genres – speculative fiction, secret history, critical fabulation, imaginary literature, autofiction. Or simply theoretical fiction.

In this collection of ten yarns, I have reconceived the 1990s slush pile in my filing cabinet as a deposited counter-cultural sediment containing trace memories of the 1960s. In my mind, it now contains rich and strange artefacts which share many common themes – dead rock stars, sectarian youth cults, paranormal activities, Anglo-American pop music, Continental theory and conspiracy theory. I have gone on to imagine that I tracked down the entirely invented authors of these lost creations, that I interviewed them and, in each case, got their story. And that I then wrote up these stories – the lives and the works – into the instances of theory fiction gathered here.

I would like to claim that *Pop Heresiarchs* is a portmanteau novel. It does, after all, have a consistent feel. It explores a terrain characterised by alienation from social milieu, political saturation of consciousness and intimations of a common culture rapidly slipping away. The narrator is unnamed, but I invite you think of him as a loose version of me.

S.B.

Hove, June 2023

BONA MAXI GREY

Choreographer of the Bowie Kabbalah

I FIRST GOT TO KNOW MAXI GREY in the summer of 1992. He used to sit by the window in Maison Bertaux, drinking his coffee, holding court with the Jarman boys, sketching out dance moves in his Muji notebook. He looked glamorous, but frail, a bit other-worldly. His hair was cropped like Sinead O'Connor's and his lips were painted blue. He sucked on the end of his gel ink ballpoint, looking out at the Soho street for inspiration.

I used to breakfast at the Greek Street patisserie on a Sunday morning, with a girl I was seeing at the time. She worked in costume design for Palace Pictures and was on nodding terms with Maxi. The first time I spoke to him, he had just pulled an all-nighter on the sound edit of *The Crying Game* at De Lane Lea. He was wearing a tweed calf-length skirt, almost military in its precision, with combat boots. His black Gucci bag was slung over his shoulder like an ammo pouch. He was high and bright and – unusually for him – alone. We got chatting and soon discovered we had a shared interest in David Bowie, whose career was in a lull at the time.

Maxi asked whether I knew that the American cover of *The Man Who Sold the World* featured an image of Cane Hill Hospital, the Victorian asylum where Bowie's half-brother had been confined in later life. Sure, I said, licking the back of my coffee spoon. Everyone knows that Bowie feared going mad, like his older brother. Freud would have said they were locked in an Oedipal struggle for their mother's love. Terry got all the attention, I said, because he was troubled. Bowie must have wondered how crazy he would have to be to turn the tables on his brother.

Maxi shook his head, with a self-satisfied and slightly annoying smile. No, no, no, he said. Bowie wasn't resentful of his brother. Quite the opposite. He idolised him. Terry was the handsome one, the clever one. He introduced the young Davie to the beat poets, jazz, Zen Buddhism – all lifelong influences. Bowie could not allow himself to outshine his brother while the dude still had his own chance of making it. It was only when Terry was institutionalised, shut up inside the dark wards of Cane Hill, that Bowie felt able to have his first hit single. Before "Space Oddity" was successful in 1969, Bowie had struggled for five long years in the deep recesses of the London music industry. On some level, said Maxi, he had deliberately blocked himself.

It was an interesting idea. Little did I know at the time that Maxi had filched most of his interesting ideas about Bowie from an old childhood friend. Nor that his understanding of human psychology was based on Rene Girard's take on Dostoevsky.

Maxi asked me another question. What did I think of Bowie's early Lindsay Kemp mime routines, the hands-flat-against-the-invisible-wall act, the one-man dumb-show depicting China's invasion of Tibet? Embarrassing? I said, remembering the reports of how Bowie had been booed by the Bolan fans when he opened for Tyrannosaurus Rex on their 1969 tour. Maxi shook his head again. I figured what was coming next. Here was a bloke who obviously specialised in offering contrarian opinions on the great pop star. Maxi looked me in the eye. Kemp taught Bowie the power of the stylised gesture, he said. The movement of the head and the neck, the positioning of the torso, the actions of the hands and fingers. All these are yoga techniques for channelling and projecting cosmic energy. Maxi raised his hand, closed the fingers on his palm and snap-turned his wrist, executing a perfect little mudra.

I grinned in delight. Maxi shrugged and went back to his coffee. He said that the art of magical gesture was the root of Bowie's power as a star, the foundation of the stagecraft, the Mick Rock photo-shoots, the album cover poses, all that. Maxi raised his hands, tilted his head forward and did the head-shot pose from the *"Heroes"* album cover. I gave him a little clap. Thank you! said Maxi. Other people in the patisserie were beginning to notice him. He was doing a turn.

It was only later that I learned Maxi had trained as a dancer throughout his youth, from the age of 3 to the age of 18. It was what gave him that strange combination of inner steel and manifest grace. I learned things from Maxi. He told me that the oldest surviving text on stagecraft in the world was the *Natya Shastra*, which dated back hundreds of years before Christ. He said that the mudras in Indian dance, the *asana* postures in yoga, had an occult significance. They were magical gestures used for the summoning and binding of cosmic entities. Bowie understood this, said Maxi, in a stage whisper.

In a late night phone call some time later, Maxi told me that Bowie had first been turned on to demonology by fellow musician and notorious occultist Jimmy Page. As a teenage boy, he had been a member of a secret brotherhood run by Page which devoted itself to the teachings of Aleister Crowley. It disguised itself with a jokey name, he said. The Society for the Prevention of Cruelty to Long-Haired Men. But it was known to insiders as the Society for the Preservation of Crowley's Law of Hermetic Magick.

I remember in one of our sessions at Bertaux's, we got into the arcane details of Bowie's occult period in the mid-'70s. It was all there in the photo on the back of the *Station to Station* album. Bowie, stick-thin, dressed in a diagonally striped black-and-white costume, like a man confined in an institution, half-lying on the floor, sketching out a mystic diagram before him. The diagram was of the kabbalah. Maxi asked me what I knew about it. This was some years before the ancient Jewish spiritual discipline became a mainstream psychotherapeutic practice courtesy of celebrities like Madonna. As a result, I hemmed and hawed a bit. That was okay, though, because Maxi had plenty to say. He told me that Bowie had got the kabbalah from Crowley and the Hermetic Order of the Golden Dawn, that they had got it from Madame Blavatsky and the Theosophists in the nineteenth century, and that she had got it from the secret brotherhood of the Rosicrucians in the seventeenth century. It went way back, he said.

Maxi flipped open his notebook at his table in Bertaux's and pointed to the diagram he had drawn. His own interpretation of the kabbalah. I saw there were four circles in a line, flanked by three circles on parallel lines either side. The circles were variously connected by arrowed lines. Maxi said the ten circles – or "stations", as Bowie had called them – represented states of cosmic existence while the lines were the psychosomatic pathways between them. The whole was a calculus of psychological transformation. I saw that Maxi had annotated the ten circles in his diagram with various names. At the bottom was "Davie Jones", at the top was "David Bowie" and in between I caught sight of "Major Tom", "Ziggy Stardust", "Gouster", "Thin White Duke"… the showbiz alter egos Bowie had used during the 1970s. Maxi closed the book. His croissant had arrived.

I was later to learn that the notebook contained the libretto for a dance-piece titled *The Man who Touched the Sun*. It was based on Bowie's life as a pop star from "Space Oddity" at the end of the '60s to "Let's Dance" at the start of the '80s. The basic idea was that Bowie had self-consciously plotted out the best part of his career according to the kabbalah. Sometimes it had gone to plan, other times not. The story had a three-act structure, with an initial crisis, a series of abrupt confrontations, a climax and a final resolution. Maxi had produced his own dance notation to describe the specific poses at each station of the kabbalah and the dramatic movements between them. He once photocopied some pages for me to review. I remember the scene-by-scene mapping of hand gestures and dance steps, done in differently-coloured gel inks, the poetic lines of dialogue and abbreviated stage directions, the kabbalistic number system. It was a beautiful work of art in its own right, way beyond my ability to understand. The names of the dance steps were particularly enigmatic – "Chime Rinpoche Pirouette", "Tulpa Jete", "Psychic Self-Defence Kick", "Coulsdon South Exit".

It's a shame Maxi never got his libretto into the hands of a Michael Clark or a Matthew Bourne. It would have made a wonderful contemporary ballet. At the very least, it would have made a decent rock musical, certainly better than the dismal production

Ben Elton and Arlene Phillips created for the Queen back-catalogue. But Maxi had his own psychological blocks to contend with.

Born in 1962 in the Midlands to chocolate factory worker Don Grey and his domineering wife Ruby, Maxwell was an only child. Ruby snatched little Maxi from the orbit of poor old Don as soon as he was born, dressed him in homemade lederhosen and sailor suits and signed him up for ballet school in Bournville at the age of three. Ruby was a dark-haired beauty from Anglesey. An ex-singer and dancer on the cabaret and revue circuit in London, she had once performed with the Dougie Squires Dancers on television. She always told Maxi that the reason she quit showbiz was that "women didn't have the same choices as men". She was determined that Maxi would succeed where she had failed.

Maxi was an excellent student. He enjoyed the exercises at the barre and learned the various classical poses – the arabesque, the croise. He excelled at mime and spent many distracted hours in the cold hall at Bournville, running around pretending to be a helicopter or fluttering his hands together like a butterfly. He wasn't bad at tap, either. But he lacked what his teacher, a formidable woman with solid connections to the Royal Academy of Dance, called "finesse". Unlike his best friend Richie. Almost a year older than him, with a gorgeous head of red hair, Richie was instinctive, charming and agile. He had finesse in spades. When Ruby saw the two boys on the mat together, she frowned and said that Maxi needed to do better, that it was no good being what she called a "clodhopper".

The theme of brotherly love is central to *The Man who Touched the Sun*. Maxi's libretto gives due significance to the bond between Bowie and his half-brother Terry, stressing the fact that Bowie felt guilty for succeeding where his brother had failed. But it also highlights Bowie's close fraternal relationship with Iggy Pop. Time and time again, Bowie came to the rescue of troubled American rocker Jim Osterberg, producing his records, taking him on tour, covering his songs and kicking him out royalty cheques. Bowie, as Osterberg said, laid some "good karma" on him. In Maxi's kabbalistic libretto, Iggy Pop is considered a shared persona occupied by Bowie and Osterberg, a Dostoevskian rock primitive that is the Binah to Ziggy's Netzach, the understanding that comes with self-overcoming.

Maxi started serious dance training at the age of 11. He managed to improve his grades by training in the garage at home. But he still couldn't touch Richie, who was always the centre of attention at ballet school. His mother was unimpressed. It was always "Richie this" and "Richie that". Maxi began to hate the older boy. He dreamed of ways to sabotage his performance. Cutting the strings of his ballet shoes, slapping him a bit too hard on the back in the changing room. He soon joined the group of girls who liked to get together and slag Richie off for being a cruel and exacting dance partner. They all had a secret crush on him, of course. Everyone loved Richie.

Oddly, Max's first memory of Bowie was not seeing him in his Ziggy jumpsuit doing "Starman" on *Top of the Pops*. He missed that. It was seeing the "Jean Genie" pop video on TV. Even then, it wasn't the red-haired Bowie that caught his eye. It was the narrow-waisted blonde girl in the background. Cyrindra Foxe.

He loved the way she stepped so gracefully in and out of her theatrical pin-up girl poses, exposing the difference between a line
of movement and an explosive stopping-point, the direction and
discharge of sexual energy. This, for Maxi, was star power. His
father, watching the screen from the sidelines of the living room,
was pleased to see his son's flicker of interest in a pretty girl. He
made a coarse remark and Ruby scolded him. Maxi just liked to
be friendly with girls, she said. That was all.

Maxi's next encounter with Bowie came when he was 11 and
the girls at ballet school gave him an Aladdin Sane makeover.
They copied the look from the Brian Duffy photo on the album
cover. First, they sprinkled his face with white powder. Then,
they got out the lipstick and eyeliner. Carefully, so carefully, they
painted a red-and-blue lightning bolt on his face, so that it zig-
zagged down from his left temple to his right jaw-line. Everyone
thought he looked beautiful. Even Richie did. But Maxi's mother
was horrified. She said he had defiled himself with the logo of
Oswald Mosley's British Union of Fascists, which her father had
warned her against in her youth. She made him scrub it all off at
the kitchen sink. Don said she the boy didn't mean any harm. She
was over-reacting.

It was around this time that Ruby, perhaps suspecting that
Maxi might never cut it at ballet, began to steer him more into
tap. Once his voice broke, she began to teach him the show tunes
she knew — showbiz standards like "They Can't Take That Away
From Me" and "Blue Skies", songs that were old even in her day.
And then she pushed him into doing a song-and-dance act at
local talent contests and music events. Maxi hated it. Over 20
years later, he still remembered the shame of being forced to do

a spot singing "Joanna" at the Tower Ballroom on grab-a-granny night, standing there on the stage in his ill-fitting tux, his hair slicked down and his ears pinned back, throwing his cane from hand to hand like Ernie fucking Wise. His mother loved it.

In 1975, Maxi saw the *Cracked Actor* documentary on TV. It took Bowie seriously as a performing artist and revealed him shucking off his glam-rock image as he toured the *Diamond Dogs* album in America. Bowie had explicitly retired his Ziggy Stardust persona a year before at the Hammersmith Odeon, but the documentary showed old habits dying hard as the pop star struggled to reinvent himself. The last scene of the film was a coup de grace. It showed Bowie transformed on-stage, debuting a slick new persona, the Gouster, a white soul singer.

Maxi was stunned by the idea of such a dramatic metamorphosis. When he spoke to Richie about it the next day, though, his friend was much less impressed. He said that Bowie's move from glam rock into black American music had been telegraphed the year before by Marc Bolan. Bowie was always ripping off his rock-star rival, said Richie. Ziggy Stardust had been a blatant copy of Bolan's T. Rex act, two years after the fact. Likewise, Bowie's new soul-man image was just a copy of what Bolan had achieved with his album *Zinc Alloy and the Hidden Riders of Tomorrow*. Why, said Richie, Bowie had even copied Bolan by getting himself a black American girlfriend. Bowie benefited from Ava Cherry's knowledge of Philadelphia soul, just as much as Bolan had benefited from Gloria Jones's knowledge of the Motown back-catalogue.

Maxi didn't know how Richie knew the details of Bowie's private life, but he was suitably awed. He was also a little anxious.

They had both been such huge fans of Bowie, but now Richie seemed to be turning his nose up at their old pop idol. He was talking about Be Bop Deluxe. He was hanging out with a gang of new boys. Maxi felt the pangs of jealousy. He became even more depressed when Bowie's soul album *Young Americans* scored him the kind of big American hits that Bolan had never been able to achieve. It suggested in an obscure way that Richie was on the right track and he, little Maxi, was being left behind.

Bowie's rivalry with Bolan is one of the big themes in Maxi's libretto. It seems safe to say that he developed it from Richie's initial thinking. The story fills the early pages of his notebook. Maxi was interested in the doublings, reversals and competitive dramas between the two men. They had known each other since 1964, when they were both teenage pop hopefuls managed out of the same office on Denmark Street. They used to hang out together in La Gioconda coffee bar, watching the comings and goings of Tin Pan Alley. Here was the ground-floor of the London music business — Malkuth, in Maxi's kabbalistic reading. Mark Feld said he was thinking of changing his name. Perhaps to Mark Bowland. The young Davie Jones took note. He thought Bowie was even better than Bowland. In August 1965, Marc Bolan signed to Decca.

Until he met Bolan, Bowie had wanted to be the next Mick Jagger, said Maxi. He had watched Jagger perform on-stage when the Rolling Stones played the Brixton Odeon in 1963. He had formed an R&B group and named it after a Muddy Waters song, just like the Stones. But even esteemed session guitarist Jimmy Page couldn't help the Manish Boys get a hit, said Maxi. He recorded a Bobby Bland number with them in 1965, but it was a flop. It wasn't until Bolan took Bowie to see Pink Floyd at the Marquee in 1966 that Bowie changed his tune. After that, Bowie shared Bolan's ambition of becoming the next Syd Barrett. The Floyd front-man's psychedelic nursery rhymes, jaunty melodies and fantastical costumes became a model for them both.

Maxi's libretto sketches the battle for pop star dominance between Bolan and Bowie as a tango, characterised by a close embrace, teetering steps and syncopated rhythmic footwork. They fight over the damaged body of Barrett, eager to pick up his discarded halo.

Bolan gets there first. He seizes Barrett's white Fender Stratocaster, steals his girlfriend June, and adopts his signature curly perm. Two years at the top of the charts follow. Bowie fails to dent his old pal's fame with "Space Oddity", even though he sports his own version of the Barrett fro. And then comes Ziggy Stardust. A science-fiction mutation of Barrett's psychedelic troubadour persona, it puts Bolan off his stride. When Bowie picks up Barrett's old lensman Mick Rock as his own personal photographer, his fame is secure.

Maxi wanted to dramatise Bowie's victory over his rival by recreating a couple of emblematic pop moments. The first was the night at the Rainbow Theatre in August 1972 when Bowie dedicated "Lady Stardust", his lament for a tragic rock star, to Bolan by projecting a picture of him on a large screen. The second, more brutal version of essentially the same fratricidal moment, occurred when Bowie made a guest appearance on Bolan's TV show, *Marc*, in 1977. The two men were meant to do a song together, "Standing Next to You". Bolan felt fat and depressed, aware that in his glam-era eyeliner and nail polish he actually looked very uncool next to Bowie, who was poised, svelte, *contemporary*. He fell off the stage.

Maxi's tango sequence ends with Bolan lying dead in a car crash. The road accident happened mere days after he was blown off-stage by Bowie. The clear implication of Maxi's libretto is that Bolan had been fatally star-struck by his old friend.

When I talked to him about the scene, Maxi said it had been influenced by Girard's reading of Freud in *Deceit, Desire and the Novel: Self and Other in Literary Structure*. In fact, he had based the psychological aspect of his whole libretto on it. Girard stated that Oedipus wanted his mother not because she was desirable in herself, but because his father wanted her. And Oedipus wanted to be like his father. Human desire, for Girard, was always based on imitation, said Maxi. And imitation always had a fatal logic. After all, Oedipus killed his father in the end.

In 1976, the ballet school put on a production of *Alice in Wonderland* at the Palace Theatre in Redditch. Richie got the star part as the Red Queen. Nobody was surprised, except Maxi's mother. She petitioned the school's principal for Maxi to have a second audition, much to his embarrassment. But the casting director's decision was final. Maxi had to content himself with playing the role of Humpty Dumpty. He felt useless and depressed.

Richie tried to make it up to Maxi by buying him a copy of *Station to Station* when it came out. They listened to it together at Maxi's place when his parents were out, lying on the living-room floor of the brick maisonette, tonguing each other. Richie had already had sex with two of the girls at ballet school. He said he was bisexual, like Bowie. He had all the moves. Maxi felt himself falling for his friend, like a stupid little ballerina. He hated himself.

Station to Station saw the debut of a new Bowie persona, the Thin White Duke, a ghoulish dandy and sinister Euro-fascist. Richie said the character was based on the tabloid image of Aleister Crowley, whose occultist practices had earned him the label of "wickedest man in the world". Richie went on to say Bowie and his old recording partner Jimmy Page were engaged in a secret duel to be the next Crowley. He said that when Bowie had recorded *Station to Station* in Los Angeles, his occult ambitions had sent him crazy. He imagined that a coven of black girls were attempting to seduce him so they could steal his jizz and gain magical power over him. He traced protective swastikas on the windows of his villa on North Doheny Drive. He drew the kabbalah on the floor and kept the TV on day and night. He stayed awake by taking cocaine. He failed to eat. He became convinced the demon Lucifer was lurking somewhere in the bottom of his swimming pool. He even hired a white witch to exorcise it.

Maxi said that messing with Crowley was probably never a wise idea. Richie said Jimmy Page hadn't done too badly out of it. He had bought Crowley's old manor house at Loch Ness in Scotland, collected Crowley manuscripts and ephemera, done black magic. But none of it had damaged him. Quite the opposite. He had made a fortune with Led Zeppelin and was ranked the greatest guitarist in the world. He had also shagged loads of nubile young girls.

It was at this point that Richie introduced Maxi to the idea of "sex magick". The two of them could be spotted the next night at a disused location on the Birmingham Canal, spunking into the water as they made an occult pact with each other. Maxi grimaced when he told me this.

It wasn't until a few years later that the boys got a chance to see Bowie in concert. He appeared at New Bingley Hall in Stafford as part of his 1978 world tour. Maxi told me that what he remembered most about the gig was Bowie's forceful stage presence. He held himself inside a cage of fluorescent white light, in snakeskin jacket and baggy white pants, like a reptilian angel. Richie and Maxi both studied his moves. Striking a pose with one foot forward, arms held away from the torso. Edging a little bit left, a little bit right.

On the train home, Richie dissected the stage move Bowie had made when singing "Station to Station", his song about the kabbalah. When intoning the line "one magical movement from Kether to Malkuth", Bowie had brought his raised left hand down to the ground in a swooping gesture, as if he were unzipping the air. Richie said it was a mudra. Bowie was signalling a transit of spiritual energy from the top to the bottom of the kabbalah, from the top to the bottom of the world. It represented the fall of the angel Lucifer from the abode of God, said Richie. An occult sign, a summoning of demonic energy as powerful as a lightning bolt. Bowie knew what he was doing. He was one of the enlightened ones, one of the "supermen" he sang about on *The Man Who Sold the World*, a follower of Lucifer who believed his true existence lay in a higher dimension. His whole approach to stardom was based on that occult understanding.

Maxi didn't say anything. But he listened. Years later, his libretto bore the imprint of Richie's gnostic take on Bowie. *The Man Who Touched the Sun* resignified Bowie's swooping Kether-to-Malkuth gesture as a projection of future stardom by the struggling artist Davie Jones, a drawing-down of the power of rock god David Bowie from an imagined peak of global fame. It was first used by Bowie in his 1969 pre-stardom pop promo for "Let Me Sleep Beside You". And Maxi suspected it was older than that. In fact, he considered it was a stylised re-enactment of an actual Luciferian invocation Bowie had made long years before.

This brings me back to the strangest leitmotif of Maxi's Bowie kabbalah, which is the rivalry between Bowie and Jimmy Page. In Maxi's version of their story, Bowie and Page had been involved in a struggle for occult dominance since 1964. *The Man Who Touched the Sun* stages their duel as a choreographed dance-off complete with macho struts, crouching runs, prominent bare-knuckle displays and taunting air-kisses. Their dance competition is judged by the demon Lucifer, whom they have summoned to decide who should be the greatest rock'n'roll star in the world. Lucifer sits on his throne at the centre of the stage, on the painted mark of Daath, the hidden extra station of the kabbalah, the eleventh station where enlightened souls go to die.

The dance duet is full of striking little touches, with the action flowing first one way and then the other. Page is so confident of victory that he gives Bowie one of his guitar riffs when they record together in 1965. Page hits it big with Led Zeppelin in 1969, when Bowie is still third on the bill doing his mime act in support of Tyrannosaurus Rex. Bowie claws his way back with his own heavy metal act, but *The Man Who Sold the World* — even with Page's gift of a riff — is no match for the biggest rock'n'roll band in the world. Page has it sewn up. He thumbs his nose at Bowie and releases *Led Zeppelin IV*. So sure of himself is he that he makes public his magical name – actually, a Luciferian sigil – on the cover of the album. Bowie is taken aback. Even name-checking Crowley on his next album can't save him. It looks like it's all over. Lucifer comes to collect. He wants Bowie's soul.

It's part of the libretto's genius to imagine Bowie's various personas – Major Tom, Ziggy, Halloween Jack – as the fake souls he offers Lucifer in an effort to evade capture. Maxi's stage directions show Bowie racing round the kabbalah painted on the floor, jumping from one station to the next. Lucifer chases him, but can never quite catch him.

I think Maxi might have got the idea for this sequence from the back cover of *Scary Monsters (and Super Creeps)*. Here, Bowie's old personas – Aladdin Sane, the Thin White Duke – feature as photographic insets, slightly whitewashed, as if fading into oblivion. I also wonder how far he was influenced by the Bowie nights he used to attend with Richie at the Rum Runner in Birmingham. This would have been in 1981, just after Duran Duran had quit their residency at the club for London and pop stardom. I can just imagine Maxi and Richie watching the pretty boys on the dance-floor, as they competed with each other to be the best homemade version of their favourite Bowie persona. All the Bowie ghosts, throwing shapes in sequence against the mirrored nightclub walls.

Richie passed his Ballet Rambert audition with flying colours and went to live in London. Maxi didn't even make the audition. His school merely acknowledged that he had acquired the "discipline" necessary for a career in dance instruction, or perhaps television commercials. He felt sick. He promised himself he would never dance again.

Maxi followed Richie to London and got work as an editor in the emerging video industry in Soho. He heard that Richie was doing well in his chosen profession, mixing with Michael Clark's people at the Riverside Studios, hanging out with Leigh Bowery and Cerith Wyn Evans, a protégé of Derek Jarman. Maxi avoided opportunities to meet his old friend. When he wasn't working, he became a creature of the gym and the gay club scene. He hung out with the wild boys from the Warren Street squats at Asylum, on a Thursday night at Heaven. Furious sex in the toilets became routine. He wore highlighter and bronzer to give himself a slimmer face, he dyed his hair blond with the black roots showing. When he looked in the mirror, he didn't recognise himself.

One night, Maxi spotted Richie leaving the Cha Cha Club alone. He was wearing a loose paisley shirt, combat trousers and tennis shoes — the whole look set off with silver bangles and rings. Maxi followed him along the railway arches under Charing Cross Station. He jumped him at a secluded spot. He put him in a choke-hold, cracked his spine and took him from behind. He gave him a full load. Richie didn't resist. The stars shone down on them just the same. Richie called out Maxi's name. It was a question. Maxi let him go and ran away. He was sobbing.

There was a confrontation between Bowie and Jimmy Page in February 1975. Page had hunted for Bowie across the island of Manhattan. He finally tracked him down to the West 20th Street apartment of his girlfriend Ava Cherry. They talked about Crowley, rock music, sympathetic magic and Kenneth Anger. All this, according to Ava Cherry in her memoir.

Maxi gives this meeting a slightly different take in his libretto. Page, at the peak of his powers with the release of *Physical*

Graffiti, had corralled Bowie in his hidey-hole on Gevurah, the sixth station of the kabbalah. Page gave the secret sign and Lucifer leapt from his throne at Daath. But Bowie disappeared and left him with only the image of the Gouster. He fled to Chesed, the seventh station of the kabbalah, in Los Angeles. Here, he took to wearing a gold crucifix and carrying a *mezuzah*, a Jewish occult talisman. On North Doheny Drive, he would create his last and greatest persona, the Thin White Duke.

By the early 1980s, Maxi was working for Aldabra, a pop promo company created to cash in on the MTV boom. He helped make videos for the likes of OMD, Human League, Flock of Seagulls and Wang Chung. He was good at coming up with scenarios – a band busking on the zebra crossing at Abbey Road, a singer wrapped in cling-film suspended upside-down from the ceiling at Heaven. He met Derek Jarman. He came to understand that, unlike Richie, he was more comfortable behind the camera than in front of it. He was making good money.

The climax of Maxi's libretto comes with Lucifer's pursuit of Bowie to Los Angeles. He stalks the Thin White Duke around his white-cubed villa. He tries to lure him into the indoor pool, to drown him. Bowie phones his publicist, back in Manhattan, and asks for help. She gets in touch with Walli Elmlark, a Wiccan priestess at the New York School of Occult Arts and Sciences on West 14th Street. Elmlark has long black hair, with dyed green highlights. She flies to Bowie in Los Angeles. She performs a belly dance in the shallow end of the pool, with much chanting, implied nudity and clicking of finger-cymbals. Lucifer is seduced. He agrees to her request. He vanishes.

It's true to say that after 1975, there was a reversal of fortunes between Bowie and his rock nemesis. Page got hooked on smack, his playing suffered and Led Zep released only two more albums before calling it a day in 1980. Bowie, by contrast, clawed his way back to sanity over those five years. He was on the way to finding popular success on his own terms – free from personas – as the greatest rock'n'roll star in the world.

In 1983, Bowie signed a $17 million deal with EMI and released his multi-platinum selling album *Let's Dance*. The London press launch was held in Claridge's. Maxi watched a clip on the TV news. Bowie preened and pranced in front of the cynical music journalists. He looked tanned, healthy, glowing. He said he had found himself. He had bleached blond hair. Too young for him, Maxi thought. For the first time in his life, he was bored with Bowie. He wished he had Richie to talk to about it. So he got his number and gave him a call.

After a four-year gap, the two young men picked up their friendship without skipping a beat. There was no mention of the assault at Charing Cross. Maxi was ashamed. But also resentful that Richie was gracious enough to silently forgive him. He was back to being the lesser fellow, as always.

And as always, Richie had a good take on Bowie, the new global mega-star, one that would make it into Maxi's libretto. He said that Bowie was back to copying Jagger, his boyhood idol. When Bowie had been in talks with EMI the previous year, Jagger had been in talks with Columbia Records about a solo career, apart from the Stones. He was enthralled by New York's downtown club scene, where punk rock and disco had reached an uneasy truce, and wanted to do a dance record. He basically, said Richie, wanted to be the white Michael Jackson. It looked like Bowie had got there first.

In Maxi's libretto, the rivalry between Bowie and Jagger is the final theme of the dance-piece. It's staged as a mambo, loosely based on the Latin-flavoured routine Bowie and Jagger performed for their "Dancing in the Streets" video, with alternations between tight ballroom clinches and freestyle kicks and points.

Bowie and Jagger going head-to-head, their foreheads touching, or swaying back-to-back, reference the early '70s period when the two men were hanging out together. Maxi's notes indicate that once Ziggy had propelled Bowie to rock stardom, he took up residence at 89 Oakley Street, a Chelsea address just a little bit less fashionable than Jagger's own at 48 Cheyne Walk. The two swapped make-up tips, clothing labels and girlfriends. Bowie was always the more insecure. He played Jagger a demo of "Jean Genie", which was quite Stones-y, eager for his approval. He stole the commercial artist Guy Peellaert from Jagger's contacts book and got him to do the cover design for *Diamond Dogs* before he had a chance to work on *It's Only Rock "n Roll* for the Stones. He was always popping up into Jagger's space.

By 1985, though, Bowie has trumped his rival. Jagger releases his own dance album, *She's the Boss*. Like Bowie on *Let's Dance* two years earlier, he uses Nile Rodgers as producer. Unlike Bowie, he fails to get the worldwide sales. Maxi references this triumph by recreating the moment in the "Dancing in the Streets" video where Bowie does his signature Kether-to-Malkuth gesture, dropping his body low, and Jagger does a feeble imitation of the move, not quite getting it. It's Bowie who is the greatest rock star in the world. And it's Jagger who could never bring himself to break up the band.

Richie's back had been giving him problems. Maxi felt guilty. The ballet company benched him, he was no longer their lead male dancer. He was 26 years old. Maxi got to spend more time with him. It was almost like the old days.

Richie still had the looks. He got work as a model, doing shoots for swimwear companies. He got a bit part in a pop video for the Pet Shop Boys, playing a King's Cross rent boy. Maxi used to dress him up and parade him at the clubs. Richie was promiscuous and a dreadful flirt, causing Maxi a lot of heartache. They had knock-down, drag-out fights at their home in Brixton. More than once, Maxi found himself going into work with a black eye.

It was at this point they started to hang out with Jarman's entourage at Bertaux's. Maxi was popular with the crowd. They called him "Bona" Maxi. He would stumble into the patisserie bleary-eyed, after finishing a 20-hour shift in the Soho video production hive. He would listen to the talk. That's how he heard about the visit Bowie paid to Jarman in 1981 at his Charing Cross Road flat. The meeting was ostensibly to talk about casting Bowie in *Neutron*, a reimagining of the Book of Revelations as a science-fiction film, complete with angels and flame-throwers. It would be Bowie's answer to Jimmy Page's collaboration with the occult film-maker Kenneth Anger on *Lucifer Rising* ten years earlier. Actually though, said Richie, turning his head to look at the door, the meeting was about something entirely different.

Whispers followed. Bowie had been summoned to Phoenix House so that Jarman could initiate him into the Rosicrucians. There, that was it. Bowie had been chosen to become a member of the secret society of artists and adepts who were guiding the spiritual evolution of the human race. He was to sit on the permanent inner council. Richie pressed his hands on the table. Bowie was to be taught the secret of spiritual ascent beyond the mortal plane, the art of making the difficult passage beyond this universe to the hidden realm of the black sun.

All this was told to me by Maxi at our final meeting at Bertaux's. It was as if he were saving the best of his Bowie lore till last. He sipped his espresso. The interval was filled with the chinking of cups on saucers and the rustling of the Sunday papers. Right Said Fred's "Deeply Dippy" played in the background. My girl was pulling at my sleeve. She wanted to go. There was a guy in a wheelchair outside, wanting to get in. He glared at us as we opened the door for him. He was wearing a single feather earring. Maxi hooted at him in delight. Richie. It could only have been.

Years later, I learned that Richie had developed MS. It was 2013 when Maxi told me this. I bumped into him on Old Compton Street. He looked well. We stopped for a drink in Soho House. He said he was looking after Richie. He wiped an imaginary speck of dust from his shoulder. Tending to his every need. He crossed his legs, satisfied with himself.

I asked about his libretto. Bowie had just released *The Next Day* after a ten-year silence. It had surprised everyone. Maxi said the album's direct re-use of the old *"Heroes"* album cover art showed that Bowie was now competing with no one but himself. I thought all this might have galvanised Maxi into publishing his libretto. But he said he hadn't finished it. He was waiting for Bowie to die.

Bowie needs a dramatic exit, he said. His career's been flat for years. After his peak success in the mid-'80s, he had nothing left to prove, no one else to imitate. He drifted, coasting his way through a 20-year cycle of greatest hits albums, stale reunions and tame makeovers, charity appearances and film cameos. Never plumbing the creative depths of old. Stuck at the highest point of self-actualisation on the kabbalah, said Maxi. Banging his head against Kether. Where else is there to go once you've reached the top? He shrugged.

We parted on good terms. And then, just three years later, Bowie made his final brilliant career move, surely the most accomplished kind of exit Maxi could have hoped for. I tried to contact him, to discuss *Blackstar*, an album about death and eternal life released by Bowie just 48 hours before his sudden demise from cancer. I wanted to point out that in the video for the single "Lazarus", Bowie was sporting the same black-and-white striped outfit he had been seen wearing on the back cover of *Station to Station*, where he had been sketching out the kabbalah on the floor of his Los Angeles apartment. In the video, the costumed Bowie creeps out of a wardrobe, almost as it were some kind of time machine, into a tiled room where a version of himself lies dying in bed. He hurriedly writes something in a book before retreating back to the wardrobe. Is he completing the kabbalah he started in Los Angeles? I was sure Maxi would have a good theory. However, he failed to respond to any of my emails. Someone said he was working in San Francisco.

And then, out of the blue, he dropped me a voice-mail. He said he had finished his libretto. The ending was obvious. Bowie perfects his transit through the stations of the kabbalah and moves on. He quits the godhead of Kether by following wily old Lucifer out through the hidden escape-hatch of Daath, mysterious eleventh station of the kabbalah, known only to those ascended masters who have raised and purified their souls. He disappears. And makes his way to his own version of the Rosicrucian black sun, his personal star at the centre of things, where all past lives are remembered and all discarded personas saved. From here, he would journey to another universe, another planet, where a forgetting could descend and a new life begin. A new life and a new transit through the kabbalah. It was all there in the "Blackstar" video, said Maxi. Bowie himself had put the only question worth answering. "How many times does an angel fall?"

LADY SARAH-JANE POCKET

Maker of the TOPY Sigils

I CAN'T REALLY TALK ABOUT SARAH-JANE POCKET, or "Lady" Sarah-Jane as I knew her, without declaring an interest. I was in love with her. There, I've said it. I'm not sure if she was ever really in love with me. She had an assortment of lovers – male, female and all points in between – and I was one of them. All of us, I suspect, were more like her accomplices than her partners. But then "Lady" Sarah-Jane found it hard to get close to people, especially those who cared for her.

Sarah-Jane Pocket was an extraordinary woman with an extraordinary mind, one that had been shaped by many abusive pressures. She sported the conventional signifiers of outsiderdom. Black hair, black nails, black boots. Listening to Nine Inch Nails and Psychic TV. Reading books about serial killers. But she also wore tailored jackets and Pucci scarves. She soothed herself to sleep with songs by Isaac Hayes. She read late Foucault alongside self-help books. Overall, I would say she had a philosophy of life that was materialistic, antagonistic and romantic.

She once told me that there was nothing to stop her from buying a can of petrol at a service station and pouring the contents over a small boy left in a buggy outside the super-market. Nothing. Why shouldn't she do it? She might take great delight in killing a child, much like Gilles de Rais. Why shouldn't a woman experience the sensations that lay beyond the bounds of Abrahamic law? she said. There was no good reason for a woman, a truly liberated woman, to be left holding the baby when the Devil came calling. Why not throw the infant in the fire and enter the gates of hell alongside men like Ian Brady and Fred West? Why not follow the example of Brady's fearless girlfriend Myra Hindley, of West's angry wife Rose? Why not go all the way? That would be the really militant feminist position. It was not enough, she said, for a woman to refuse to be shamed for neglecting her children. She had to be strong enough to abuse children, to torture children, to kill children – all without the slightest trace of mercy. Only then would men finally get the message that women were their equal.

So this was "Lady" Sarah-Jane being provocative. She was always searching for the limit cases of liberal freedom and arguing in favour of them. Her logic was irresistible and her passion was frightening. I was never entirely convinced she wouldn't take the final step and go on a minor killing spree. Which was why I was relieved when I found out she had made scrapbooks about Myra Hindley and Rose West, her twin obsessions. If she were expressing her murderous fixations through precise symbolic gestures – the pasting together of broadsheet newspaper headlines, found photos and hand-written journal entries – surely this meant she wouldn't act on them in real life. So I liked to believe, anyway.

In the end, I got to examine just one of Sarah-Jane's many scrapbooks, the one on Thee Temple ov Psychick Youth. More committed than a joke religion like the Church of the SubGenius, but less fanatical than the *Hitlerjugend*, TOPY – as it was familiarly known to its members – was a cult built around an electronic rock band. In one sense, it was Psychic TV's fan club, run by mail-order from a squatted address in the London borough of Hackney. In another more imaginative sense, it was an occult sect with its very own temperamental guru – Psychic TV's frontman, the frivolously self-named Genesis P-Orridge. It also had a panoply of secret signals, initiation rituals and criminal saints. Sarah-Jane's TOPY scrapbook – titled *My Perfect Cult Hell* – was a fantasia of sensational sex, transgressive violence and invented ethnography that read like a screen-play for a mondo exploitation film. As an artistic treatment of excessive alienation, it was up there with *American Psycho* or *Suite Venitienne*.

It was no surprise when "Lady" Sarah-Jane told me, rather grandly, that she came from a long line of criminals. Her grandfather had been arraigned at the Old Bailey for fraud. She didn't know if he had done jail time. Meanwhile, her father Benjamin had been involved in dodgy diamond dealing in South Africa. He had made enough money, she said, to buy a suburban villa in the stockbroker belt outside London. Brambles, it was called. He married a young woman when he was in his fifties and starting to tire of adventure. It was the second time round for Stella. She had tried bohemian in North Kensington, now in the early 1960s she was trying bourgeois in Camberley. She was equally unhappy in both. Stella was a notable beauty in the 1950s mould – tall, statuesque, imperious. She craved male attention. When she couldn't find it in a string of bit parts in the lower rungs of the British film industry, she found it in a string of lovers. Eventually, said Sarah-Jane, she drowned her disappointments in Smirnoff vodka.

Sarah-Jane's older brother Sterling was the real piece of work in the family, though. From what I could make out, he was a criminal psychopath. Five years older than Sarah-Jane, he liked to torture small animals and set fire to empty houses. Finally, one dismal afternoon by the lake, he graduated to hurting little girls. The episode was kept out of the papers but Sterling's life-course was set. By the time I met Sarah-Jane many years later, he was in jail. "Lady" Sarah-Jane, with chilling satisfaction, said it was where he belonged. She had a child-like sense of natural justice.

Still, her brother was a great influence on Sarah-Jane. As a delinquent middle-class punk in the late 1970s, Sterling was a fan of the early Genesis P-Orridge in his pre-Psychic TV incarnation as front-man for Throbbing Gristle. Whereas Psychic TV played with the idea of the cult, TG was an industrial music band that played with the idea of the company. Its records were packaged as "annual reports" and it saw itself doing research and development in the marginal and forbidden sectors of culture. Child abuse, serial murder, Auschwitz, secret military experiments – all were up for grabs as topics for songs, record sleeve designs or press releases.

Genesis P-Orridge – or "Gen" as he was nicknamed – was the moving spirit behind it all. In my view, he was essentially a prankster. He learned the tricks of his trade alongside his inamorata Cosey Fanni Tutti in the publicly-funded performance art world. Here, he had not been above using fake blood in his stomach-churning exhibitions of self-harm. I always saw his work in the music industry as a continuation of the old avant-garde game of epater-ing la bourgeoisie. By all accounts, though, that's not how Sterling saw things. Gen was his idol, a transgressive culture hero, an outsider. He wrote to the old scoundrel at his squat in

Beck Road and was pleased to receive back much swag — the Industrial Records newsletter, a black T-shirt adorned with the legend "DEATH FACTORY", glamour postcards of a pouting Cosey and a personal note from the great man himself. If there was one thing Gen took seriously, I guess, it was his mission to corrupt the youth.

Sterling paraded around the Surrey streets in a black leather jacket and SS arm band, frightening the little old ladies and intimidating the young school girls. At home, he entertained his mother with discourses on high crime as low art, a proposition he'd lifted directly from Gen. He claimed that when Ian Brady had tape-recorded the screams of the little children he murdered, he was documenting a work of performance art. He was affirming the value of life by giving death its full due.

Stella was dazzled by her son's borrowed eloquence. She pointed him out to the boy's father and said they had a young lawyer on their hands, a future Queen's Counsel, no less. Sterling beamed. Benjamin rustled his copy of *The Times* and said that the boy's scurrilous proposition was nothing new. De Quincey had got there a hundred years ago. Tears came to Sterling's eyes. He rushed to his bedroom, howling.

Even at the tender age of 15, Sarah-Jane was intrigued by the grinding rock music that emanated from her brother's room. When he was out, she snuck into his sanctum and looked through his collection of TG records. She was thrilled by the cool and austere design of the sleeves for the band's double A-sided singles. Here was an ambivalent juxtaposition of black-and-white photos, a neutral use of type, which took tabloid themes of sex, crime and violence but refused to sensationalise them. Instead, it cooled them down, turning them into specimens in a display case. The same was true of the design of the Industrial Records newsletter, which treated taboo cultural themes with a quasi-institutional collage aesthetic. These gestures of detachment had a great effect on Sarah-Jane's budding sensibility.

She made her first scrapbook when her mother took Sterling away for a holiday to Lindisfarne, just the two of them. Sterling had said he wanted to see the ruins of the priory, where the Vikings had slaughtered the Christian monks. The boy's psychiatrist had advised Stella that it might be a good idea to take him there, so he could release his repressed anger in a quiet, isolated place. She thought it would be a good excuse to get away from her husband for a while. In their absence, which was bliss for Sarah-Jane, she found a half-filled photo album in her father's cabinet, removed the pictures of her mother and brother, cut them up and reassembled them in sexual poses on the blank pages. She also stuck in ripped adverts from her mother's copies of *Country Life*. She identified a hunting theme and elaborated upon it with illustrations of farm animals from her old nursery books. She pressed the images together with her big thumbs, feeling a great sense of satisfaction.

Inspiration of a different kind was available in the old porn mags under Sterling's bed. He'd dutifully collected the editions of *Fiesta* and *Knave* which contained photo-shoots by an unsmiling Cosey in stockings and suspenders, displaying herself enigmatically to the gaze of thousands of anonymous men. Her genitals had been obliterated by Sterling's biro scrawls.

When Stella and her son got back from Lindisfarne, if that is really where they had been, Sarah-Jane told her mother about

Sterling's secret porn stash. Stella exploded with rage. The beloved Sterling, however, was not the target of Stella's abusive behaviour. Instead, it was Sarah-Jane who had to fend off the flying plates and cutlery. Stella called her daughter a little sneak. She said she was always stirring up trouble within the family.

Sterling was triumphant when he visited Sarah-Jane in hospital. He said that she'd got what she deserved for trying to turn their mother against him. He picked at the extravagant basket of fruit Benjamin had brought his daughter. He said that she was just like Cosey Fanni Tutti. A bitch. Cosey, he said, had left Gen after he'd made her a pop star in Throbbing Gristle. She'd moved out of Beck Road and left him alone. But she still expected to be in the band. Outrageous! Poor Gen was so upset he had attempted suicide. She drove him to it, the overdosing on tranquillisers at the Cryptic One Club, the rush to hospital after he finished performing.

Lightweight! said "Lady" Sarah-Jane. What do you mean? said Sterling, shocked. A rock star killing himself live on-stage? she said. That would have been a first. It would have made Genesis P-Orridge bigger than Elvis. An honest-to-God rock martyr. But he bottled it. She smirked. Sterling scowled. He said he was upset by the news that Gen had broken up Throbbing Gristle. But there were rumours he was going to form a new band. One without Cosey. He put his half-eaten apple back in the basket and left.

I don't know the full story of what went on behind closed doors at Brambles. I do know that "Lady" Sarah-Jane destroyed the first scrapbook she made, fearful of another beating if her mother found it. In her later teens, she was in and out of children's homes, where she picked up the admonishing "Lady" sobriquet. She had a particular horror of going to Duncroft, where she was told the really bad girls were sent. And she once joked to me that she couldn't have fared much worse if she'd run away to live at 25 Cromwell Street, the Gloucester lodging house where Fred and Rose West had run their informal sex trafficking ring and murder farm during the 1970s and '80s. There was a newspaper photo of the Cromwell Street property – a narrow three-storey terraced house – in the Rose West scrapbook she assembled many years later. I remember seeing it as she flashed me the pages one night.

Sarah-Jane's life changed irrevocably in 1984. She reached the legal age of majority and both her parents died, one after the other. Benjamin succumbed to cancer and Stella, after a lifetime of failed and highly theatrical suicide attempts, finally understood that her audience was gone and took a massive overdose of sleeping tablets. Sterling contested the will and the family estate got eaten up by lawyers. Sarah-Jane moved to a rented room in North London and was shown how to apply to the council for housing benefit.

The housing co-op on Grosvenor Avenue was full of young middle-class people who were all failing in their different ways. She consoled herself with the thought that at least with her it was involuntary. She kept herself apart from the Hare Krishna devotees and the speed freaks, the various maniacs rushing in and out. She was quite aware that if she let herself go in any one direction, she would be lost, fallen into an abyss of despair. No drugs for "Lady" Sarah-Jane, no risks, no attachments. She got into body modification and had her tongue pierced by Mr Sebastian. She called herself a lesbian and got a job as a fetish wear model for *Skin Two*. The magazine knew it could rely on her to sport the more extreme leather bondage hoods. She enjoyed the discipline of having to control her panic attacks.

She also attended a Psychic TV gig, mainly out of curiosity. A couple of her house-mates were going to Thee Fabulous Feast Ov Flowering Light festival at the Hammersmith Palais in 1985. She tagged along. It was a Sunday in May. They arrived in the evening and Sarah-Jane felt a thrill at the sight of the neon-fronted dance hall with its confident angular lines and promise of modernity, pleasure and ease. Inside, it was cavernous and dark. They had completely missed the appearances by Kathy Acker and Derek Jarman. The Virgin Prunes had just quit the stage. Sarah-Jane found herself unexpectedly excited as she waited for Psychic TV to appear. She had only gone to the gig so she could say she had seen Gen perform on-stage. It was something her brother had never done. But once she was there in the mosh-pit, among the moonfaced young men in their rolled-up jeans and second-hand jackets, the angry girls with the pleading eyes, she found herself caught up in atmosphere of exultation.

When Gen hit the stage, he was nothing like the lumpy, sullen creature Sarah-Jane remembered from the TG press shots Sterling had collected. He looked fabulous, like a proper pop star. He wore black leather trousers and a filmy psychedelic shirt, teamed with a matching head-scarf. His hair was growing out from the severe Krishna cut of a few years back and his eyes had a sparkling, mischievous quality. He posed at the mike with bass slung at his hips, unafraid to bask in the adulation of his audience, quite unlike his punk days, when he had confronted his fans from behind a wall of amps. "Lady" Sarah-Jane could feel herself almost swooning. She couldn't take her eyes off the man, who seemed half-girl at times, like David Bowie or Lou Reed.

In its many years of existence, Psychic TV had a mercurial line-up. Whereas Throbbing Gristle were a cohesive four-piece band, with Gen as front-man, Psychic TV were much more like Gen's ad hoc backing band. On the evening Sarah-Jane saw them, though, they almost amounted to a post-punk super-group, featuring as they did Soft Cell keyboard player, Dave Ball, and one half of Strawberry Switchblade, Rose McDowall. They brought a bright, psychedelic-pop feel to the early part of the set, supporting Gen's seething chants with guitar jangles, synth chimes and sweet high-note carolling. Sarah-Jane found herself dancing to "Godstar" and "Roman P" with the rest of the audience. She was delighted by how trippy the music sounded, like the Velvets crossed with New Order. The later part of the set saw the band slow down, with the sounds becoming darker and more menacing, less structured, a bit like the sounds she remembered coming from the record player in her brother's bedroom. Gen leaned into the audience on his mike stand as he howled and crooned, like some lounge act at the end of the world. The final number, "Ov Power", saw Gen get himself together to lead audience chants of the song's title over a repetitive funk bass-line. The band left the stage to the sound of Gen's echoing voice on tape-delay. "Lady" Sarah-Jane clapped and cheered along with everyone else. She had been converted. Much to her surprise, she was now, like her brother before her, a Genesis P-Orridge fan.

That was the night when Sarah-Jane discovered Thee Temple ov Psychick Youth. From conversations with ecstatic Psychic TV fans waiting to go home at the bus-stop in Hammersmith, she learned that the gig she'd just attended was actually a collective ritual, dedicated to the celebration of TOPY's spiritual ideals – escape from the guilt and fear traps laid down by authorities like the Catholic church, liberation of forbidden desires, revolt into neo-pagan discipline. One of the TOPY lads showed off the occult logo tattooed on his back. It was a three-barred cross, much like the papal cross, except he called it a "psychick" cross. "Lady" Sarah-Jane was suitably impressed. A girl in fishnets and T-shirt said that Gen was a modern shaman, leading his followers into a new phase of human evolution. Everyone else – the "pod people", as she called them – would be left behind. A boy at the back of the queue told her she was making a fascist statement. Gen was not their leader, he was merely first among equals. EDEN Numero 1. Shush! said the girl. That's a secret, not for outsiders. Besides, you're only at Ratio 3. What do you know? An argument broke out. Then the bus pulled up.

Sarah-Jane sent off to Beck Road for a copy of the TOPY bible. It cost her 23 pounds. When *Thee Grey Book* arrived in the post, she was impressed by its size and weight. Its cover was embossed with the same occult logo she had seen tattooed on the boy's back at the bus-stop, the three-barred psychick cross. However, she was disappointed by the book's contents. Reams and reams of badly-formatted text, with muddy black-and-white photos of shadowy figures and bodies in distress. There was nothing like the provocative collages of text and image, the atrocity-under-glass aesthetic, of Throbbing Gristle's newsletters and album sleeves. She thought that, given the chance, she could do a much better job of designing the volume.

It was soon afterwards that Sarah-Jane made her Myra Hindley scrap-book. In this, she was partly inspired by the fact that Throbbing Gristle had recorded a song about the Moors Murderers ("Ian Brady and Myra Hindley, very friendly"). She found a second-hand copy of an old true-crime paperback on the Moors Murder case in Chapel Market. It contained a slim cache of black-and-white photos. Sarah-Jane cut out the pictures of Hindley, who for her was one of those rebellious '60s girls, much like Marianne Faithfull, attempting to reinvent themselves through the medium of glamour. Of course, Myra's paramour was a killer rather than a singer. She chose badly. But even so.. Sarah-Jane juxtaposed her Myra Hindley photos with headlines from *The Face* magazine. She also wrote in accounts of her dreams, in which she and Sterling were posing the bodies of the children they'd killed, fixing a button here, a tooth there, taking photographs.

During the late 1980s, "Lady" Sarah-Jane made a name for herself as a professional submissive named Sweet Fanny Adams. At that time, the London fetish scene was still a demi-monde of contact magazines, rented rooms, Torture Garden nights at the Paradise Club on Parkfield Street and sporadic police raids. The dismal results of Operation Spanner were rumbling their way through the law courts and RE/Search had just published their *Modern Primitives* book on body modification, which included an interview with Gen himself. Sarah-Jane was familiar with it all. She found herself in high demand among a clientele of highly-educated bankers and civil servants, older gentlemen with complex sexual needs who appreciated her tact, good humour and stamina. She made a decent, if precarious, living.

But she was restless. She enjoyed being hidden. And yet she also wanted to be in the world. How could she resolve the contradiction? She remembered Cosey Fanni Tutti, who in addition to her porn actions performed a series of striptease actions. Could that work for her? thought Sarah-Jane. She already had the beginnings of a stage persona, with her "Lady" monicker. She took the plunge. "Lady" Sarah-Jane did a series of bizarre strip shows in the back-rooms of London pubs and dragooned a tame male companion into taking pictures with a large-format camera. One thing she knew about performance art was that an action wasn't art unless it was documented. Already, she was thinking about the requirements of an application to art school.

She did a show at the Seven Stars in Brick Lane where she stripped off a dress stitched together from sides of raw beef. The performance was a nod to Francis Bacon's life-long fascination with Chaim Soutine's paintings of animal carcasses. The art-world references went over the heads of the broken-down old men drinking at the bar, of course. But they appreciated the fullness of Sarah-Jane's figure. There were always quite a few pounds in the jug that went round — much to Sarah-Jane's annoyance.

The Flying Scotsman at King's Cross was by contrast a noisy strip pub, filled with raucous and cheerful young men from Euston fire station. The girls who paraded on-stage were proud of their charms and taunted the punters. "Lady" Sarah-Jane had a specialty act. She performed wearing a strap-on latex vagina, covered in horsehair, which she would shake in front of the men, daring them to stick their fingers inside. As they made a grab for her, she would switch on the sex device to make it vibrate and, at the same time, activate the tape recorder slung round her shoulder. As the sound of a screeching chain-saw kicked in, the men quickly backed off. They spilled their drinks over themselves. They laughed and swore at "Lady" Sarah-Jane. It was all quite farcical. Joe Orton would have loved it.

At the gay club nights hosted at the Shipwright Arms on Tooley Street, "Lady" Sarah-Jane put on a more conceptual show, one appropriate for an audience more intimate with the concealed meanings of pain. She attached one end of a fishing line to a rafter and inserted the other, which had a hook, into her vulva. When she stood on tiptoe, which was stressful for any extended period, the line was quite loose. When she became tired and had to stand on her feet, the line pulled taut, causing her to wince with pain. The performance lasted as long as it took her to remove her bra and panties. Sometimes, she wore stockings and suspenders, just to make the predicament more difficult. The wounds she received were minor, but the blood was real. The audience watched in appreciative silence, then drifted off.

In 1992, Sarah-Jane followed the trail of her anarchist housemates to Hackney. She found lodgings in a housing co-op in Brougham Road, next to London Fields. One in a row of Victorian terraced houses overlooked by high-rise council estate blocks, it had been ear-marked for demolition by the local authority in the 1970s. But the money had run out. Now it was part of an unsettled urban landscape which was slowly gentrifying, but still partly derelict. It suited her own sense of indeterminacy. At the age of 26, she was still in many ways not quite mature. But then, that was not untypical of her generation.

Sarah-Jane soon discovered that Beck Road, Gen's old stomping ground, was just a few streets away from where she lived. However, he no longer lived there. The gossip in Broadway Market was that he had been chased out of his fortress compound by Special Branch. He had been running a religious cult which had brainwashed runaway teenagers and turned them into sex slaves and serial killers. There was talk that he had left behind a stack of Nazi literature and occult videos at 50 Beck Road, that people were reluctant to live there because there were dead children living in the walls and that its basement was a compost of manure, rotting remains and blood. "Lady" Sarah-Jane shivered when she heard this. She imagined how Sterling would have loved playing in such a place as a boy. And she wondered about the secret life of the lithe creature she had seen writhing on-stage at the Ham Palais.

It was only a bit later Sarah-Jane found out that there was no basement at Gen's old house in Beck Road. The feverish local rumours about his Satanic blood-letting activities were largely invention, the mischaracterisation of an old TOPY performance art video which had been chopped out on the TV news and labelled a homemade kiddie porn tape. It was true that there had been a Special Branch raid on 50 Beck Road, but this was back in the 1970s, during the time Gen's mail was being opened by the Post Office. Gen had actually moved out of Beck Road many years ago, in 1987.

Even so, the local legend of Genesis and Thee Temple ov Psychick Youth died hard. It became part of the gothic back-story of London Fields, along with the plague pits and the *Luftwaffe* bombing raids, casting a spell of sinister glamour over an area which by 1993 was being colonised by the likes of Tracey Emin and her young-British-artist pals.

As the trains clattered over the arches towards Liverpool Street on the old Great Eastern Railway, Sarah-Jane found out some of the truth about the Temple from the old boys who lingered in Brougham Road. They became animated when she brought out her copy of *Thee Grey Book*, pointing out the most useful pages, reading bits out aloud, talking of Austin Osman Spare, chaos magick and the value of occult belief as a tool for self-determination. She learned that there were five religious grades within the Temple, known as "Ratios", and that she was at Ratio Zero, because she had not been initiated.

When Sarah-Jane asked what someone had to do to become a member of the Temple, the old boys looked at each other with pained expressions. One, whose occult name was EDEN 36, said that Gen had dissolved the Temple a couple of years ago and even hired lawyers to protect the use of its logo. He was living in America now. Another old boy, EDEN 35, scoffed and flashed his signet ring, which was mounted with the three-barred logo. I'd like to see Gen take that away from me, he said. The scumbag! EDEN 35 said that the Temple was still going, Gen couldn't shut it down, it belonged to its members. The rituals were still intact. There was nothing to stop anyone from doing the rituals themselves.

So what do I do? said Sarah-Jane. She was curious. EDEN 35 shifted on his haunches and said that she had to write down her most obscene sexual fantasy in a letter addressed to TOPY. It doesn't have to be sexual, said EDEN 36. It can be any kind of fantasy, so long as it excites the deepest part of yourself. So it can be a homicidal fantasy? said Sarah-Jane. She had decided to test the old boys. EDEN 35 had got up to beg for spare change from passers-by. EDEN 36 leaned in close to Sarah-Jane. His breath smelled of peppermint. You just have to be honest with yourself, he said. That's the real magic, naming your unconscious desire. EDEN 35 was back, empty-handed. Cunts! he said, shaking his head at the disappearing couple.

Once you've written the letter, you have to seal it with your own blood, said EDEN 36. Menstrual blood! said EDEN 35. Technically, yes, said EDEN 36. Menstrual blood. Combined with your own piss and spit. I see, said Sarah-Jane. And you have to do it on a night of the full moon, said EDEN 35. Well, not necessarily, said EDEN 36, noting Sarah-Jane's bafflement. It's really about creating a suggestible atmosphere, something that opens your mind and enables your unconscious desire to be launched into the world. EDEN 35 snorted. That's a weak explanation, he said. The bodily fluids, the moonlight – these are vitally important. He looked into Sarah-Jane's eyes. The initiate, he said, has to call up the forces of the cosmos and press them into the service of his or will. That way, the circuit will be complete and their deepest desire will be fulfilled. EDEN 35 rocked back on his heels.

"Lady" Sarah-Jane's legs were hurting from squatting on the pavement for so long. Sounds a bit too good to be true, she said. Magick works, said EDEN 35, shrugging. It's true, said EDEN 36. Nobody really knows why it works, not even Gen. But as Crowley said, if you do certain things, certain results will follow. Sarah-Jane stood up. Can I keep this? said EDEN 35 about her copy of *Thee Grey Book*. Sure, said Sarah-Jane. Don't forget the most important thing, said EDEN 35, looking up. The charm of numbers! You have to do the ritual 23 times, each instance on the 23rd of the month. EDEN 36 was shaking his head again. And then you'll have done it. You'll be a TOPY member, like us. Will I be called EDEN? said Sarah-Jane. No, you'll be a KALI, said EDEN 35. Girls are called KALI. But we don't know what number she'll be, said EDEN 36. Nobody's keeping count since Gen closed the membership list. Scumbag! said EDEN 35. He spat on the pavement.

Sarah-Jane lingered, her back to the wall. Did she want to trade being a "Lady" for being a "KALI"? She noticed some old graffiti on the sun-lit brick-work, "TG" painted in white. No doubt why the old boys were squatted here. She listened to them talk. You remember how much fan mail Gen used to get? said EDEN 36. The filing cabinets were over-flowing at Beck Road. I remember the letters from TOPY applicants, said EDEN 35. All those kids wanking away their lonely nights at boarding school. You shouldn't have opened their letters, said EDEN 36. Hey, don't blame me, said EDEN 35. Gen shouldn't have opened them either. They were meant to be used, sealed, as mediums of cosmic energy in TOPY rituals. That's right, said EDEN 36. But then, Gen was always allowed to break his own rules, wasn't he? said EDEN 35. He had a special dispensation. He did what he wanted.

Sarah-Jane drifted away from the two squabbling priests. She found herself in front of 50 Beck Road. The front door was still painted black, but now there were curtains in the windows. The whole road was smartening up. She had been told that Helen Chadwick, an old friend of Cosey's, a fellow artist, continued to live on the street somewhere. "Lady" Sarah-Jane fantasised about meeting her, perhaps at the bus stop. She had read somewhere about the bronze sculptures Chadwick had cast from the holes she had made in the snow one night, when she squatted outside to piss. The whole performance intrigued Sarah-Jane. Here was a way, she thought, for a woman to make a statement about the human body without having to expose her own body. It was a performance, but also an avoidance. A way to exhibit yourself, thought Sarah-Jane, without having to deal with the gender issue which always dogged women. It was at that moment, outside Gen's old place, that she decided to retire "Lady" Sarah-Jane from the stage.

She packaged up the 35mm slides of her striptease actions and submitted them to the Royal College of Art as part of her application to do an MA on Fine Art. As it turned out, Helen Chadwick was on the interview panel, sporting glossy black bob and Russian Red lipstick. She asked Sarah-Jane a question about Bataille and Sarah-Jane answered with an anecdote about how Soutine used to haul animal carcasses into his studio from the Paris slaughterhouses. That went down well. She was accepted by the college. One of her ex-clients arranged for her fees to be paid from an oil company bursary. She felt that her life might be finally coming together.

I met "Lady" Sarah-Jane during the first year of her course. We literally bumped into each other one week-day afternoon in the ICA bookshop, a circumstance which could have felt like the forced hand of chance at work, were it not for the fact that the space was so cramped. I was flipping through the cyber-culture books on the new releases table. She was slipping a volume into her big hand-bag. Our elbows touched. There was a quick apology on my part. She glared at me and stalked off. I paid the cashier for the stolen book.

I caught up with her at the empty bar and gave her the receipt. She was contemptuous of what she imagined to be my gallantry, saying that shop-lifting was righteous theft. But she let me buy her a drink. A Britvic orange juice. I had a non-alcoholic drink as well, not wanting to appear a lout. She perched on a bench in the corner, like a delicate little bird, her solemn eyes viewing me from over the rims of her big, black glasses. She was draped in a red Westwood jacket. Her whole look was precarious, an obvious construct. I could see it collapsing around her at any moment. I feared for her safety.

She showed me the book she had taken. *The Kristeva Reader*. I said something about the exhibition of abject art at the Whitney in New York a few years before. I mentioned Mary Kelly's dirty nappies. "Lady" Sarah-Jane shook her head. She said someone like me could have a mere abstract knowledge of abjection. She said that the display of shit, blood and guts at the Whitney was more than a pile of refuse. It was a reminder of lived reality for some people. I nodded. She laughed and flashed me her broken teeth. The silver stud in her tongue seemed to wink at me.

Intellectuals don't really understand abjection, said "Lady" Sarah-Jane. Abject materials, in Kristeva's formulation, were products of the body that had to be considered waste in order for the mind to be sure of its own domain. Piss and blood, she said, in their power to disgust, had an almost built-in psychological authority, a counter-authority to that of the mind. This was all connected at the deep level, the Freudian level, with the child's struggle to free themself from what they felt to be the mother's threatening body – the hairy cunt, the milky breasts, the scratching finger-nails. Ugh! "Lady" Sarah-Jane shivered. She said that some mothers, of course, fully matched the nightmare image their children had of them. What do you do with that? she said.

I shrugged. You make a symbol out of it, she said, running her tongue against her teeth. A feminist symbol. I wanted to point out she was contradicting herself, but held back, out of courtesy. Sara-Jane's eyes were closed, she was ecstatic. I wondered, quite absurdly, if she were having an orgasm. She opened her eyes and smiled. Kristeva wouldn't like that, she said, as if reading my mind. Turning the fantasy of the all-consuming mother into a Jungian symbol. But I think we have to symbolise female-based anxieties at some point. Otherwise, we're just left playing in the blood and the dirt. We have to find a way to beat men at their own game, eh? She gently punched me in the arm.

I asked what she thought of the painting of Myra Hindley which was on show at the Royal Academy on Piccadilly, a huge portrait of the child-killer based on her police mug-shot. Myra wasn't a mum, she said. But she played the role of the mother with Brady's victims, she coaxed the kids into his embraces. So, yeah, I approve of the work. It gives us the symbol we need, as a culture, to model the fear of the archaic mother, the killer mother, what Sylvia Plath called the "mother of shadows." But I don't like the fact that the painterly marks on the canvas are composed of a child's hand-prints. There's a note of Christian moral protest creeping in there. Sickening! As if women are not loaded up with enough guilt. She was angry.

"Lady" Sarah-Jane packed up her bag. The yelping oscillations of the Chemical Brothers' "Private Psychedelic Reel" blasted out of the bar's speakers. The sitar loop broke over the surging noise and "Lady" Sarah-Jane did a little wiggle. She smiled at me and left.

We saw each other many times after that. We entered into a sexual relationship. But that's not what I want to discourse about here. I want to focus on her TOPY scrapbook, *My Perfect Cult Hell*, which she was working on for her degree show project. In her first year, she had already received good notices from her tutors for her Rose West scrapbook. They nodded when she said it was an exploration of the mythos of the "mother of shadows" based on Fred West's story that it was his wife and not he who had murdered their 15-year-old daughter Heather. They nodded even more when she said she intended to reclaim a traditionally female collage aesthetic from the dismissive gaze of powerful male critics.

For her TOPY project, she upped her game. Her so-called scrapbook was actually a black leather portfolio with a brass lock. She showed it to me one evening at Brougham Road. I examined its contents under the kitchen light. There were 23 works on paper, each bagged inside a polythene sheath. "Lady" Sarah-Jane explained the concept behind the work. It was what she imagined Heather West might have fashioned if she'd applied to join Thee Temple of Pyschick Youth in 1986.

Okay, I said, as I leafed through the portfolio. The works featured various found items — music paper items on Psychic TV, photos of a naked female slumped in bins and basements, her head wrapped in layers of tape, repeated uses of the school portrait photo of Heather West, the one where she looks out nervously at the world from beneath her gypsy-black fringe, photos of the forbidding black door at 50 Beck Road and lots and lots of typed notes. Each work was smeared with a dark substance which I could only assume was blood. I didn't know what to say. "Lady" Sarah-Jane watched me squirm. She knew the work was good.

In the end, she took pity on me, brought a chair next to mine, sat down, and took me through the work in detail, her beguiling profile just inches away. She explained that each work was a fantasy, from Heather's point of view, of what it might be like to lead a fulfilled life at 50 Beck Road as a TOPY member. In a more technical sense, each work represented an idea of a TOPY ritual. "Lady" Sarah-Jane explained that she had invented these ideas based on a late-night viewing of *Mondo Cane* and a quick dip into Frazer's *Golden Bough*. She said that in her version of TOPY, there were five initiation rituals. Her fingers had stopped at a work featuring a photo of the naked hooded female — immediately recognisable to me as "Lady" Sarah-Jane herself — suspended by ropes from a ceiling. They were slip knots, she said, giving me a reassuring touch.

She said that the title of this particular work was *Ascension to Ratio 5*. Heather was dreadfully abused by her mother, she said. And I imagined her wanting to replay those traumatic experiences in the controlled environment of Beck Road, where she could give them a new, positive meaning. "Lady" Sarah-Jane smiled. She was quite serene.

"Lady" Sarah-Jane turned to the next work in the portfolio. *Collective Worship of the Master*. It featured a newsprint column review of a Psychic TV gig, together with a candid Polaroid photo of an off-stage Gen merrily gurning. There was also a black-and-white newspaper photo of a crowd of excited kids in jeans and nylon jackets being held back by police outside Dewsbury Magistrates' Court. One of the children at the front had her face scrawled out with a biro. The whole work was soiled with bloody thumb-prints. "Lady" Sarah-Jane told me this was one of a number of works devoted to the idea of Gen as a cult leader.

She flipped to another work. A mating ritual, she said. It featured passport-sized photos of Heather West and Gen, side by side. There was shit smeared everywhere. *The Marriage of KALI and EDEN*, said "Lady" Sarah-Jane. She said she'd also done works on what she thought Heather might imagine to be a TOPY conception ritual, a TOPY baptism ritual and a TOPY infanticide ritual. Infanticide? I said. Naturally, said "Lady" Sarah-Jane. A beautiful and loving ritual conducted on behalf of KALI when she has to kill her child. Why would she have to do that? I asked. The portfolio closed before me. Because she might not want it, of course. An infanticide ritual would have to be conducted before the child was baptised into the faith of the Temple. *In utero*, ideally. But not necessarily, I said. Right, said "Lady" Sarah-Jane. Not necessarily. Although I haven't worked out the technical details. She was gritting her teeth.

Was Sarah-Jane trolling me? I couldn't tell. She asked whether I'd seen Helen Chadwick's show in Edinburgh a couple of years before, her last show, put on just before she died. I confessed that I hadn't. "Lady" Sarah-Jane said I should look up the catalogue. Beautiful photographs, she said. Taken at the IVF clinic at King's College Hospital. Photographs of dead human embryos. Makes you wonder what kind of photos could be taken at an abortion clinic, doesn't it? she said. Does it? I said. Why shouldn't abortion be made into a sacrament? she said. That's part of what I'm trying to say with *Infanticide Ritual for KALI*. Do you want to see the work? She made as if to re-open her portfolio. I grabbed her by the wrist, said I'd had enough. She remained silent.

Our relationship ended soon afterwards. I guess she wanted a sexual partner with more of an appetite for her work, whose libertinism had an almost Gnostic flavour. Or maybe she was secretly looking for a strong man, an uncomplicated man, to finally put an end to her self-development. Either way, I was too feeble.

I didn't go to her degree show. I heard *My Perfect Cult Hell* got bought by Saatchi. It apparently sat in a warehouse in East London for many years. Before it had a chance to be exhibited in his gallery, it got burned up in a fire.

I kept looking out for Sarah-Jane's name in *Frieze* during the noughties. But she seemed to have faded from public view. One November night in 2016, I waited outside the Shepherd's Bush Empire and watched all the grey-faced, middle-aged people file inside to see Psychic TV perform one last time. This was a year before Gen was diagnosed with the leukemia that would go on to kill him. He sported long blonde hair and said he was "pangender". He went by a variety of pronouns. Some of the old mischief was still there, no doubt. But "Lady" Sarah-Jane was a no-show. When the doors of the Empire shut, I ripped up my tickets and went home.

For many years, I had a recurring dream about Sarah-Jane. We are trapped in a flooded basement, trying to get out. The water is up to our waists and there is an old corpse bobbing about in the

darkness, somewhere. We are arguing with each other, screaming in each other's faces. In the end, I push "Lady" Sarah-Jane up
against a wall and start to fuck her. She sobs in my arms. She calls
out Gen's name. Then I wake up.

BILLY DE VERE, ESQ

Designer of the Beatles Tarot

MY MOST ENDURING MEMORY OF BILLY DE VERE is of a big English-man striding across the motorway landscape gardens of Cobham Services as if he had just come down from the Surrey Hills. With his long black coat and his frizzy hair knotted in ribbons, he cut an imposing figure against the orange glow of the slip-road sodium lamps. There was the flash of his belt-buckle, the flit of his rings, as he leaned into the open windows of the parked cars to hawk his wares. It was a summer's night at the back-end of the '80s.

Billy dispensed more than tabs of MDMA and wraps of amphetamine sulphate. He also — as I was to learn — had the inside dope on the '60s counter-culture, its myths, legends, sick jokes and tall tales. The teenie girl psychos of the Manson Family, according to Billy, were the Beatles' most adept disciples. Their killing spree in the Hollywood Hills was the purest manifestation of Beatlemania. While the Beatles themselves were an occult psychological operation. The long hair! The blasphemy! The promotion of drugs! The celebration of black music! The teen girl frenzy! It was all intended to break the morale of the United States Bible Belt. Billy had developed a crackpot Beatles mythology way more detailed than anything dreamed of by Lyndon La-Rouche. And I was to hear more about it than I ever wanted to know. That night, though, I was with a gang of pals and we just wanted to get off our heads.

Our car was stopped on the forecourt of the shuttered petrol station, next to the pay-phone booth. John Boy had just bought his Ford Escort XR3i. It was black and shiny. Amy and I sat in the back. "French Kiss" was churning out of John Boy's tape-deck. The groove was infectious, unrelenting, punctuated with sudden tempo changes and the orgasmic moaning of a female vocalist. We all nodded along. We were waiting for the pay-phone to ring. It would give us the location of the local farmer's field where the unlicensed rave was going to be held.

Billy poked his head in our window. All sorted for billywhizz? His weather-beaten face was trimmed with a moustache and mutton-chops. He looked like an old hippie biker. John Boy turned down the music and bought some Es off the guy, mainly to get rid of him. But Billy had taken a shine to us and was hanging around. Better watch it, people, he said, thumbing his Zippo to light a giant-size spliff. I seen the Old Bill prowling around over at the McDonald's. Fuck! said John Boy. Calm down, said Amy. Maybe they're just going for an Egg McMuffin at the end of their shift. Aye, maybe, said Billy, laughing. And maybe they've been paid off by the posh-boy promoters who are making thousands of pounds off the acid house party you'll be wanting to go to. A faint Merseyside lilt was detectable beneath the Estuary English vowel sounds. You ever think of that?

Billy was all smiles but his eyes were solemn and dark. He passed the joint to John Boy, who took a token drag, coughed, and passed it back to Amy and me. Billy smoked hash rather than weed, which was a bit of a change for the three of us. But we coped. Soon, John Boy had opened the car door so the joint could go round more easily. It was then that Billy, with his "I am the Walrus" badge and anarchy-logo pendant, zoomed into focus for me as more than just a shambling relic from subcultures past. He was a survivor from London's underground scene, a stroller of the freak-ways, a collector of old dope tales.

The Baphomites want you young ones to get used to living in fields on a diet of pharmaceutical drugs, he said, licking the edge of his rolling paper. The Baphomite Order was his name for it, that secret nexus of controlling social forces which Ken Kesey had called the Combine and which was known more simply by us as the System or even just the Powers That Be. Billy had pieced together a whole political philosophy of the Baphomites, but he didn't get into it all that night. Instead, he gave us a few tantalising fragments. The Baphomites were actually pretty cool with big illegal raves happening in the disused spaces around London's M25, he said. It was part of a secret resettlement plan. The raves were just the start of it. A rehearsal for future living.

Bring it on, I said. A world without work where we can party all day and all night. A rock'n'roll utopia! Could be, could be! said Billy, who was already building another monster spliff. Or it could be a disco version of Khmer Rouge collectivisation in the countryside. An urban population decanted into the muddy trenches beyond London's orbital motorway system, struggling to survive while being bombarded with a steady stream of hypnotic sounds and catch-phrases. He winked at us.

That's cra-azy, man! said Amy. Is it, is it? said Billy. Once Bush has won the Cold War, the Baphomites will move in and run the whole world as one big Peoples Temple, heavier than anything

Jim Jones could have imagined when he was doing his suicide rap in front of the faithful in the jungles of Guyana. It'll be a real trip! A new world order of sex, drugs and recreational killing, he said. That will be the time when the Baphomites will come out into the open and decriminalise all of its global rackets.

Putting you out of work, I said. Billy shrugged. He said he could always get a consultancy gig. He had plenty of experience. The second spliff went round.

The thing is, said Billy, that the Baphomites expect to rule through the imposition of polymorphous perversity, see? And that's because they are basically a bunch of degenerates. Look at Bush. He was a member of the Skull and Bones secret society at Yale University and their initiation rituals were loaded with gay sex and black magic. Amy shot me a warning look. Not that there's anything wrong with gay sex and black magic, said Billy, noting Amy's reaction. He drew heavily on the spliff. Quite the contrary. It's just that the Baphomites pretend they're so bloody virtuous when they're probably, let's face it, into Satanic ritual child abuse and shit like that.

Gross! said Amy. I said that Billy was pushing a sinister conspiracy theory. He shrugged. The Baphomite Order, the Grand Lodge of London and Westminster, the Order of Saint John, call it what you want he said. They exist and they run things behind the scenes. Like the Elders of Zion? said Amy, who was becoming a tiny bit angry. No need to bring God's special people into it, said Billy, with an offended air. If you want to get sociological, look instead at the British aristocracy. Ever wondered why they have those buck-toothed equine faces? It's because they're actually Dutch. They came over with King Billy when he invaded

Britain in 1688 and have been busy little bastards ever since. Shell, Unilever, right? Both creations of the Anglo-Dutch oligarchy. He expelled a pillar of smoke from his wide nostrils.

Good gear, said John Boy, who had the joint. Tell me about it, said Billy. Here's my pager number. He gave John a playing card. Wow, cool man! said John, turning it over to inspect the design. Let's have a look, I said. Billy passed the card back to me. And that was my first introduction to Billy's Beatles Tarot. An experiment in magical thinking which, while almost disastrous for Billy personally, represented an intriguing addition to the ever-expanding folksonomy of the world's most famous rock band.

On one side of the card was a circle containing the famous drop-T BEATLES logo and the word TAROT spelled out in the same typeface. At the base of the card, was a name — BILLY DE VERE, ESQ — and contact number scrawled in red magic marker. On the other side of the card was a pencil tracing of the famous photo on the sleeve of the "Red Album" of the Fab Four looking down over the stairwell in EMI House. Clean black lines on a white background, with minimal detail. The legend at the bottom of the picture read simply: "EMI: The Chariot".

Nice, I said, handing the card back to John Boy. But what does it mean? It means you should remember to call my number the next time you want to get sorted, said Billy. No really, though, I said. I was already getting hooked on what Billy had to tell me about the secret meaning of the Beatles.

Electric and Musical Industries were the vehicle chosen by the Baphomites to launch the Beatles in the US, said Billy. 73 million views on *The Ed Sullivan Show* in 1964. A third of the American population. The biggest exercise in mass media brainwashing the world had ever seen. Made the Nuremberg Rallies look like a chimps' tea party. And all delivered on a tiny budget by the cultural warfare boffins at EMI House.

Okay, I said. I'll bite. Cultural warfare. An aspect of the Cold War, right? The active ingredients of the dope were rearranging certain parts of mind. I was now prepared to believe Billy had discovered a great secret about the British record label which had signed the Beatles in 1962. Not Cold War, said Billy, his voice burrowing into my ear. The American Civil War. Uh, okay, I said. The war that never really ended, said Billy.

You see? said Billy, who had settled on his haunches in the car-park. The American Civil War was essentially a trade war between the Baphomite Order and Abraham Lincoln's Republican Party. The Baphomites were in favour of free trade on a global scale. Always have been. While Lincoln was an upstart American protectionist. He threatened the investments the Baphomites had made in the cotton plantations of the South, okay? You know, through their Yankee banks in New England and New York — or should I say New Amsterdam, huh? He winked again.

The Anglo-Dutch oligarchy, John Boy said, obediently filling in the blanks in Billy's discourse. Exactly, said Billy, slapping his thighs. Exact-a-fucking-mundo. The Beatles were a part of the Baphomites' secret war on FDR's New Deal, okay, which was trying to make good on Lincoln's old promise of industrial development for the South. Don't you get it? The Beatles spearheaded the return of Anglo-Dutch laissez-faire capitalism in the US.

So, I said, joining up the dots in my head, the Beatles were an emergent form of Reaganite neoliberalism? Um, said Billy, suddenly baffled by the implications of his own logic. He looked over at the distant glow of the McDonald's, as if for inspiration. There are rumours that John Lennon was a closet Reagan supporter in 1980, said Amy. Exactly, said Billy who was up on his feet. He appeared distracted.

Hey, can I have a card as well, said Amy, sensing Billy was about to leave. Sure, little dudes. Have one each. He flung a couple of cards into the back of the car. Just think of me as the Fifth Beatle, he said. And with that, he was gone. Are the cops coming? I said. Nah! said John Boy, looking into his rear-view mirror. He pulled the car door shut.

Hey, I've got Ringo, said Amy, looking at the card she'd just picked up from the back-seat. "The Fool". What have you got? she asked me. I picked up the third card, which had landed at my feet. It showed a black-and-white pencil portrait of Paul McCartney with the legend "The Twins". McCartney's face had been split down the middle and the then swapped around, so there were two half-portraits side by side, as if he had dissociated. I showed it to Amy. It's the sleeve design from Macca's second solo album, she said. Amy was a bit of a rock geek. The back-cover, in fact.

Are the pictures all takes on Beatles album covers? said John Boy. Amy showed her card around. Think so, she said. The card featured a pencil sketch of Ringo's face from the *With the Beatles* album cover, the one where he was set apart from his band mates, his white face half obscured in shadow — looking like a turtlenecked Harlequin, a mod trickster. Ringo the Fool, I said.

He was certainly a lucky bugger, said John Boy. I mean he landed the job of drumming for the band just seconds before they broke big. And all because EMI didn't like the look of Pete Best. Poor bastard! Fancy getting stabbed in the back like that. The Beatles wouldn't have lasted as long as they did without Ringo, said Amy. His jokes and stupid antics eased the tensions in the band. Without Ringo, the band would have broken up years earlier. She asked me what I thought. I shrugged.

Hey, anyone know what Ringo's favourite Beatles song was? said Amy, still pushing her knowledge of rock trivia. The one about the Octopus? said John Boy. The one about the Walrus, I said. Neither, said Amy. It was "Rain". Never heard of it, said John Boy. The B–side of "Paperback Writer", said Amy.

I said that the coolest thing about Ringo Starr was his name. It was a throwback to the Larry Parnes era of manufactured rockers like Billy Fury and Marty Wilde. But it also felt a bit like a proto-punk move, a self-invented alias to rank alongside Captain Sensible or Joe Strummer.

Better than Richard Starkey, anyway, said John Boy. He looked a little glum. You both got good ones. Why couldn't I have got John Lennon? Or George Harrison? No one gives a shit about EMI. Don't forget it's the Chariot in the Beatles Tarot, said Amy, as if she were already an expert in Billy's system. Must be a reference to your new car. Holy shit, said John Boy. Have we just got a reading for the evening? The XR is going to take us to a magic place where we'll meet a couple of sexy twins and a clown. We all laughed.

The police arrived a few minutes after Billy's departure. They dispersed all the cars parked at Cobham Services with a flurry of cautions and radio chatter. If the call had come later that night, we wouldn't have known about it. It would have rung out from the pay-phone over an empty forecourt.

Looking back, Billy's Beatles Tarot was almost a joke religion, like Discordianism or Church of the SubGenius. At least, that's my hope. I like to think of it as a culture-jamming tactic designed to undermine belief in any and all magical systems — especially ones focused on an elite cabal of occultists running the world. What it was to Billy remains an open question.

But then, Billy was a difficult man to get to know. He even went by a fake name. Billy de Vere, who claimed to be the impoverished younger son of English landed gentry, was actually Billy Freedman, the son of German Jewish refugees. Michael Friedmann and Hannah Rubenstein both came to Britain from Nuremberg in 1939 as a result of the Refugee Children Movement. Eventually, they married and settled in Sefton, a well-heeled Merseyside suburb, where Michael became a psychoanalyst. Hannah's uncle Maurice joined them in Liverpool after the war. He had survived confinement in Belsen. Hannah's husband offered him a room in their family home, but Morrie, as he was known, preferred to take a bedsit in Toxteth, saying he liked to be close to the Princes Road Synagogue for its beautiful architecture. Billy came along in 1955, the youngest of three children.

Billy was mad on the Beatles when he was a kid, just like everyone else. However, Billy had the distinction of joining the fan club, signed up as he was by his teenage sisters. *Help!* was the last Beatles album they brought home. After that, they stopped buying pop music. Soon enough, Billy started going to Merchant Taylors' Boys' School. The next time the Beatles entered his life was when Morrie brought him a copy of *Sgt Pepper's Lonely Hearts Club Band* in hospital.

Crohn's disease was the bane of Billy's life, though when he was first admitted to Myrtle Street Children's Hospital at the age of 13 it was called a chronic inflammation of the digestive tract. Billy told me that for many months he was confined in a small dark ward suffused with the sickly-sweet smell of unopened bowels and floor wax. He was subject to a regime of laxatives, barium meals and X-Rays. He lost a lot of weight.

An old porter used to hang around his bed a lot, asking him which of the nurses he fancied and sneaking him cigarettes. One night, he offered to take Billy down to the Myrtle Street basement on a tour of the pathology department's collection of specimens. Jars and jars of dead babies there were, he said. Dating back years. One of the sisters on the ward over-heard him and shoo-ed him away. She told Billy to take no notice, as she plumped his pillow. The old porter was a drunkard and should have been sacked years ago.

Morrie came to visit Billy in hospital to teach him the Talmud. Billy's parents didn't go to shul and weren't particularly religious. Morrie, however, maintained that studying for bar mitzvah offered the most rigorous mental fitness test possible for a young man, one that could not be bettered – even by the Jesuits. Morrie himself was an old communist, a Trotskyite in fact. He still carried his KPD card and spoke of the Reichstag Fire as if it had happened yesterday. In fact, much of what passed for Billy's education in the Talmud was Morrie's imaginary settling of old scores with the high command of Nazi Germany. He said that Hitler hated the Jews only because he envied them. After all, said Morrie, the Jews were the original master race. Our rituals select men for their brains and women for their beauty. Those that could never make the grade, like Hitler, those were the real *Untermensch*. Which is why it was important, said Morrie, for Billy to memorise the 613 laws of the torah.

When Billy complained to his mother that he found the visits of great-uncle Morrie a bit disturbing, she said the family had to make allowances for him. She said Morrie had been through a lot in the camps, that his wife was missing, presumed dead, and that he was suffering from what psychiatrists called "survivor guilt". When Billy put this to Morrie, he snorted in derision and said that the goyim would take any chance they could to feel sorry for the Jews. When we have inspired all the great political revolutions in history! he said. His shock of white hair almost crackled in the daytime twilight of the ward. And do we get any thanks for this? No, of course not. But that's probably just as well. He was calming down. Why make yourself a target? Better to stand at the back.

The copy of *Sgt Pepper's* was a gift from Billy's eldest sister. Morrie watched Billy open it. There was no record player on the ward, but Morrie said it didn't matter. The latest Beatles album was not that different from any other Beatles album in his opinion. Billy was shocked. He objected as vehemently as he could. Morrie raised his voice. He said Billy should read Adorno's note, "On popular music". All pop music was standardised. It was the same simple chord progressions over and over again. In the super-market, on the train, on the radio. Billy needed to open his ears to some twelve-tone serialism.

In a way, Morrie was right. Billy didn't need to listen to *St Pepper's*. But only because the collage-based sleeve design offered rich enough pickings for the imagination on its own. It featured the Beatles posing in Edwardian military uniform, alongside cut-outs of fifty or so figures drawn from mass culture. Billy recognised Monroe, Brando and Laurel and Hardy. Years later, he discovered that John Lennon, in typically provocative fashion, had wanted Hitler on the cover. Billy was only too pleased that the record company had slapped him down, otherwise he couldn't imagine the tirade it would have prompted from Morrie. As it was, Morrie was quick to pick out Marx, Einstein, Freud and Jung. But he still had complaints. Why no Adorno? he said. Why no Marcuse? They surely belonged in any secret society worth a damn.

Billy explained that the Beatles weren't interested in outing a cabal of hidden persuaders. They were playing a game of influences. And maybe not even their own game. They appeared on the cover as a fictional band, after all. But Morrie was having none of it. If Sgt Pepper's Lonely Hearts Club Band was a front-group for the Beatles, he said, then who were the Beatles a front-group for? Billy admitted it was a good question.

The nurses swished around Billy and his precious copy of *Sgt Pepper's* when Morrie wasn't there. They told him stories about how Myrtle Street had treated each of the Beatles at different times when they were children. George had been admitted with a swollen kidney when he was 12 or 13, said one. No, said another, that happened at Alder Hey Children's Hospital up the road. She knew that because her aunt worked there and the nurses had had a whip-round to buy the young lad his first guitar. Her aunt had known Paul's mum, who had trained at Alder Hey. One thing all the nurses agreed on, though, their rubber soles squeaking on the terrazzo floor, was that Ringo had been in Myrtle Street when he was a nipper. This very ward, in fact. His appendix burst and he was in a coma for weeks. The doctors only just saved his life. Imagine! they said. No Myrtle Street no Ringo, no Ringo no Beatles, no Beatles no *Sgt Pepper's*. So where's our credit? said one, tapping the cover of the album.

Morrie collected Billy from hospital when it was time for him to leave. He couldn't wait to get him out of there. Billy remembered standing outside waiting for a taxi, looking back over at the unforgiving Victorian barracks of Myrtle Street, with their soot-covered red-brick walls and tall mournful windows. The rounded frontage seemed to plunge straight into the ground, guarded as it was by thick iron railings. Billy wondered about the racks of specimen jars in the underground corridors. Was such a thing possible? Morrie spat out a strange word. *Kinder-Konzentrationslager!*

Things changed quickly after that. Billy's father moved away, his mother went out to work and Morrie disappeared from his life. He never did do his bar mitzvah. He didn't even take his O-Levels. When Paul McCartney announced the break-up of the Beatles in 1970, Billy dropped out of school. That summer, he hitch-hiked his way to the Phun City festival on the south coast of England and never went home again. He shared a tent on Ecclesden Common over the July weekend and rocked out to the MC5. He picked up a copy of *FRIENDS*, the one which labelled Enoch Powell an "enemy of the people" on its front cover, and followed the hippy caravan back to London. He had, as Morrie later put it, "run away to join the circus."

Billy was a fixture on the Ladbroke Grove squat scene in the early 1970s. He hung out at the Mountain Grill in Portobello Road and made himself useful to the underground crowd – a little bit of speed dealing, spots of graphic design under Barney Bubbles, some roadie work for Hawkwind. He scribbled a few cartoons here and there after studying the work of *International Times* cartoonist Ray Lowry, whose scratchy visual style he much admired.

One of his favourite places to go was the flat above the head shop in Blenheim Crescent. Its outlandishly painted frontage was a beacon for freaks from miles around and Billy used to love browsing its esoteric collection of books and pamphlets. There were Mike Moorcock science fiction novels, a Paladin copy of Barthes' *Mythologies*, books on occultism, alternative technology and druids, and also various stapled items of kook literature – UFO sighting bulletins, British Israelist almanacs, "orgone energy" pamphlets and Lyndon LaRouche parapolitical zines. Billy filled his head with it all but never managed to systematise it. Like many an autodidact before him, he was long on knowledge and short on judgement.

Billy used to steal some of the obscure items that took his fancy. He was particularly struck by the lurid Evangelical sermons contained in Jack Chick's tracts, miniature action-packed comic-books which portrayed a world full of paranoia where nothing was what it seemed and everything was a potential Satanic plot to lead the unwary to hell. Tools of the devil included the Catholic Church, the Freemasons – fingered by Chick as worshippers of Baphomet — and rock'n'roll bands. On that last note, Billy also ripped off a copy of David A Noebel's 1965 pamphlet "Communism, Hypnotism and The Beatles", which characterised the Fab Four as a Soviet brainwashing operation designed to incite American youth to riot against the government and desecrate the Christian churches.

It was in Ladbroke Grove that Billy came up with his de Vere alias, as a way of either dodging the drug squad or smudging his Jewish origins. Certainly, it was on the fringes of the music business that he encountered for the first time specific resentments associated with the usual generalised anti-Semitism. Bitter anecdotes circulated about how Allen Klein had ripped off the Beatles and Don Arden had burned the Small Faces, with the cynical coda that any Jewish music exec could be expected to do the same to any artist they represented.

To lighten the mood, Billy used to entertain his companions with renditions of scabrous rock'n'roll fables. The one about Led Zep and the dead groupie. Black Sabbath and the haunted album cover. Keith Richards and his mobile blood bank. The one that got the biggest laugh was that the CIA had created the Manson Family as a secret mind control experiment. It's true, Billy would say. They set up a free medical clinic in Haight-Ashbury to attract the hippie runaways and junkies.

It was at this time that Billy began riffing on the myths surrounding the Beatles. He obviously got a lot of mileage out of the notorious "Paul is dead" legend. The original myth-makers claimed Paul had been covertly replaced by a lookalike after a fatal car crash in 1966, a lookalike named Billy Shears, like in the title track on *Sgt Pepper's*. Billy de Vere went a step further.

He reckoned the lookalike was in fact a secret McCartney twin, born alongside Paul in the Liverpool hospital where his mother had worked. Cue much groaning and laughter at the Mountain Grill. Billy insisted with a straight face that the McCartney twin had a longer nose than Paul.

Another of Billy's rhetorical tricks was to join the dots between various Beatles scandals. This was how he concocted his story that "the Beatles are Moloch". He started with the banned cover photo for the US Beatles album release *Yesterday and Today*. It showed the four grinning mop-tops posing in butcher's coats with cigarette-burned doll parts and joints of raw meat. Paul had said, somewhat half-heartedly, that the cover was a protest against US military involvement in Southeast Asia. Billy made the connection instead with John's blasphemous claim that the Beatles were bigger than Jesus. Meaning that the offensive butcher cover, with its suggestions of pagan idolatry and infant sacrifice, was actually an image of Moloch, the Babylonian demon king.

Billy was making all this up for laughs, of course. But he thought enough of his stories to scribble them down on postcards, accompanied by doodles and scratchings, and send them to Bob Rickard's Fortean newsletter, *The News*.

In the white parts of mid-1970s Ladbroke Grove, the end of the hippie scene was morphing into the start of the punk scene. Billy barely changed his style. He didn't even trim his fro. He dealt speed for the Deviants and the 101ers and hung out in the Elgin, a pub notorious for its preening and pretension. He watched Woody Mellor come and Joe Strummer go, he nursed his pint, he put the years on. He went from being the youngest freak on the street to being the oldest hipster in town. He knew it was all over when he got beaten up at a Clash gig.

Bitter and resentful, Billy retired hurt from the scene, burrowed deep into a flat in St Stephen's Gardens and smoked a lot of dope with the curtains drawn. He decided it was time to write a novel. He figured he could manage it, some kind of whacked-out counter-cultural science fiction novel like *The Illuminatus! Trilogy* or Mick Farren's *Texts of Festival*. He could make it a semi-satirical novel about the secret history of the Beatles, he thought. That should shake up all the young punks!

It all clicked for Billy when he discovered that the Beatles promo videos for "Rain" and "Paperback Writer" had been filmed at Chiswick House. This, he discovered, was a fancy villa in West London which had been designed as an unofficial lodge for the Freemasons in 1729. The videos showed the band playing outside in the ornamental gardens, posing languidly among the huge Grecian urns and sightless Roman statues. They wore black suits and turtlenecks, sometimes sunglasses, looking for all the world like the high priests of some enigmatic cult. The Beatles as project of the Freemasons? This, for Billy, was a more promising line of enquiry into a Beatles conspiracy theory than the idea they were the result of some Soviet lab experiment. He remembered Jack Chick's proposition that the Freemasons were secret worshippers of a demon king. Not Moloch, but Baphomet. How would that do?

Billy scrambled for one of the stolen books on his shelf. He flipped the pages until he found Eliphas Levi's famous sketch of Baphomet. Illustrated alongside the monstrous horned god was an image of the Devil card from the Marseille tarot. It showed the horned god attended by two grotesque imps. Billy noticed the tarot devil had an additional face in its belly. Meaning the picture card featured a total of four faces.

Billy had seen *The Manchurian Candidate* and knew from late-night conversations in Blenheim Crescent that the core psychiatric concept of Cold War brainwashing programmes was the group-oriented personality. In the movie, Laurence Harvey's sleeper agent character was easy to manipulate because he was part of a platoon that had been captured and hypnotised. Billy wondered if something similar had happened with the four young men in the Beatles.

He lit a joint and let his mind wander. He reminded himself that the members of the Beatles had all started out as psychologically vulnerable boys in postwar Liverpool. George was only 15 when he joined the band. Paul was motherless. Ringo had an absent father. As for John, he was both motherless and jettisoned by his father, the most neurotic of them all in many ways. They were certainly ideal candidates for psychological manipulation, thought Billy, through their shared membership of a deliberately manufactured and semi-isolated *pseudo-family*.

That was when Billy, his mind racing to join all sorts of hidden dots in the counter-culture, noticed that the picture of the Devil on the tarot card in the book on the floor had an extra set of eyes. Yes, they were definitely there. Eyes on the knee-caps. A fifth face, a hidden face.

This was when Billy first understood the occult significance of the "Fifth Beatle". It manifested the role of the missing mother in the pseudo-family. A role occupied most obviously by Brian Epstein when he stood at the back of the Cavern Club watching his young charges with a glow of pride. But also a role discovered quite intuitively by Astrid Kirchherr in the Kaiserkeller when she dressed her little dolly boys in Reeperbahn leather jackets. A structurally open role then, one played with by George Martin in the Abbey Road studio and exploited by press agent Derek Taylor in the days of the Apple corporation.

In fact, so far as Billy could tell from his gnomic utterances, it was Taylor who had the real handle on the workings of the Beatles as a psychological operation. He reckoned that as a concept the Beatles would only be complete when all four of them had died. So it was early days, thought Billy. And Taylor also understood that the Beatles mythology — with all its fan fiction, rumours and legends — defined a system of archetypes with potentially universal application. Just like the tarot, thought Billy.

Then one day, he got the phone call. Great-uncle Morrie had had a stroke. A minor one. Arrangements had to be made. Once Morrie got out of hospital, Billy ended up caring for him in his little flat. He was back in Liverpool.

Now the roles were reversed. Morrie was in his pyjamas, surrounded by books. Billy was at the bedside. They fell back into their old arguments. Morrie had got into Lyndon LaRouche conspiracy theory, that strange blend of Marxism, anti-Semitism and American nationalism which found a cult following in the 1970s among the intellectually dispossessed. Morrie said that the Jews had always done the dirty work for the European nobility, acting as their tax collectors, bootleggers and extortionists. And what had they got for it? All of the guilt and none of the glory. Billy said he had skimmed a few LaRouche publications in London and that as far as he could tell, LaRouche fixed the ultimate blame for global gangster capitalism less on the Jews and more on an a post-1688 Anglo-Dutch oligarchy. Pfaw! said Morrie

Billy felt that he had to prove to Morrie that his fixation on the historical banking activities of the Montefiores and the Goldsmids and the Sassoons and the Rothschilds was a mistake. He referred to the emerging influence of the Adam Smith Institute and said that LaRouche's Anglo-Dutch oligarchy's success in opening up global markets was based on economic liberalism plus gunboat diplomacy. Not on the Rothschilds. In fact, said Billy, the development of international credit systems – with all that meant for invidious interest payments, exploitation and blackmail – could actually be traced all the way back to the Knights Templar. Here were the original private bankers to kings and popes.

What did the Templars know? said Morrie. They were pagan idol-worshippers! Maybe so, said Billy, remembering his Jack Chick tracts. They were accused of worshipping Baphomet, said Morrie, as if reading Billy's mind. Sodomites! Baphomites! said Morrie, suddenly possessed of all the zeal of an Orthodox rabbi. And weren't they also practitioners of alchemy? Yes, said Billy, now quite glum. Making them either idiots or charlatans, said Morrie. He raised his finger triumphantly.

It was impossible to win against Morrie, Billy knew that. But he gave it one more go. The Templars understood that their letters of credit had value only as a matter of confidence, he said. In themselves, yes, they were worthless pieces of paper. But they could be redeemed for gold at a Templar exchange. Something for nothing. That was the basis of the myth about Templar alchemists. Billy was now definitely making things up, but it all sounded quite plausible.

Even if that were true, said Morrie, the Templars stole the secrets of banking from the Jews when they fled the destruction of Jerusalem in 70 AD. Billy gave up. He remembered what his mother had said about the need to make an exception for Morrie. He had, after all, been through a hell that few would ever experience.

When Morrie died from a massive second stroke in 1987, all arguments were over. Billy helped his family sit *shiva* on comfortable chairs in his mother's large suburban home. His sisters lit the candles and fussed over him. He didn't know what to say.

On the last night of mourning, Morrie came to Billy in a dream. They were back in the old children's hospital on Myrtle Street. The ward was dark and warm, the curtains were closed. Morrie was sat at the bedside of a young boy, six or seven years old, who was pale and weak. The boy wasn't Billy. The name on the clip-board at the end of the bed read "R. Starkey". Morrie wore a white coat. His name badge carried the insignia of the Baphomite Order.

Billy watched, like a ghost, as Morrie showed the boy the Rorschach ink-blots, one after the other. Butterfly, clown, cowboy hat, said the boy. Really? said Morrie. He slapped the boy's face. The little fellow's lower lip trembled. Morrie made coo-ing noises and gave the boy an American comic-book. He flashed Billy a look and said they were testing boys from broken homes. The little boy was sucking his thumb and looking at the action panels in *The Ringo Kid*.

Then they were all downstairs in the toilets of some dank nightclub. A poster on the wall announced that Rory Storm and the Hurricanes were appearing at the Kaiserkeller. The flimsy walls shook from the pounding they were taking from "Blue Suede Shoes" played live upstairs. Slumped against a piss-streaked wall next to the urinals was a gorgeously pompadoured young man, drunk, his collar awry. The drum-sticks were still in his hands.

Morrie had set up a film projector in the stall next to the young man. He was screening an old cowboy film on the lightly painted brick wall opposite. Gregory Peck played a gunfighter by the name of Jimmy Ringo. A left-handed gunfighter. He draws his weapon in a duel at the bar and shoots down the bratty young kid, who was asking for it. "He's got three brothers", warns one of the cowboys in the saloon. Ringo is unconcerned. Morrie plays the scene again. The fatal shot sounds again. Ringo had to do it, said Morrie to the befuddled young man lying on the floor. He was not to blame.

Next, a four-man beat group is wowing the girls at a hall somewhere in the Home Counties. It's the Beatles, no doubt about it. The young man from the Kaiserkeller sits at the drum-kit, hitting the snare left-handedly. Ringo Starr, obviously. Morrie stood at the back of the hall in his white coat, talking to the glossy-haired Brian Epstein. He said the replacement drummer was settling in well. The pseudo-family was complete. Epstein nodded, though whether to Morrie or the beat, Billy couldn't tell.

CBS wants to launch them in America. Morrie was speaking into Epstein's ear so as to be heard above the din of the screaming girls. I've spoken to their top man. William Paley. He was in psy-ops during the war. What? Said Epstein. He's one of us, said Morrie. And at this he turned to tip Billy the wink. All the best people, he said.

Billy woke with the duvet in a tangle. He was sweating. The dream had been so vivid! He lit a last candle for Morrie and let it burn for a day and a night.

It was then that he realised there was no way he could write some wild and crazy novel about the secret history of the Beatles. Even though he certainly liked the sound of the Baphomites as a clandestine sect. He just didn't have the patience to nail down a long-form conspiracy fiction. He preferred to think in anecdotes and images.

Soon after this epiphany, Billy created the first of 22 planned picture cards from his Beatles Tarot. "John Lennon: Death". He lifted the album cover image from Yoko Ono's *Season of Glass*, which featured a photo of Lennon's blood-spattered glasses propped on a window sill next to a half-empty glass of water. In the background was a blurred view of the New York skyline. Yoko had taken the picture from the apartment she had shared with Lennon in the same building outside of which he had been shot and killed only months before by a demented fan.

The second card Billy created was his favourite of them all. "Paul McCartney: The Twins". It seemed to fit. Not just in terms of the Billy Shears lookalike story but also in terms of the many aliases and personas Paul had adopted throughout his career. Signing into hotels as Paul Ramon. Making music as Apollo C Vermouth or Bernard Webb or Percy Thrillington. Writing liner notes as Clint Harrigan. And that was before any consideration of the various roles he had contrived to play down the years — Paul the film-maker, Paul the music mogul, Paul the vegetarian activist, Paul the professional Scouser, Paul the reclusive laird tending his estate on the Mull of Kintyre just south of the Isle of Jura… the identities were legion.

In fact, thought Billy, wasn't multiple personality disorder one of the symptoms associated with people who had been through – or imagined they had been through – secret mind control experiments? He shuddered, thinking that his tarot system was almost starting to convince him of the occult truth of the old Beatles legends.

Billy emerged from suburban exile and returned to London in 1988. He was only in his thirties, but in sub-cultural terms, he was ancient. He dealt ecstasy to the midnight ravers in the rammed warehouse club on Clink Street. He stamped his feet on the cobbles to keep warm and danced in and out of the steam that poured from the gaps in the brick walls. It was then that his tarot cards first started to circulate.

The only other card I really remembered from that time was "George Harrison: The Hermit". It appropriated the photographic portrait of Harrison which was featured on the poster which came with his first solo album. There he was, the Krishna devotee in a black hat, long-haired, bearded, standing in front of the leaded glass windows at his neo-gothic country pile in Oxfordshire. He looked like a male witch.

Billy followed the rave scene out to the forgotten fields beyond the M25. He lived for a time at Cobham Services. But when England's wild and free acid house parties were tamed by 1994's Criminal Justice and Public Order Act, the scene moved back to London and other cities. At that point, it was money-spinning super-clubs that ruled the night. The drugs trade at these new leisure and entertainment venues was controlled by criminal gangs. And they certainly had no place for an independent entrepreneur like Billy. He managed to bump along, though. He told me he was dealing for the K Foundation.

By this time Billy and I had encountered each other enough times on the London launch party circuit to be on speaking terms. He even sent me raw chunks of his autobiography in the hope, as he put it, that I might "polish it up" for publication. I tried to help him as much as I could, but after making enquiries it was clear to me that much of what he had written was fiction. Billy said Feral House wanted to publish his book in the US. But then he lost interest in the whole thing. He went quiet.

I met Billy one last time. It was in the early days of the year 2000, in Borders on the Charing Cross Road. He flopped down beside me on the sofa, looking a bit distracted. His hair was matted and his rings were gone. He said he'd popped into the bookshop to consult the latest revised edition of Ian MacDonald's *Revolution in the Head*, specifically the Beatles chronology at the back. He wanted to check up on Brian Epstein's movements in 1967 in the weeks before he died. I asked whether Billy had done a tarot card for Epstein. No, not yet, he said. He's either the Moon or the Sun, I can't make up my mind. He ran his fingers through his hair.

I asked Billy what was bothering him. He started in on a long monologue about a newspaper story he'd seen a few days before. A frenzied knife attack. On George Harrison at his country house in Oxfordshire. By a maniac. There was blood all over the walls. Billy counted off the coincidences on the fingers of his left hand. The attempted assassin was a Beatles fan. In fact, he thought of himself as the real Fifth Beatle. He was from Liverpool. He'd been in and out of hospitals. And worst of all, he had a Jewish name.

So what, I said. So, said Billy, what if the Baphomite Order – or some CIA equivalent – is using the Jews to take out the Beatles? Had no one thought of that? I pointed out that John Lennon's assassin wasn't a Jew. In fact, he was a Jesus freak. Billy ignored me. He said he thought he might have been brainwashed when he was in the Myrtle Street Children's Hospital. Like in *The Manchurian Candidate*? I said. I'm not fucking joking, said Billy. He said he kept dreaming of Paul McCartney. What did that mean? He was worried he might bump into Paul on the street. What would happen then? Would he, Billy de Vere, be triggered into committing some murderous action?

Perhaps it was inevitable that Billy would find a reason to insert himself into the magical Beatles system he'd created. He'd drawn the Devil card from the tarot deck once too often and spooked himself into a paranoid revisioning of his past and apocalyptic projection of his future. Either that or he was telling one last Beatles sick joke with me as the only audience.

About a year after that strange encounter, Billy came back into my mind. George Harrison had just died from lung cancer. But it wasn't that which had caught my eye in the newspapers. Instead, it was the rash of sensational headlines about the old children's hospitals in Liverpool: "Scandal of the Organ Hoards", "The Basement of Horrors", "The Baby Butcher". A government inquiry had concluded that post-mortem organs had been stored at Myrtle Street for study by an erratic pathology department. There were stories about children's hearts and eyeballs being pickled in jars stored in underground vaults, thousands of them.

It all suggested the existence of a medical culture whose attitudes dated back to the days when corpses were dug up from paupers' graveyards for use in the anatomy theatres.

I wondered what Billy would have made of this. But he had disappeared. All his old haunts in Ladbroke Grove were luxury pit-stops for trendy millionaires and ambitious young Tory politicians. There was no further place for him in England. And so, like a bad dream, he was gone.

HIS MOST REVEREND HIGHNESS D J MENSAH

Creator of the Scratch Perry Space Opera

WHEN I FIRST MET DEREK MENSAH it was 1990 and the British comicbook industry was going through a boom. Brash new action-adventure titles like *Deadline* and *Crisis* were on the newsagent shelves alongside *2000AD*. *Revolver* had just come out, with its stylish neo-psychedelic reworkings of 1960s British pop culture. Independent comics shops Gosh! and Comics Showcase were thriving in London. The Virgin Megastore on Oxford Street had opened a comics section on its first floor. And Forbidden Planet had moved from St Giles High Street to larger premises on New Oxford Street.

I had been invited to FP's Christmas party and was mingling. Dick Jude was busy managing affairs in the background. Igor Goldkind was working the room. Someone said they had spotted Neil Gaiman, but there were a lot of leather-jacketed geeks around that night. People were swapping scurrilous stories about Alan Moore. He was the first British comicbook writer to succeed in America, but had recently quit DC Comics in high dudgeon. I bumped into Derek at the new releases section. He was wearing a Halo Jones T-shirt and leafing through the Christmas issue of *Revolver*. I said I liked the way Grant Morrison had Dan Dare battling a thinly-disguised version of the Thatcher government. He nodded. He said he himself was a fan of Rogan Gosh, Milligan and McCarthy's blue-skinned time traveller from the future.

Derek was down from Bristol, visiting his family in South London. He had blagged his way into the party to promote his self-published comic, *Adventures of Super Ape*. He gave me a copy of the latest issue. It was a black-and-white stripzine with a colour wraparound. The front-cover featured an image of a giant ape, like Mighty Joe Young, battling a humanoid razor-fanged reptile, like the Lizard from *Spider-Man*, except dressed in a velvet top-coat rather than a lab-coat. The break-out cover line read "Storming the Slave Pits!". In the background was a neo-medieval fort with whitewashed walls and long elegant stairways. Derek explained that Super Ape was on a mission to rescue his fellow apemen from Croaking Lizard's lair.

I flicked through the comic. Science-fiction action scenes jumped from planet to planet in a larger cosmos inhabited by apes, lizards and lions. I could see that Derek was borrowing a trick from Art Spiegelman's *Maus*, which had used the tradition of animal comics to create an allegory of obscene history — in his case, the Holocaust of the Jews. It was apparent that Derek might be doing something similar with the history of the transatlantic slave trade. I asked him some questions. He explained that the black lions — who I could see had dreadlocked manes — originally came from Planet Zion, but had been captured by the lizards from Planet Satan. I nodded. The lions had been transported to Babylon, said Derek, which was a planet inhabited by apes. Here, they had been turned into apemen themselves. Super

Ape emerges as a prophet of Zion whose mission it is to rally the apemen and return them to their home planet.

The visual panels were full of baroque spaceships and machine-like skyscrapers. I said they reminded me of Jack Kirby's "Fourth World" comicbook series. Derek was delighted by the comparison. His long, elegant index finger rested on the credits box adorning the splash page. "Story by Mensah & Walker", it read. Derek said that Nicky Walker was a visual artist from Bristol. He had been busted for graffiti offences the previous year. Should be a good journalistic angle, no? Derek was leaning into me. I shrugged. So why Super Ape? I asked. A King Kong take on Superman?

Lee Perry, said Derek. Lee Scratch Perry? The record producer and chat-artist involved in every genre of Jamaican music from ska to rocksteady to reggae. The man who had popularised the whole idea of the dub version of a hit single, its experimental B-side, the alternative version of a song drenched in sound effects. Derek was almost rapping himself. Super Ape? He looked at me as if I were retarded. The man behind Bob Marley in the early days, the king of the mixing-desk. The living legend who produced "Complete Control" for the Clash.

I got snappy and said I knew who Lee Perry was. In truth, though, I couldn't have named one of his albums. Derek gave me a squeeze round the shoulder and laughed. It's okay, man. He reached into his bag and gave me a promo 12" in a feature-less sleeve. It was a version of "Any Love", an old Rufus and Chaka soul number. Just to give you an idea of the new Bristol sound, he said. I nodded. At that stage in my career, people were always giving me free stuff. I was used to it. No way was I ready to be impressed by a dance track which had been cut two years ago. Plus, the name of the band seemed a bit suspect. Massive Attack.

Nevertheless, I played the record when I got home. The track was built around a bass-heavy breakbeat with a reggae vibe. But it had an uplifting female vocal that made it feel like a house anthem. I saw it was produced by Smith & Mighty, which reminded me at once of a comicbook credit – like Milligan and McCarthy or, indeed, Mensah and Walker.

Three months later, Massive Attack blew up big with their debut album *Blue Lines*. That made me dig out Derek's creation and give it a proper read. It was then that I noticed the comic's Rasta sub-text. Its freewheeling space-opera storyline barely concealed a deep religious narrative, one which seized upon the fragmentary transatlantic history of the African diaspora and attempted to put it back together in an imaginary homeland.

I had underestimated Derek. I wondered if he would take a follow-up call. He did. In fact, he was very gracious. I said that his comic fitted the graphic novel trend. It was obviously tackling serious themes. We bonded quite quickly after that. Those were the days when comicbook fans still felt part of a secret society, one where the names of its pen-and-ink illuminati were known only to an initiate few. Derek told me his story.

He was born in South London in 1961 and christened Derek Jojo. It wasn't until he was a student that he moved to Bristol as a student. His parents, Emmanuel and Christine, had flown into London from Accra soon after Ghana had gained independence from the UK. The bitter memory of those times hung heavily on his father throughout Derek's childhood. Emmanuel was still railing against the "totalitarian dictatorship" of Nkrumah years after the President of the first republic was ousted in a military coup. He never forgave Nkrumah's socialist government for nationalising – or "thieving", as he put it – his palm oil business. Derek's father taught geography at a public school housed in a grand building on the Victoria Embankment. But he was often away from London on mysterious missions to Sandhurst.

It was left to Emmanuel's wife to get on with the business of raising the family. After Derek's sister Kwasiwa was born, Christine got a job as a midwife at Lewisham Hospital and busied herself with charity work at the local Presbyterian Church of Ghana. When her husband was absent and she needed to make an important decision, she consulted the church pastor. It was as a result of his guidance that Derek got into Battersea Grammar School. The jovial old man told him that the Ghanaians were the cleverest people in Africa. We played the British off against the Portuguese, he said. We played the Americans off against the British. And now we're playing the Soviets off against the Americans. We even, he said with a rather grim twinkle in his eye, made money out of the slave trade. Oh yes, he said, we are certainly a very different breed from the Africans who were shipped to the Caribbean plantations.

This was a distinction that was lost on Derek's white school mates. They assumed he was a second-generation immigrant from the West Indies and were surprised at how well-spoken he was. Even the old Jamaican boys in Brixton Market, clocking his neatly barbered hair and immaculately shined shoes, figured he was a "brought-upsy" young man from Barbados. Meanwhile, the uniformed thugs stationed on the corner of Brixton Road and Gresham Road regularly gave him the cut eye, as he walked past. He was never stopped and searched. But that didn't mean he didn't dread the application of the over-mighty "sus" law. In the end, Derek let all the pre-judgements and the misunderstandings wash over him. People could think all the stupid things they wanted. He didn't care. As his mother always said, the Lord knoweth those who are His.

Derek bonded with his school-friends through a shared interest in the American comic-books imported into the local newsagents' shops. More highly-produced and garish than the British action-adventure comics on the racks, the superhero titles of DC and Marvel offered an escape into a world of fantasy, sensation and four-colour printing. Derek found himself drawn to the pencil-work of Jack Kirby, whose skewed perspectives and distorted action figures dated back to the 1940s. He wasn't as keen as his mates on the photorealist style which was all the rage in the mid-1970s. He enjoyed the delirium and mystery Kirby brought to *Mister Miracle* and *The Eternals*. Soon, he was burrowing his way into Kirby's back-catalogue in the bins at Dark They Were and Golden Eyed in Soho.

Here, he discovered that in the early '70s, Kirby had developed a whole mythology – the "Fourth World" mythology – which was spread across not just *Mister Miracle* but also *The Forever People* and *The New Gods*. He snapped the titles up. The inter-linked tales told a story about a cosmic battle between good and evil represented by the worlds of New Genesis and Apokolips. The Forever People are a group of extraterrestrial superheroes from New Genesis on a mission to oppose agents of Apokolips on Earth. They teleport between planets using an inter-dimensional portal known as the Boom Tube. This idea made a deep impression on Derek. In *Adventures of Super Ape*, a version of the Boom Tube is used by Super Ape to target the apemen who are to be saved from Babylon before its doom and transport them back to Planet Zion.

While in Soho, Derek also bought a rare copy of *Fantastic Four* number 52, by Lee and Kirby. Derek was already a fan of the Black Panther stories appearing in *Jungle Action*. He was thrilled by the fact that the 1966 issue of *Fantastic Four* was where the black African superhero had made his comicbook debut. Derek fancied he saw something of himself in the enigmatic image of the Black Panther on the front cover. Here was a masked figure in a black cape leaping across a spaceship, looking for all the world like Batman's superbad elder brother. Rather than living in Gotham City, though, he came from the fabled African kingdom of Wakanda, depicted by Kirby as a gleaming technopolis on a par with New Genesis. The Accra which Nkrumuh had tried and failed to build in Ghana, thought Derek gloomily.

In 1977, there was a big change at Derek's school. It merged with a local girls' school and became Furzedown Secondary School. Derek was a hit with the more adventurous white girls. They assumed he was a bit of a bad lad. As for the *NME*-reading boys in his class, they had just been turned on to Bob Marley by the success of his Lee Perry-produced single "Punky Reggae Party". They pestered him with lots of questions. Was the single as good as Perry's seminal work with Marley ten years ago? Was it true the Clash had originally invited Perry to produce their first album? Why had Marley and Perry left Kingston for London? Was the political violence in Jamaica really that bad? Did Rastas like Marley and Perry still believe that Hailie Selassie, the old Emperor of Ethiopia, had been the Second Coming? He had certainly called himself the Lion of Judah, a Biblical term for Christ, right?

Also, why did Perry have all these nicknames? Scratch, the Upsetter, the Rockstone, Super Ape and all that? What was going on?

Derek didn't have good answers to any of these questions. He was more into synth pop by the likes of Devo and Kraftwerk. He even had a soft spot for Steve Hillage. All he knew about Lee Perry was that an old ska track of his had been used in a Cadbury's "Fruit & Nut" TV ad years ago. As for Marley, he had dutifully listened to his album *Exodus* and pieced together the fact that, like the Biblical Israelites in ancient times, Rastas expected to be led out of Babylon to a new spiritual homeland in Zion. But as to how this would happen, he had little idea. And when Marley sang about Marcus Garvey, Derek had no idea who he was talking about.

Derek's ignorance about Rastafari was understandable given that the pan-Africanism at its heart had always been something scorned by his father. Emmanuel called it the last refuge of the black nationalist scoundrel. He was no doubt thinking of his nemesis President Nkrumah when he said this. What Derek didn't understand until he went to university and studied the subject, was that Nkrumah's interest in forging a collective identity for all Africans was a matter of personal conscience. Nkrumah had picked up the pan-African bug from his youthful study of a Jamaican political activist who believed that blacks from around the world should reunite in an African homeland. The name of this activist was Marcus Garvey, the same Marcus Garvey who had inspired Bob Marley and the original Rastas.

Derek knew none of this as a boy. He didn't know much. When he saw the impassive African-Caribbean boys loitering on Coldharbour Lane in their huge tams with their straggly black beards, he felt an unexpected sense of kinship. At the same time, when his white friends asked him to take them to a blues party on the Railton Road — which they excitedly called the "Front Line" — he experienced only resentment. The truth was he didn't feel black and he didn't feel white. He felt as if he were an exception to the usual ethnic rules, a special boy who had fallen into South London from the clear blue sky, like one of Kirby's Forever People, tumbling to Earth from the Boom Tube.

Derek was expected by his family to attend a top-tier British university — Oxford, Cambridge, the LSE or, at a pinch, Durham. He got into Bristol University, which was accepted by his father only as "top of the second-tier". Derek shrugged. He moved to Bristol in 1979.

Derek had chosen to read anthropology. As a result, he was exposed to the modern idea that race is a social construct. He figured his old Ghanaian Presbyterian pastor might disagree with this, thinking instead that race was something biological. Still, Derek made pan-Africanism a special object of study at university. He understood that it positioned a utopian society in Africa as the symbolic opposite of the slave trade. But what form might this utopia take? According to Garvey, it was to be built by a scientific vanguard of the best and brightest African-Americans returning to Africa on his Black Star Line ships. According to Nkrumah, it was to be designed by the newly independent African nations. And as far as Bob Marley was concerned, it was to be delivered by a revolutionary call to arms – or at least an exaltation of Rasta consciousness.

Derek photocopied the Rasta source texts. He hypothesised that Rastafari was just as much a culture – a counter-culture, in fact – as a religion. He reckoned it could be studied using the tools of cultural analysis developed by British scholars such as Richard Hoggart, E.P. Thompson, Raymond Williams and Stuart Hall. Rastafari in Derek's view was essentially a hybrid culture. It grafted the political ideals of pan-Africanism with romantic back-to-nature beliefs, an invented patriarchal tradition and the Old Testament idea of a chosen people who had a covenant with God. Haile Selassie was a kind of Moses figure.

Derek responded well to Bristol. He found the city to be an open book compared to London. It was commonly said that without the West Indian slave and sugar trades of the eighteenth century, Bristol would be a small fishing port rather than one of the richest cities in England. And, indeed, the iniquitous history of the city was legible in the layout of its streets. Derek observed the contrast between the grand Georgian town-houses of Clifton and Redland and the decaying Edwardian housing stock of St Pauls and Easton. He noted that the promenade was home to the Society of Merchant Venturers, which had made its money from slave-trading. And he couldn't help but notice the bronze statue of Merchant Venturer Edward Colston in the city centre.

One of Derek's close-to-campus haunts was the Dug Out Club on Park Row, half-way between the trendy post-punk scene in Clifton and the shebeens of St Pauls. Derek spent many late nights mixing with other kids in the tiny bar. Here, the city's contradictions played out on the dance-floor in a kaleidoscope of DJ mash-ups and patchwork youth cults. Derek rubbed shoulders with blue-eyed soul boys, white Rastas, post-punk autodidacts, high-fashion black kids and student misfits. He even played a few records as "His Most Reverend Highness" D J Mensah. His thoughts whirled. He developed a crush on this fierce little white girl, who was always rushing around the video lounge, berating the cool guys and spilling their drinks. She wore her dreadlocks tight.

Her name was Millie. But Derek didn't know that until he bumped into her in Revolver Records on Clifton Triangle. He had made the pilgrimage to Bristol's hipster record shop to update himself on the legacy of the city's punk scene. He was clutching a copy of the Pop Group's debut album and making his way past one of the little shop's many tottering piles of vinyl. She had her back to him and was going through the reggae bin, sliding out the vinyl imports from their homemade packaging to inspect the labels. As she put a Mikey Dread record under her arm, she jabbed him in the ribs with her elbow.

For fuck's sake! she said. Derek apologised. She turned to give him a piece of her mind. But when she saw his dazzling smile, she softened. She stood there teasing out her locks, posing for him. She touched the record in his hand. It was good, she said, that he was into the Pop Group. They were the only white band who knew how to do dub properly. Mark Stewart was an undoubted genius. But it was bad, she said, that Derek was buying the album a full six months after it had come out. That showed he was a bit out of touch. She pursed her lips.

Derek asked what music she was into. She tapped him on the chest. War Ina Babylon! she said. Ark of the Covenant! Rescue Jah Children! Derek put up his hands, in mock surrender. He didn't realise that she had just flung the titles of three roots reggae tracks at him. All produced by Lee Perry. It was only later on in their relationship that he found out she was a true believer in Rasta livity. When they huddled under the covers in her bedsit, she gave him a lesson in Jamaican politics. The country had been independent for little over a decade and already its socialist government was being undermined by Anglo-American plutocrats. Blood-sucking vampires, she called them. She said that a Day of Judgement was coming, an Apocalypse. Babylon would crumble and the Rastas would inherit the earth. A new age of peace, justice and love would dawn. Open up the gates of Zion, sang Millie. Africa we wanna go.

Derek was smitten by Millie. He loved the softness of her skin, the quickness of her speech. He also loved the uninhibited way she lived out and put to the test the anthropological idea that race was a social construct. His tutors had taught him that a black man could be British, no doubt. And the white punks he had met in the Dug Out undeniably had a right to express their alienation using the roots concept of Babylon — it came from the Bible, after all. But could a white girl be a Rasta? Millie certainly took shit from a vocal minority of St Pauls girls when she went to see bands play in the smoke-filled shebeens on Campbell Street and Stapleton Road. They said she should stick to the diluted reggae of Bob Marley, who cut his sounds with bluesy guitar riffs and disco rhythms. The likes of Black Roots and Restriction were not for her. When Millie retorted that Restriction were a racially mixed band, the mean girls changed tack and said she had no right to wear locks, which were a hair-style belonging exclusively to blacks. She replied that locks were a sign of Jah's universal power, exercised over the bodies of white and black people alike, and the girls should read their Bible. This got her only the sucking of teeth in return, made more vehement by the fact that Restriction's guitarist had a deep appreciation for Millie's talents as a viny scout.

All this prompted Derek to consider the possibility that blacks and whites might discover common meanings in their shared urban plight. If Kingston was no different from Babylon, was Bristol so different from Kingston? Might white kids enter the gates of the city of Zion? Could pan-Africanism become a post-racial political ideal? These were radical new questions.

Derek smoked dope for the first time in a punk squat, round the back of the Full Marks bookshop in Stokes Croft, on the edge of St Pauls. Millie had insisted on rolling the spliff. She used the green buds rather than the black hash. When Derek took a hit, his mind blew up. As if from a great height, he saw the Lee Perry-produced dub reggae albums scattered all over the floor. Max Romeo's *War Ina Babylon*, The Upsetters' *Super Ape*, Junior Murvin's *Police and Thieves*, The Heptones' *Party Time*, the Congos' *Heart of the Congos*. The interlocking cover designs formed a mosaic of late 1970s Jamaica, one whose political fevers were mere months away from breaking.

Every morning the black sun rise, sang Millie. She span some vinyl. The needle hit the groove and the heavy bass jumped out of the home-built speaker stack. Derek choked with euphoria. The drums hit low on the third beat of every four, while the first beat was left unstruck. The dub music was punctuated by sound effects — echo, reverberation, the artful dropping of vocals in and out of the mix. The empty spaces in the music seemed to add up in the room. Derek put his thoughts in there, thoughts about his father and Nkrumah, about Kirby's New Gods, about alien spaceships and distant planets.

Derek picked up the *Super Ape* album. The drawing of the giant ape-like monster on its sleeve had the same graphic impact as a cover image from *The Incredible Hulk* comics he had read as a kid. Here was a monster on a rampage, brandishing an uprooted tree in one hand and a huge spliff in the other. Brightly-coloured captions glossed the image. The Super Ape fed on ROOTS and MAKKA. It faced off against its mortal enemy, CROAKING LIZARD, a creature which inspired much superstitious fear in the Jamaican countryside. Derek noted there was a pastiche certification mark in the top right-hand corner of the sleeve. It mimicked the Comics Code Authority badge which had appeared on all Marvel and DC superhero titles. The legend inscribed on the badge read: DUB IT UP BLACKER THAN DREAD.

Derek could hear Scratch shouting instructions to the musicians in his Kingston studio, he could hear the noises from outside its open door. There was the crying of babies and the barking of dogs, the singing of birds and the sound of thunder, water flowing, bottles smashing. The dub mood was light and edgy. Every so often, a voice spoke, a Jamaican voice, ranting about God and the Devil, four hundred years of colonialism, the bondage of Babylon and the saving grace of the Ark of the Covenant.

Every morning the black sun rise, sang Millie. It shines out the Ark of the Covenant. What the hell does that mean? said one of the stoned punks. Millie turned down the music. The Black Ark was Scratch's recording studio, said Millie. What like Noah's Ark? said the punk. An ark for black people, is that it? Partly, said Millie. She drew on the spliff and was knocked back for a minute. Derek spoke up. God instructed Moses to build the Ark of the Covenant to house the Ten Commandments, he said. Uh? said the punk. The tablets of stone he brought down from Mount Sinai, said Derek. Uh! said the punk. The end of the spliff burned brightly. Moses and the Israelites were wandering in the desert after quitting slavery, said Derek, memories of Sunday school returning to him. God promised them a new land if they followed the Ten Commandments. That was the deal. Exactly, said Millie. The Israelites are the Rastas, Moses is Scratch and the Promised Land is Ethiopia. Or Jamaica. She was building another huge joint.

In those days, news about what was going on in the recording studios of Kingston was hard to come by. The good information was all mixed up with rumour and innuendo and hearsay. Homemade mythologies sprouted up overnight.

So if Moses is Scratch, what are the Ten Commandments? said the punk. The records Scratch made in the Black Ark, said Millie, quick as a flash. Hundreds of them. She was licking the adhesive on her papers. Imagine if all these records were made of stone, said Derek, gesturing to the albums on the floor. How would we play them? He giggled. Stalactite lithophones, man, said the punk. Exactly, said Millie, her eyes blazing. Rocks carry a message from Jah when they are struck, just like Black Ark vinyl does. Scratch knew that. When he was a boy, he used to throw stones against the rocks in the Jamaican countryside. In the din which reverberated around the gullies, he heard the voice of Jah telling him to go to Kingston. She passed the joint along. And when he worked in the Black Ark, she said, he blessed his recording equipment and blew the sacred ganja smoke on to his tapes because he wanted to make Jah feel welcome. What if God didn't come? said the punk. What if the Devil came calling instead? What then? Millie lifted her right buttock and farted. Exactly! said the punk, before nodding out.

March saw the high-point of the punk infatuation with postcolonial politics when the Pop Group released their second album, *For How Much Longer Do We Tolerate Mass Murder?* Racism and greed keep the people in need, sang Mark Stewart. It all made Derek wonder again how different Jamaica was from England. Haile Selassie might not be the Second Coming of Christ, but he had the same messianic pull as Che Guevara or the Red Army Faction – both of which featured on posters in Bristol's student halls. Was the Pop Group's antinomian socialism so different from Lee Perry's Rasta beliefs?

Millie didn't think about any of these questions. She was too busy dancing like crazy to the album's ferocious mix of raw funk, atonal jazz and disturbing found noises.

Vigilantes in St Pauls, Handsworth and all, sang Mark Stewart. Twelve days later, the St Pauls riot kicked off. Derek told me he was in the Student Union bar in the middle of a Thursday when Millie rushed in to give him a first-hand account of the trouble. Of course she had been right in the middle of it. The words spilled out of her. She'd been with the kids outside the Inkerman when they'd ambushed the police van taking the crates of lager away from the Black and White Café. So what if the café owner didn't have a licence to sell alcohol? He was storing the booze for a private house party. Completely legal, man! The police raid was just another example of the usual state violence and racism. War Ina Babylon! Millie's eyes were lit with righteous fury. The cops had run away from the mob. She laughed. They'd overturned the cop van and liberated the Red Stripe. And then it was down to William Street to help set fire to the overturned police car. It'd been a great crack! she said. The black and white youth standing shoulder to shoulder. And at the forefront, leading the way, the Rasta men, local elders like Clifton Mighty.

Millie had apparently left St Paul when the fire brigade arrived. But not before she'd helped them unfurl the hoses. She didn't want the kiddies coming home from Cabot School to get hurt, she said. And she hadn't taken part in the looting and arson which followed later on in the evening. Derek thought she sounded a bit aggrieved, as if she'd left a party too early and missed the best bit. She dragged him down to Grosvenor Road that afternoon. They joined the victory dance with other kids on the patch of grass opposite the Black and White. The sound system played Lee Perry's "Beat Down Babylon" and everyone sang along. Whip them, whip them! The Rastas smoked ganja in the open air. The police stayed clear.

Looking back, Derek told me in 1991, the St Paul riot marked a generational dividing line in Bristol youth culture. It was the moment of peak militancy for the 1970s Rasta-dominated roots reggae scene, its political high-water mark. The riot made the national newspapers, Parliament began the process of repealing the "sus" law and Clifton Mighty and his co-defendants were acquitted of riotous assembly at Bristol Magistrates' Court.

Everything, everywhere, changed at once. Jamaica's socialist government was swept from power in a landslide election. A right-wing government came to power in America. Bob Marley, Rasta's great international ambassador, died of cancer. The British government accepted that youth unemployment was a fact of life. And a new bunch of wild kids came out to play on the streets of Bristol.

With the police now avoiding the area, St Pauls was chock-a-block with turntables and speakers. A new sound system culture emerged. It mixed Jamaican dub and punk with the new hip hop sounds coming in from New York on cassette-tape. The Wild Bunch, City Rockers, 2Bad, UD4, Three Stripe and other popular street crews played all-nighters, rocking abandoned warehouses and packing out clubs like the Tropic and the Moon. The old live music scene faded out.

Derek was in the thick of it all. Newly graduated and planning to do a PhD, he took a year out from his studies and ran round Bristol with a graffiti posse known as the Crime Incorporated Crew. He hit up the city's whitewashed walls with flashy comicbook panels and baroque letter-forms. He wasn't above lifting captions from the old Kirby titles he loved so much. WAHUM! WAHUUM! Sometimes, he'd steal whole lines. THE GODS HAVE RETURNED!!! His pieces got painted over by the council, but he'd be back the next night, to do them over. THE BOOM TUBE HAS PENETRATED TO EARTH! He never got caught and he had a lot of fun. He signed his pieces "HMRH".

By this time, Derek had a new girlfriend. He saw Millie only now and again. She still followed Restriction on the gigging circuit. Occasionally, she would pop up at a Three Stripe do, where

Clifton Mighty's brother Ray preserved some of the old-time roots-reggae religion, toasting about peace, love and unity over a low-end mix of break beats, soul tunes and dub effects. On the whole, though, she was sad. The death of Marley had hit her unexpectedly hard. She detested the new Jamaican fashion for dancehall slackness, with its emphasis on materialism, sex and glamour. Where's the spirituality gone, she said? She was particularly upset by the dark rumours surrounding Scratch Perry. People said he'd gone mad and burned down his recording studio. The Black Ark, with its famous portrait of Haile Selassie over the entrance, was now a blackened ruin. People said Scratch had quit Jamaica. He was living in Amsterdam, America, London. They said he believed that Marley had been killed by demons, unleashed by the Queen of England.

Maybe the Devil really had come calling at the Black Ark, said Derek one afternoon as he sat with Millie in the Arnolfini. She had trimmed back her locks and thrown them up into a headband, Slits-style. She looked poised, grown-up. She stirred her coffee. Something went down in the Black Ark, she finally said. Something bad. Scratch tried to fight it off. I heard he built a protective chicken-wire fence round the drum booth, she said. He scribbled hexes on the walls, hid his precious tapes in the earth and struck the ground with a hammer to exorcise unclean spirits. He walked backwards, to confuse the Devil. He even gave himself a new name. Pipecock Jackxon. None of it worked. She licked the end of her spoon. So, said Derek, he had to burn the Devil out? Was that it? Millie shrugged. Maybe he just wanted a change, she said. Why not? Everything changes. She herself was getting into Buddhism.

Derek spent a lot of time working on the proposal for an anthropology PhD at Bristol. He was using Raymond Williams' 1978 essay on "Utopia and Science Fiction" to speculate about a futuristic idea of pan-Africanism which was not in hock to the Rasta myths of the past. He based it on the science-fiction album-cover art of Scratch, fellow King Tubby dub protégé Scientist and American funk artist George Clinton. He called it "Afrodiasporic Futurism".

Prime exhibit in his case was the album sleeve art for *Mothership Connection* by Clinton's band Parliament. The front cover showed a clownish image of Clinton in silver space suit, platform heels and pharaonic kilt, rodeo-riding a flying saucer through the cosmos. The spaceship glowed. The back cover showed the saucer hovering above a street in the black American ghetto. Clinton was at the door of the ship, one leg over its side. Was he getting out or getting in? thought Derek. Was the funky black messiah of 1970s America about to lead his chosen people to take over Washington DC and turn it into the party capital of the world? Or was he signalling it was time for black folks to liberate themselves from America and take their groove into outer space?

Answers to these questions were encoded in the tiny cartoons and felt-tip liner notes which adorned the albums of Clinton's other 1970s band, Funkadelic. The artwork, Derek learned, was the creation of one Pedro Bell, a self-taught visual artist who combined the epic sweep of a Jack Kirby with the freakish detailing of a Robert Williams. Bell's nightmare insects, obscene aliens, giant naked women, threatening robots and outer-space back-drops were garishly coloured and extensively annotated. Derek was particularly intrigued by the cover of *The Electric*

Spanking of War Babies, which showed a partially occluded image of what looked like a naked woman shackled inside the berth of a spaceship. Was that it? Derek squinted. He couldn't quite tell.

Piecing together Bell's hieroglyphic fragments as best he could, Derek gained insight into a bombastic mythology where "funk" was a cosmic sexual energy animating all things. Clinton, along with Sun Ra, Jimi Hendrix and Sly Stone, had been made an "apostle" of funk by the "Cosmic Strumpet of a Mother Nature" and been expected to restore "Order Within the Universe". He had "descended from the Original Galaxy Ghetto" to Earth, where his mission was to "cleanse the wayward souls" who infest the "PIT OF PENTAGON" and other bastions of the military-industrial complex.

This quasi-apocalyptic battle between Clinton's funky "swash-bucklers" and the "POLLUTING ENTERPRISES of capitalistic pimpism" was given a slick, upscale feel by the commercial artist Overton Loyd on later Parliament albums. Loyd even produced an eight-page comic book for the inner sleeve of *Funkentelechy vs. the Placebo Syndrome*. Derek didn't much care for it. He wondered what Kirby would have done with the same material — especially the epic duel between Star Child, with his "bop gun", and the pimptastic Sir Nose d'Voidoffunk, with his "snooze gun". It was a shame Clinton and Kirby never collaborated.

Another key reference for Derek's PhD proposal was the cover art for *Scientist Encounters Pac-Man*. Here was another pastiche comicbook cover in the mould of *Super Ape*. The young dub artist, in a reprise of the video-game action of his first album *Scientist Meets the Space Invaders*, squares off in his Kingston recording studio against a giant Pac-Man robot. He wears a skintight superhero jersey. The robot is in the process of devouring him. He is horizontal, dreadlocks flying. His reel-to-reel tape recorder has smashed to the floor. All Scientist can do to save himself is reach for the dials of the mixing desk. Is it too late? Beyond the flimsy glass screen of the control room gather a lugubrious crew of vampires and B-movie monsters. For Derek, the meaning of the image was clear. Dub was a sonic medium which could be haunted by evil spirits, just as Scratch had intuited.

Derek argued in his proposal that "Afrodiasporic Futurism" established an aesthetic holding place for a pan-Africanism struggling to reinvent itself as a counter-culture for a postmodern world. Similar to hip hop artist Afrika Bambaata's post-racial notion of the Universal Zulu Nation, it gestured towards a utopia which could accommodate new ideas of individual creative identity as well as old collective salvation myths. After a short delay, his proposal was rejected by the university for being "novelistic". They said it "substituted wish-fulfilment for field-work" and suggested that his talents might be better served by studying the "anthropology of utopia" in the context of Colonel Gadaffi's *Green Book*. Derek snorted with derision.

After that, Derek drifted. He hooked up with Millie now and again. She was working part-time for the Three Stripe record label set up by Ray Mighty with old Restriction guitarist Rob Smith. She said Smith & Mighty, as they called themselves, were getting into new areas of production. They were layering melancholic Erik Satie piano riffs on top of heavy, squelchy basslines. It was wild! He said he was working on designing a new typeface, based on New York graffiti styles and Jack Kirby's early lettering. She gave him a thin smile.

In 1987, The Wild Bunch went to London and got a record deal with Fourth & Broadway. Derek approached them with some ideas for album cover artwork. But their debut single bombed. They disbanded. Three of them returned to Bristol and started up Massive Attack. Derek got a graphic design job in Temple Meads. He worked long hours. As he toiled away with scalpel and glue, his mind drifted. Clinton's mothership and Scratch Perry's Black Ark fused in his imagination into a fantastic new science fiction device… something akin to Kirby's Boom Tube, a tunnel between worlds which appeared out of thin air with a mighty bass clap. He called it the Sonic Time Capsule. He imagined it as a combination of time machine and recording studio with a flight deck. It was equipped with microphones to pick up signals from the times it travelled back to and its cargo bay was filled with reams of cryptic messages collected on tape and on disc. Derek began to draw sketches of the machine.

Soon, he had invented a whole Afrofuturist mythology of his own. He planned out a twelve-issue run of comicbooks and drafted in some of his old graffiti pals to help with the visuals. Together, they managed to create three issues of the *Adventures of Super Ape*. The splash page of the first issue depicts Super Ape setting up the microphones in the Sonic Time Capsule he had built next to his home in the suburbs of twentieth-century Babylon. He has been commanded by the King of Planet Zion to create the Dread Book of Life, a long-playing record which lists the names of all holy apemen on Babylon. They are destined to be turned back into lions and transported back home to Zion in a spacecraft. Super Ape builds his recording equipment from the radioactive stones and rocks which have fallen to earth from

Planet Zion. The upper ranges of his mikes are tuned to the Holy Spirt frequency. The lower ranges pick up crackly interference from the Satanic dimension. Super Ape puts on his head-phones. As the sounds pass through his mixing desk, he employs various means to test them for holiness.

Reverb. Super Ape springs the sound around to mix and match frequencies. An act of intensification. The holy names sing in his cans.

Echo. Super Ape delays the sound to double-check its sanctity. Repetition, repetition, repetition. The names of the holy few decay in an infinite half-life.

Drop out. Super Ape turns a dial and banishes the wicked information. Purification. Only the sacred noises remain, names encoded in rhythms which sound like drum and bass.

Super Ape puts it all down on his four-track machine. The filtered sounds are pressed on top of each other, with five, six takes squeezed into one track. The psychomagnetic tape on his reel-to-reel is overwritten many times.

There is a hidden space on his four-track, space for an extra track, an occult space where the bad information is dumped. Here, the unholy names accumulate, the names of the demons, the names of the damned. Gonna put on an iron shirt, chase Satan out of Earth. So sings Super Ape. He is creating the Satanic flip-side of the Natty Book of Life, known as the Book of Death. It is a record full of doom.

BOOM! Super Ape hits a dial and his Sonic Time Capsule disappears from Cardiff Crescent. KA-BOOM! It reappears on a thin strip of brown sand in eighteenth-century Babylon. Through his viewing-screen, Super Ape clocks the flying saucers of Satan.

They hover just beyond the boiling white surf, firing their guns in a deafening salute. At his back, his mirrors show the deep green line of the jungle, full of squawks and alarms. He adjusts his mikes and starts recording…

I've still got the first issue of *Adventures of Super Ape*, which Derek posted me after our encounter in Forbidden Planet. It explains how Super Ape's mission is to redeem the missing history of the transatlantic slave trade by making a proper record of all those who died in transit. A fantastic idea, worthy of Borges! Derek's homemade strip should really have been picked up by *Deadline* or *Revolver*. The timing was good. I fully expected Derek to follow in the footsteps of Neil Gaiman, Grant Morrison, Jamie Delano and Peter Milligan and find work in America. *Adventures of Super Ape* would have been perfect for DC's hip 1990s imprint Vertigo. But it was not to be. Was the comic too experimental? Too African-Caribbean? Maybe the window of opportunity was just too narrow. The British comics boom stuttered to a halt soon after I met Derek. *Revolver* and *Crisis* folded in 1991. *Deadline* staggered on for another few years. And then the charmless *Tank Girl* movie killed the whole proto-Britpop action-adventure comics scene dead. A shame.

I lost touch with Derek in the 1990s. I heard he'd moved into video game design and was working for Sega. Meanwhile, Millie traveled the world with the More Rockers crew, reinventing herself as a DJ who mixed soulful drum'n'bass with old-skool dub effects and St Pauls breakbeats. The last I heard, she was living in Los Angeles.

As for Lee Scratch Perry, he moved to Switzerland and settled into a long, self-imposed exile from Jamaica. He gave up smoking ganja and married a blonde Swiss dominatrix. He built a new recording studio, the Blue Ark. But it wasn't the same. Severed from his Rasta roots, Perry became more showman than shaman. His records lacked the old dread vibe. In a sly mockery of his previous beliefs, he referred to himself as an "elf", an "extra-terrestrial", and played the madman when music journalists came to call. His critical reputation soared in 1997 with the release of his Black Ark compilation album *Arkology*. He spent much of the noughties impressing the international music festival circuit with his bag of tricks, decked out in medals and rings and patches like some modern-day harlequin.

I wondered what Derek would have made of this slightly degrading spectacle. Probably, he would have loved it, the idea of Scratch becoming a fashion icon. I couldn't help but think the old man was going through the motions, an idea reinforced by the fact that in the 2010s, his schtick was picked up by the art world – always the place where good religious ideas go to die. His 2019 show in New York featured totemic artworks he had originally fashioned in the Black Ark as aids to the recording process. There were old CDs and obsolete laptops, cordless phones, a TV screen surrounded by a pile of rocks, mirrors, lion statues, toy monkeys, postcards, cryptic prayers to Jah from his Pipecock Jackxon days, plant roots, sticks and stones.

Appearing like so many fetish objects gleaned from the ruins of the Black Ark, they were in a forlorn state. Here were the fragments of a collapsed eschatology reassembled as a hermetic collage. I desperately wanted to reinterpret them as the magical components of the Sonic Time Capsule envisioned by Derek in *Adventures of Super Ape*. But I knew such hope was poor consolation for anyone mourning the demise of Rastafari. Derek's idea of Afrodiasporic Futurism as an inverted stand-in for pan-Africanism had been curated to the point of extinction. I wondered how much it would cost to buy one of Perry's painted rocks.

In 2020, Edward Colston's statue was toppled by local antiracism protestors and chucked into Bristol harbour. I dug out my copies of Derek's comic once more. His depiction of Super Ape's nemesis, Croaking Lizard, looked like Colston from certain angles. I noticed the use of Bristol street names – Blackboy Hill and White Ladies Road – I'd missed the first time around. Even the names of Super Ape's pals, I realised, echoed the names of the famous old sound systems from Bristol – 2Bad, City Rocker, UD4, Excalibur. I am afraid I've not really done Derek full justice in my account of his work.

One thing I can report with confidence is that Scratch Perry returned home to Jamaica to die. He was buried in the parish of Hanover, where he was born. His baptismal name is Rainford Hugh Perry. Rainford, for what it's worth, is a small village in England.

LITTLE BROTHER RIFAAT

Scribe of the Lost Songs of Syd

WHEN I FIRST MET RIFAAT SAMSON it was 1994 and he was jammed up in the back of Megatripolis, sporting an Edwardian smoking jacket and astrakhan hat. He wasn't doing much trade. The crusty kids and the Mondo dudes were not much interested in his display of WWI-era bayonets, English herbal tinctures and chapbooks published by Hangman Books and King's Shilling Press. They were looking for guarana tablets and VR manuals, back-issues of *2600*, quick fixes for strung-out minds, cyberpunk short-cuts to nirvana.

The Prodigy's "No Good (Start the Dance)" was playing when I picked up a copy of *Syd's Long Last Album* from the stall. This was my introduction to Rifaat's book of poems, his only book of poems, his homemade magnum opus. The photocopied pages were filled with scribbled lines of verse in a free hand and bound in cheap board. The poems were short and had memorable titles— "Curly Fred", "Sant Mat Blues", "If You Go, Don't Be Slow". I remember Rifaat leaned in beneath the din of the speeded-up female soul vocals, the tips of his walrus moustache quivering in earnest. He smelled faintly of cologne. He said the book was one in a limited edition of 400. His mournful eyes stared into the strobe-lit abyss.

I gave Rifaat a few coins for his volume. It would eventually take pride of place on my book-shelf alongside *Les Champs*

Magnétiques and *Hexentexte* as one of the finest literary specimens of automatic writing. Something I couldn't have anticipated at the time of buying.

Rifaat and I got talking, as best we could, in the noise and the heat of the club, yelling at each over the beats of the *Streets of Rage 3* soundtrack. I can't recall much of what Rifaat said at this time – our real conversations came later – but I do remember I was impressed by the way he spoke in complete sentences, with none of the redundant verbal filler, the "y'knows" and "kindalikes", so typical of youth sub-culture speak. I was also impressed by his companion, a young Japanese woman in an over-large white shirt and motorcycle boots, strikingly mysterious as all Japanese girls in London were back then. She did the geisha thing of lighting her male escort's cigarettes all night and leaning on his shoulder. Rifaat ignored her, for the most part.

I later came to know that Rifaat, like his poetic subject Syd Barrett, had always been popular with women. Maybe it had something to do with the fact that his mother Irene had spoiled him as a child, calling him her "little prince", and the surfeit of love had given him an unusual self-confidence. Irene was a Turkish Cypriot immigrant who thought she'd married beneath her when Bob Samson transported her from the jazz clubs of Soho to the "wilds", as she put it, of the Isle of Sheppey. Bob was a train driver on the Chatham Main Line between London and Ramsgate and a steadier hand could not have been imagined. In 1956 Irene gave Bob a son, Christoph, and then banished her husband to his allotment on the Kent coast. When a younger son arrived six years later he was a happy surprise, not least to Bob.

His mother named him Rifaat, after a favourite great-uncle who had died somewhere in the Libyan desert during the war.

When she wasn't claiming obscure descent from Ottoman royalty, Irene styled herself as a gypsy clairvoyant and was much in demand after funerals. She did have some minor talent at reading the tea-leaves and sometimes even boasted, with faint annoyance, that the dead spoke to her on the radio. When she was having a particularly bad day, the neighbours would pop in with odd bits of shopping, only to be accused by her of snooping. Rifaat took it all in his stride and even used to help out at his mother's seances. He took the warm cup in his tiny hands and solemnly swirled the leaves three times. Anything to the left of the tea-cup handle was this life, he learned, while anything to the right was the next life.

It was the older brother, poor fellow, who couldn't take his mother's eccentricities. Forever imagining her as suffering from some congenital mental defect or family curse, he kept his distance from her, playing records in his darkened room while worrying about the day when he would come into his true inheritance. His school-mates teased him for his distracted air and gave him the nick-name Doc. It stuck.

Doc left school at 16. He earned money doing odd gardening jobs around Sheerness. But mainly, he drifted. He was often absent from home in his late teens. He took trips all round the country, courtesy of his father's British Rail card, to see Jethro Tull, Robert Fripp, Kevin Ayers and other second generation prog rock acts. Sometimes, he took his little brother with him. In fact, Rifaat says he has a cloudy memory of seeing Syd Barrett perform with his band Stars at the Corn Exchange in

Cambridge, still doing the old songs like "See Emily Play" and "Baby Lemonade", but with his guitar now detuned and his voice a pitiful bark, the '60s glory days of trance-inducing psychedelic rock now far behind him.

As we talked, Rifaat did his best to defend Syd. He said that with his long, tangled hair and raggedy beard, Syd looked like a freak and wouldn't have seemed out of place in the Gong line-up. He claimed that Syd was actually well on his way to becoming a punk rocker at that time while his old band Pink Floyd, with their increasingly overblown orchestrations, their insipid tragical-comical-historical compositions, were struggling to fill the void created by the enforced departure of their leader four years earlier. Rifaat said it was a shame that Syd had stopped making music after the appearance with Stars. He saw the long silence that followed not as notice of an expiration date on genius but as a deliberate internal exile, the principled refusal by a true artist to mortgage his imagination to the market-place.

I appreciated Rifaat's enthusiasm for late-period Barrett. It was a familiar manifestation of the Syd cult, which enshrined a romantic legend of doomed poetic youth as powerful as that of Chatterton or Keats. Here was a prodigious lyric talent who as a child named Roger Barrett had always sung to himself and as a teenager had become notorious among the Cambridge Brahmin set for his word games and his charm. It didn't take him long to create a beatnik alter ego for himself – the weirdo Syd Barrett – and go on to achieve fame in London. In a handful of songs, he single-handedly reinvented rock music, grafting elements of English nursery chant, Edwardian pastoralism, Eastern mysticism and sardonic humour to its Mississippi blues-based melancholy. He became a cult figure among fellow musicians, took daily doses of acid to reach a higher state of consciousness and, as they used to say, blew his mind. After that, he quit the music scene, drifted through England's '70s freak demi-monde and cogitated. Eventually, he shut himself away in a rented room in London's Chelsea Cloisters, just off the King's Road, surrounded by uniformed porters and locked gates.

Rifaat said that one of his fondest memories as a child was listening to Doc reading to him from the pages of the Syd fanzine *Terrapin*. Are you ready, Little Brother? Doc would say from high up in his leather-backed armchair, looking down at Rifaat sat cross-legged on the floor. The boy nodded. Then I shall impart this day's lesson, said Doc. And he would read out a juicy bit of gossip from the pages of the zine.

Rifaat especially enjoyed hearing about the various Syd sightings of the 1970s. Syd seen working in a chicken factory, hitch-hiking round France, busking outside Ely Cathedral. Syd seen buying a bag of sherbet lemons in Harrods, Syd seen strolling on the King's Road in a Crombie over-coat and floral-print dress. The light slanted through the closed curtains in Doc's room. He used to smile at "Little Brother" Rifaat's delighted laughter, but made no comment on the veracity of the stories, as if he and Syd were in on some great cosmic joke.

Syd's appearance at the Corn Exchange was one such sighting, one that had the added distinction of actually being verifiable. I understood why Rifaat would want to place himself at the scene of the legendary rock star's last gig. It was a way of directly participating in the Syd cult. But it was also a way of honouring his big brother. For Rifaat could surely not have attended this gig.

He would have been all of ten years old at the time. Much more likely was that Doc had been to the Corn Exchange in 1972 and told his little brother about the gig when he got home to Sheerness.

This is all a roundabout way of saying that it was Doc, not Rifaat, who was the real Syd buff. Indeed, he developed an obsessive mythology about his idol that rivalled any of the maniacal pop fan fictions compiled by the Vermorels years later in their *Starlust* anthology. For Doc, Syd was an old soul in a youthful body, a pagan mystic in Chelsea glad rags, a Confucian governor of the English counter-culture. And it was Doc who initiated Little Brother Rifaat into his occult Syd lore in the twilight of his bedroom, with solitary lamp burning and the 33 long-player spinning on the turntable.

Syd was the great bringer of names, said Doc. He named himself as a pop star, going from plain Roger to the more unisex Syd. And he came up with the name for his band one lonely night, conjuring it from the liner notes of an obscure Blind Boy Fuller album, where the old blues musicians Pink Anderson and Floyd Council were mentioned side by side. He called his cats Lucifer and Samael after the gnostic old gods, wrote the song "Lucifer Sam" about a witch from the Cambridge fenlands, his soul-mate, and, Doc went on, with his call to "Huff the Talbot" on the prophetic song "Octopus", he had invoked an ancient English spectre associated with altercation and civil war. Little Brother Rifaat soaked it all up.

Doc hated the post-Syd Pink Floyd with a vengeance, claiming they represented the worst aspects of English conformism and respectability. He reserved particular bile for Roger Waters, who he said had stolen the band from his old Cambridge school chum. Doc called him Syd's assassin, his shadow, a second Roger who displaced the first, a man whose biggest hits in the reincarnated Pink Floyd were all songs about the legend of Syd, his acid-fuelled madness, his decline and fall, his mystery. It maddened Doc, who pored over Syd's post-Floyd opus, searching for the stigmata of persecuted genius, the signs of displaced authority.

Syd released two solo albums at the back end of the '60s. *The Madcap Laughs* featured him singing in a sad voice, off-key, about his cracked epiphanies and lost loves. To my mind, he strummed his acoustic guitar as if it were a rack for his heart-strings. The bum notes, glitches and fluffs were all prominent in the mix. Doc found it very touching. He spent hours staring at the album sleeve design. The front cover featured a photo of Syd with the hair over his kohl-smeared eyes, crouched on the candy-striped floor in his Earl's Court pad. On the back cover was a similar photo from the same session, this time with a naked girl waiting for Syd in the background.

I have to say that the second album *Barrett* was a much more anguished affair, with Syd sounding alternatively maniacal and zonked out, as he strained at the limits of poetic self-expression. Here was an attempt to invent a modern English folk idiom, full of crazed acts of daring and abrupt failures. Doc preferred it to the first album. He latched on to one particular track, "Effervescing Elephant", a zoomorphic nonsense lyric set to a jaunty nursery tune, which Doc thought was a cryptic clue to understanding Syd's psychology. It told the story of a selfless elephant who, having warned the other jungle animals that a hungry tiger was on the prowl, stayed out too late and was himself eaten by the big cat.

In one of their teenage bedroom huddles, Doc told his little brother that "Effervescing Elephant" was the most sacred hymn in the Syd cult. It was the first song he wrote as a teenager in his Cambridge bedroom and the last song he performed on-stage at the Corn Exchange. It was an oracular song, Doc said, about the stalled beginning of things and the premature end of things. Little Rifaat remembered being drawn closer and closer to his big brother by all this strange Syd talk, so close their heads nearly touched. Now who is the Hindu god of beginnings? asked Doc. Little Brother Rifaat shrugged. Ganesha, said Doc, with an air of triumph. Ganesha, who has the body of a man and the head of an elephant. Rifaat nodded.

Ganesha has a sweet tooth, said Doc. Just like Syd. And he has a pot belly. Just like Syd? asked Little Brother Rifaat. Well, in later life, yes, said Doc. Though maybe that's not so important. What is important is that Syd was always really good at beginning things, like Pink Floyd, like psychedelic rock, like a specifically English and sexually ambiguous approach to pop stardom. And he influenced so many others, said Doc, from Bolan to Bowie. But he was always really bad at finishing things, things like songs, things like albums, things like his career, his life as a whole. It's as if he had been overwhelmed by blessings from Ganesha.

Doc went on to enlighten Little Brother Rifaat about one of the less well-known periods of Syd's life, his dalliance as a teenager with a Sikh variant of Hinduism known as Sant Mat. Rifaat told the story to me as Doc told it to him. I've consulted the various Syd biographies and it checks out. Back in the mid-1960s,

Syd and his clever Cambridge friends, kids with middle-class names like his own — Paul and Bridget and Andrew and Lucy and Nigel and Jenny and Lindsay — had got turned on to Sant Mat after tripping on acid-dosed sugar-cubes and doing yoga in their parents' back-gardens during the summer holidays. This was at a time when a wave of Indian gurus were spreading the doctrine of karma and reincarnation among the educated young hippies of Britain and America. There was Maharishi Mahesh Yogi and his TM cult, which attracted the Beatles and the Beach Boys. There was A.C. Bhaktivedanta Swami Prabhupada and the Hare Krishna sect, which got George Harrison to turn their mantra into a pop hit. And there was the boy guru Prem Rawat, who addressed the crowd at the first Glastonbury festival with his DLM teachings.

Sant Mat was headed up by Maharaja Charan Singh, a twinkly-eyed Indian guru with a long white beard and a self-satisfied aura of wisdom. When he visited London in the summer of 1966, many of Syd's pals travelled to meet him and were initiated into the sect. Syd, who was barely out of his teens, made the pilgrimage as well. But he was turned down for induction. Twice.

The first time, Syd was over-confident. Ushered into the Maharaja's presence in a Bloomsbury hotel room, he saw only a little old man in a turban and flowing white robes, sat cross-legged on a couch. He failed to bow. Instead, he launched into a high-minded justification of his spiritual worth as a Sant Mat candidate. He claimed that while consuming magic mushrooms in the Gogmagog Hills, just outside Cambridge, he had heard the still spreading echoes of the Big Bang, the beginning of the universe. He was now attuned to the vibrations of the cosmos, he said, and was ready to follow the path of spiritual enlighten-ment under the Maharaja's guidance. Surely, the Maharaja would agree that he was an exceptional candidate. But the Maharaja did not agree. In fact, he laughed at the young man's presumption.

Leaning forward from his couch, the Maharaja said that if Syd were accepted into Sant Mat, he would have to give up sex with strange girls, give up drugs and alcohol, stop eating meat. He would have to cut his hair. Syd froze. He was very proud of his long, tousled hair. The girls loved it. The Maharaja shook his head. He said that the path of "dakshina" was obviously not for Syd. He dismissed the candidate with a curt wave.

The next day, Sad returned to the same hotel room. He had shaved his head and looked like a Hare Krishna monk. This time, he threw himself on the floor and begged the Maharaja, the en-lightened Maharaja, to please, please, please let him join the Sant Mat sect. He was willing to renounce sex and drugs, willing to retreat entirely from the world. He would lead a simple life in a monastery cell, consuming only bread and water. He wanted to devote his life to singing the praises of the Brahman. So said Syd, his nose rubbing the carpet. The Maharaja toyed with his ceremonial dagger. He said there was no need to go that far.

Sant Mat disciples, said the Maharaja, were all expected to get a proper job, get married, start a family, run a household. Syd bit his lip. He raised his head and said he could do that. Why, he could get a job as an architect. The Maharaja said that was good but that Syd would have to give up his music or, at least, do it only at weekends and in the evenings, like any normal person. Syd scowled. The Maharaja laughed and said it was even more obvious, second time round, that Syd was not suited for the path of "dakshina". He told him to go in peace and gave him a little plastic statuette of Ganesha. Syd left the hotel despondent.

So said Doc. Rifaat later told me that he often thought about this story. It seemed to him that Syd had proved his unfitness for life under the Maharaja in all possible ways. Not only had he failed to give up the sex, the drugs, the peacock garments. But he had failed to marry, failed to have children and failed to escape from always being a lodger in somebody else's home.

All that remained from a wasted life were the songs, said Rifaat. Songs about misfits and loners, songs like "Scarecrow", "Arnold Layne" and "Vegetable Man". But even Syd's musical talent had deserted him in the end and he was unable to produce a third album.

Rifaat thought it was inevitable that his brother would drop acid himself. In the summer of 1979, he travelled to Europe to see his favourite bands, working his passage on a cargo ship running out of Sheerness to Vlissingen. He hitched around Holland, Belgium and France, sleeping under bridges and prowling around school playing fields. When he returned weeks later, he had the dishevelled look and thousand yard stare of the acid casualty. He insisted he had been given a secret mission by the Dalai Lama to scout a good location for the spiritual leader's reincarnation and that was why he had been away for so long. But Rifaat figured that what he had really been doing was following in the footsteps of his idol, a Stanley to Syd's Livingstone, searching the dark continent of the Freudian unconscious for some spark of enlightenment. It was bitter. Rifaat desperately wanted to rescue his big brother from his mental imprisonment, but he didn't know how.

During the final months of 1979, Doc took to crashing in his father's allotment. He used to slump on a deck-chair in a slouch hat, gazing out over the steely grey expanse of the Thames Estuary, humming to himself. Sometimes, Rifaat would sit on the ground beside him. Doc would talk about Syd's failed attempt to make a third album in Abbey Road in 1974. The "long last album" as Doc called it, his clanging speech patterns already starting to show signs of the echolalia associated with schizophrenia. It was a sad story, said Doc. Syd struggled to get down anything at all in the studio. He had brought fistfuls of scribbled lyric sheets to the sessions, but no one had ever been allowed to see them. Instead, his lips formed the shapes of ghostly words, his fingers moved the plectrum across a string-less guitar, the glint in his eye faded away. "Have you got it, yet?" he used to ask the engineers after one of his pantomimes.

Doc said he thought that if Syd had actually made his third album, it would have been his masterpiece, his saving grace. Doc warmed to his theme. It would have been the redemption of his youthful promise, the late flowering of '60s psychedelic culture, a justification of his chosen path in the eyes of the Maharaja and a sharp retort to the treacherous Roger Waters. Doc had removed his hat. He was turning the soft cloth over and over in his hands.

Doc was confined to the old Barming Mental Hospital in 1980. The psychiatrists told him that his over-indulgence in LSD had triggered a psychotic episode. They wanted to isolate him for his own safety. Rifaat was allowed to visit him only once. He sat silently in the day-care room next to his heavily medicated brother. Doc gazed through the window at the patients moving slowly across the grounds. The asylum was a four-floor block of grey stone surrounded by heavy walls and railings. A place full of whispers and the smell of bleach. Rifaat used to consider it his brother's version of Chelsea Cloisters, the monolithic block of flats in London where Syd was still hiding out. It comforted him to think of Syd in his lovely warm dark room, watching the soft flicker from his Dynatron colour TV set, the brand-new stereos and guitars and satin shirts and silk scarves and snakeskin boots all stashed safely in the spare flat next door, like so many grave goods in a pharaoh's tomb.

Rifaat didn't ever forget about his older brother. But he did begin to do better at school, mix with girls more and generally get on with his life. In 1981, he enrolled in a foundation course at Medway College of Design and discovered a new influence. Billy Childish. The halls still rang with talk of this extraordinarily talented young artist, an enfant terrible who had supposedly been expelled a few years earlier for obscenity, and who had since made a name for himself on the local scene as a punk poet. Billy was charismatic and had a gang of like-minded freaks who did readings with him at various pubs in Maidstone and Chatham. Rifaat became a devoted camp follower.

The Medway Poets, as they were dubbed, were always to my mind a cut above punk ranters like Seething Wells and Attila the Stockbroker. They saw themselves as artists, a caste apart, and their performances mixed lewd confessional verse with the old capers of the Zurich avant-garde reformatted as humorous pub entertainment. Marginal men — and they were mostly men — with no fixed place in society, they hid themselves among the millions of ex-industrial workers who had signed on the dole in the 1980s, doing two-week Restart courses on welding in between dashing off neo-expressionist paintings and stapling together photocopied sheets of their poems.

This was when Rifaat began to dream of being published by Hangman Books, Billy Childish's publishing imprint. He realised there was value in not being pinned down by a society that was changing too rapidly to offer any chance of a permanent role for him. He would never be a railwayman or a dock worker, he knew that. But he could be a poet. Why not? Spending his time in the company of perpetual students, malcontents, petty thieves, dossers and working girls was no wasted life, as his mother might imagine. It was preparation for a noble life of the mind, a form of poetic training.

So ran Rifaat's thoughts in his student days. He bought a tweed jacket from a charity shop, wore it over a hand-knitted jumper and a pair of corduroys and paraded the streets with a succession of pretty young art sluts on his arm. People in Maidstone used to stare. The aura of the Granada TV adaptation of *Brideshead Revisited* still hung heavily in the air and Rifaat, like many underemployed young men of the time, considered himself a revolutionary traditionalist in the line of a John Michell, a Lord Byron. He cultivated all the vices of the English aristocrat. He dabbled in many things, didn't try too hard at any of them and perfected the exhibition of an easy anti-intellectual charm. He found himself attracted to the forms of the old order – queen and country, arrogant provincialism, figurative painting, rhyming poetry.

Rifaat admitted to me that all his early poems were rubbish. He described them as Ginsbergian effusions about abstract ideas such as honour and death, lyrical observations of the Kentish railway landscape, exaltations of knee-tremblers in back-alleys.

It was only when his brother's memory started to creep into the poems that Rifaat felt he was getting somewhere. After the publication of the Griffiths Report in 1983, the old Victorian asylums began to discharge their patients into something known as "care in the community", which in Doc's case amounted to living with his exasperated mother and working part-time in a charity shop off Sheerness High Street. Rifaat remembered that his brother used to spend hours in the shop folding and refolding garments, ignoring the customers, as if working out some pristine geometrical formula known only to himself. He would wander the streets at night, in a sodium-lit inferno of distraction, chattering away. Only occasionally would he redeem himself with some devastating but painfully accurate insult hurled at an unfortunate passerby.

Rifaat wanted to believe that there was hope for his brother. He got hold of the abridged paperback copy of Michel Foucault's *Madness and Civilisation* from the college library. The book was a masterly summation of the 1960s anti-psychiatry movement. It claimed the Victorian practice of confining the insane in institutions was socially oppressive and its influence had even found its way into the Griffiths Report. Foucault made the claim that in older times the madman was seen as an esoteric source of higher wisdom, much like the holy fools in *King Lear* and *Twelfth Night*, much like, indeed, Syd at the height of the psychedelic '60s. Was it possible, wondered Rifaat, that Doc, beneath his veneer of antic malarkey, was on the same cosmic plane as Syd, thinking deep thoughts unknowable by the common man?

Rifaat left Medway College of Design in 1984. He signed on the dole, rented a room above a shop in Maidstone High Street and spent his days honing his poetic craft. In 1986, he read in the paper that Roger Waters, Doc's favourite villain, had left Pink Floyd two years earlier and was now applying to the High Court to prevent remaining band members from touring under the band name. Rifaat felt his gorge rise. He could well imagine what Doc would think about this. The man who had stolen the band name from Syd was now complaining about the band name being stolen from him. What a cheek! Syd, meanwhile, was living in his mother's house in Cambridge. He had had to quit Chelsea Cloisters in 1982 when the flow of Pink Floyd royalties reduced to a dribble. Reporters had run round to his house for a quote on the lawsuit, but Syd refused to answer the door. He had nothing to say.

But what would Syd say if he could? wondered Rifaat. It was then that he had his great poetic idea. He would channel the lyrics to Syd's missing third album, bind them in a chapbook and present the whole affair to Doc. It would be a tribute to their shared teenage memories of the lost rock star and a manifestation of Doc's greatest wish. Obviously, it wouldn't cure Doc. Nothing could. But it might make him feel better.

So one afternoon, Rifaat took the train to London and made his way to the King's Road. When he walked out of the Sloane Square tube station, he could see the place was much changed from the hippie days of Granny Takes a Trip and other psychedelic boutiques. The King's Road now had a brash and corporate feel, although it seemed to recover some of its old bohemian seediness the closer he walked to World's End. He turned the corner at Anderson Street and soon the great hulk of Chelsea Cloisters was upon him. Rifaat put on his Sony Walkman head-set, adjusted the cheap foam ear-pieces, and pressed play on the little tape deck strapped to his waist. The plaintive strains of "Effervescing Elephant" played in his head, over and over again.

Rifaat had no intention of invoking the deity Ganesha, or even some abstract notion of Syd. He wasn't that soft-headed, he told me. Instead, he was attempting to recreate a specific mental state from the past, from 1974, to be precise, when Syd had wandered the same Chelsea streets that he now found himself in, humming away while composing in his mind the lyrics to his abortive third album.

Rifaat slunk around Chelsea Cloisters as evening fell, squinting at its long horizontal lines, concrete bay windows, rounded corners and shielded glass-door entrances. He monitored his perceptions, searching for the same things Syd might have seen all those years ago. Rifaat observed the slant of the sunlight on exposed brick-work, the patterns of leaves in the trees, the signage of tatty old restaurants, the notices on the red pillar boxes, the ancient cracks in the pavement. He used these trigger-points to generate associations in his mind. He went back in time.

Rifaat carried a stubby pencil in one hand and a school notebook in the other, a sleek Clairefontaine notebook Doc had brought back with him from France. As part of his planned London trip, Rifaat had spent a week tracking down clippings and pages from Syd's known sources of inspiration. There featured lines from "Hiawatha", old sea-shanties, Lamb's *Tales from Shakespeare*, Sant Mat pamphlets, Tolkien's *Lord of the Rings*, the *Alice* books, fenland folk tales and more. Rifaat had stapled the clippings on to the left-hand pages of his notebook. And now, on his walk around Chelsea — or his derive, as he rather grandly thought of it — Rifaat would stop at random intervals and flip open the note-book, to find a likely Syd association, and combine it with the stopped thought in his mind to create spontaneous lines of free verse. He held his soft little 2B lightly between thumb and fore-finger and let it flow across the blank right-hand pages, re-morselessly filling the notebook. It was the twilight hour when the rush of words came to end.

On the train back to Kent, Rifaat patiently removed the clip-pings from his notebook so that only the pencil-work remained. He was impressed by the drift of the graphite across the smooth paper. The handwriting was looping and cursive, slightly old-fashioned, nothing like his usual style. He didn't know what Syd's hand-writing looked like. But Rifaat was impressed that in his semi-trance state he had managed to generate the words to what looked like eleven songs. They made little obvious sense, of course, seeming to be a collection of riddles, nonsense rhymes, Sanskrit phrases and jokes. But they definitely had a Barrett-like feel to them. They were stark and disconsolate, full of arresting imagery and enigmatic symbolism. And they seemed to feature an oblique running commentary on the ups and downs of Syd's life.

Rifaat went to see his brother at once. He found Doc sitting in the deck-chair on his father's allotment, watching the great floating marker buoys turn restlessly on the coastal tide. Rifaat gave him the notebook. Its title page was adorned with fat, serif lettering. *Syd's Long Last Album*. Doc squealed in delight. He care-fully opened the book and examined the scribbled pages with all the attentiveness of a Vedic scholar, his newly-acquired read-ing glasses perched on his nose. He nodded and chortled as his finger passed over the dark tracings. Of course, he whispered. Of course. Rifaat's heart leapt with joy. Some most wonderful lessons, Little Brother, said Doc.

Rifaat asked him what he thought the "lessons" were about. Doc gave his little brother a pitying look. The first thing he did was explain the meaning of the Sanskrit words. He talked about the law of "karma" and the obscuring veil of "maya", the relationship between the One of "atman" and the All of "paramatman", the outcast life of the "kapalika", the spiritual divergence between the right-hand path of "dakshina" and the left-hand path of "vama", the occult significance of a guru's "siddhi" or magical powers. Rifaat barely knew what any of it meant. Doc told him to come back tomorrow. He needed more time to examine the book. But rest assured, he said to his brother, his hand on his arm, it's marvelous.

Little Brother Rifaat did as he was told. The next day was overcast with strong south-westerlies gusting in from the Medway over the coast. Doc's hair danced in the breeze. He was in high spirits. The book lay in his lap. Doc tapped its cover in excitement. He said he had it all figured out. He had cracked the code of Syd's silence and recovered the occult wisdom encoded within his various acts of supposed lunacy. The Syd cult was not a joke, he said. It was not just some obscure rock'n'roll fan club. It was more even than a mythology. Instead, it was an honest-to-god secret theosophy, a Westernised Hindu cult with Syd as its hidden guru, Pink Floyd as the holy name of its originating sacred sound and Syd's records and music press interviews as its disguised mantras and teachings. Doc took a breath. He was having a manic spell.

It's all so clear, he said to Rifaat. Syd had been turned down by the holy Maharaja when he had asked to join the Sant Mat sect in 1966. He had been turned down twice. But according to the occult lore Doc had deciphered from *Syd's Long Last Album*, which he now took as the key to the Syd theosophy, there had been a third time of asking — kept secret by both parties — when Syd had got what he had so richly deserved. This time, Syd was neither too proud nor too humble, too hot nor too cold. He was just right. He lounged on the floor of the hotel room and wriggled his bare toes in the Maharaja's tiger-skin rug. He sang him an early version of "Effervescing Elephant". The Maharaja was seriously impressed.

It was then, said Doc, his hair flying, that the Maharaja revealed the truth about the lad Syd, the truth he had tried to protect him from in his two previous visits. Yes, Syd had an exceptionally strong spiritual aura, a powerful *atman*, the most powerful the Maharaja had ever encountered. But, no, he could not join the Sant Mat sect. And that was because his aura was toxic, polluted, tolerable in only small doses, even by the most upright persons. That was why the Maharaja advised Syd to form his own sect, a secret sect, open to only the most despised and untouchable persons, the "kapalikas" of the hippie scene.

Syd bit the rug in ecstasy. The Maharaja loomed over him. He said that Syd had committed an unspeakably hideous crime in a past life. His karmic load was so heavy that the only way to burn it off in one life-time was to follow the left-hand path of "vama". This would oblige him to squander his life force in as many directions as the world allowed. He should destroy his mind with drugs, exhaust his body with aimless wanderings and consume his spiritual energies with jealous fantasies of betrayal and treachery. And he should sing and play his guitar for as long as he could, all over the world, if possible, until he had forgotten the echo of the cosmic Om he had heard in the Gog Magog Hills all those years ago. Only then would he be done, only then would the One of "atman" and the All of "paramatman" coincide. Only then would Syd attain a state of nirvana.

Syd used himself up very quickly, said Doc. King of the London underground rock scene at 20 years of age, pop star by 21, celebrity has-been at 26. It was at the Corn Exchange in 1972 that Syd had begun "treading the backward path", as he put it in an interview. He blocked out the world, said Doc, tuning himself into the pulse of his interior being, the blood rushing in his veins, the neurons firing across his synapses, until even that, too, was gone and he had done it, got back to the moment before the Big Bang, where there is only the Brahman, the divine silence of the eternally unstruck sound, and only his skin and bones, his sunken eyes, were left as testament to his achievement.

It was deranged talk, of course. But Little Brother Rifaat, as he told me, was spellbound. And as the winds died down and the evening came on, Doc became more meditative, his voice carrying across the dark. He talked of the eight "siddhis" which he had discerned in Rifaat's book, the paranormal shape-shifting powers that any enlightened guru possessed, and which Syd had in spades. Doc said he believed that Syd had manifested them on the sly to his fans, fellow band members and, sometimes, even the most casually met strangers.

When Syd appeared on TV in rags and still managed to enthral his audience, when he knocked off mesmerising songs from the roof of his Earlham Street flat, a stone's throw from the market cries of the fruit and veg traders in Covent Garden, when he walked the royal parks of London barefoot, handing out benedictions left, right and centre to grateful passersby, what was this, said Doc, if not a manifestation of "isitva", the supernatural ability to force influence upon people?

And what of the power of infinite self-magnification known as "mahima"? said Doc. At the 14 Hour Technicolour Dream gig at the Ally Pally, Pink Floyd were on-stage when the rising sun streamed its rays through the venue's huge east-facing windows. Fans testified that at this moment, Syd dilated his body to such an extent that he blocked the sun's light, before bouncing it off the mirror discs of his white Telecaster and dazzling the audience.

At the other end of the scale, Syd had reduced his body to the size of an atom when he lived inside a linen cupboard for months on end, undisturbed by hunger or thirst, at his Egerton Court crash-pad in South Ken. The power of "anima", said Doc.

The supernatural power used most often by Syd was "prapti", said Doc, the ability to teleport anywhere at will. He was famous among his teenage friends for never failing to appear when spoken about in his absence. He often turned up mere minutes before Pink Floyd were due to open tour dates. He unaccountably appeared in the front row of gigs, guitar in hand, after he was dropped from the band. And he manifested at the back of Pink Floyd group press photos to which he had never been invited as a stricken, ghostly presence.

His most notorious act of teleportation, said Doc, involved the simultaneous use of "garima", the power to make oneself infinitely heavy. Pink Floyd were at the mixing desk in Abbey

Road in 1975, fiddling with the sound of "Shine On You Crazy Diamond", one of Roger Waters' blubbering guilt-ridden songs about Syd, when he magically appeared out of nowhere in Studio Three. At first Waters didn't recognise him, because of the paunch. Syd was sporting the shaven-headed monk look and was ready to play his guitar part. Waters dismissed him. Hitching the waist-band of his trousers over his gut, Syd looked past Waters and disappeared as mysteriously as he had arrived.

On the other hand, said Doc, Syd could become almost weightless. He used to levitate behind drawn curtains in his flat at Wetherby Mansions in Earl's Court. His girlfriends talked of it in hushed tones. A manifestation of "laghima".

The most self-punishing of the magical "siddhis" according to Doc was "prakamya", the ability to realise whatever one desires. The songs, the girls, the fame – it all came far too easily for Syd. As did the Pink Floyd royalty cheques after he had quit the band. He wasted the money as fast as he could, as if it were cursed, buying up the huge Pontiacs and Cadillacs and giving them away to fans or leaving them to rust in the King's Road.

Finally, said Doc, as the money seeped away, there was the long walk back to Cambridge, to live in the back bedroom of his mum's retirement home in St Margaret's Square, looking out of the window, with only a naked light-bulb for company. Here, said Doc, Syd would adopt the lotus position, the soles of his feet upturned like petals, and manifest the power of "vasitva", of self-mastery, waiting out the years in solitude until the last of his karma balanced out and he was ready for a positive exit.

Doc finished speaking to his little brother. It was dawn. A sea-gull landed on the allotment and looked at them both. Then it flew away.

In the weeks that followed, Rifaat gave his Syd screed a light edit and typed it up on some old sheets of legal paper. He laid it out as lines of free verse. There were about 30 pages. He kept the title, *Syd's Long Last Album*, and finally got up the nerve to submit his typescript to Hangman Books. He was surprised when it was accepted.

Not all of this was told to me that night at Megatripolis. But Rifaat let slip enough that I was keen to know more. We left the club together in the small hours, still talking, and parted under the arches of Charing Cross. The trains had not yet started their early morning commuter rumblings and town was quiet. Rifaat said he could always be contacted at Megatripolis on a Thursday night. He hoisted his canvas bag over his shoulder and walked up Villiers Street into the Strand. His Japanese girlfriend waved goodbye to me at the top of the rise and they were gone.

I thought about Rifaat a lot after that, met him a few more times at the club and got the whole story about Doc and his obsession with Syd. Then we drifted apart. The last I hard, he had reinvented himself as a painter and was exhibiting his bright-ly-coloured daubings in Tokyo, to much local enthusiasm. His brother died after consuming a toxic mix of prescribed sedatives and anti-depressants. The coroner returned a verdict of death by misadventure and his ashes were cast into the Medway.

As for Syd, he finally passed away in 2006. His family auc-tioned off his possessions through Cheffins in Cambridge and I got hold of the catalogue. I considered buying one of his old spiral-bound notebooks, the one containing a few hand-written notes on "The Philosophy of Priests". But I knew I would be out-bid. So I stayed away.

JOHNNY AGGRO

Composer of the Brian Jones Shango Baptist Routine

WHENEVER I HEAR THE NAME JOHNNY AGGRO, which is rare nowadays, I always think of a forlorn young man standing at the mike in the Tunnel Club hitting the tape keys of a chunky Panasonic boom box. His fingers skipped between pause and play as he announced his political opinions over a selection of pop songs which leant heavily on the Rolling Stones. His act was advertised as a condensed version of a 60-minute spoken-word monologue called *Jagger's Army*. And that monologue, I was to learn, was itself extracted from *Rock My Religion II*, a huge collection of tape cassettes and notes assembled by Johnny over the years. The fragment I witnessed that night in south-east London was a kind of Brechtian turn, combining as it did popular song with jokes and invective. Despite wearing the recognisable uniform of 1980s alternative comedy — a Burton's suit and a silly hat, in this case a black Pilgrim hat — Johnny failed to get any laughs. In fact, he was bottled off-stage after 20 minutes. Given the spirit of the times, though, this was quite an achievement.

I caught up with Johnny at the bar. He was being consoled by a couple of his friends, who were introduced to me as Watson and Minerva. Watson was jovial and cynical, dressed in figure-hugging lycra — club gear, basically — while Minerva was short-haired and pouty, in a black MA-1 flying jacket, fishnets and DMs. I bought a round of drinks and explained I was doing a story on the latest wave of post-punk comic talent —Vic Reeves, Jenny Eclair, Felix Dexter — to emerge from the Tunnel Club. It was 1988, a full year into Mrs Thatcher's third term of regressive modernisation, and the mood in the little comedy venue was defiant, if gloomy. Jammed in the back of the Mitre, a south London pub plonked next to a gasometer on the traffic-heavy approach road to the Blackwall Tunnel, it was a place that seemed to have no past and little future.

Watson was offering the miserable Johnny an Adornoite critique of his act. This is what struggling artists used to do in those days — demolish each other's work in a spirit of high-minded exaltation. Watson was obviously familiar with the long-form version of *Jagger's Army* and conceded it was a brilliant take on the endless recycling of the blues in Anglo-American rock music. Johnny nodded. He was sweating. But at the end of the day, said Watson, it only offered an intellectual justification for the continued existence of boring stadium rock bands like Queen and Guns N' Roses. Minerva said she hated Axl Rose. He's such a dick!

Johnny turned to me as if I were an impartial witness. He said that *Jagger's Army* traced the history of the '60s British blues scene back via the Mississippi blues and Afro-Christian gospel music to the psalms sung by the revolutionary Puritan chaplains of Cromwell's New Model Army. To that extent, he said, he was amplifying the thesis implicit in *Rock My Religion*, the film made by American artist Dan Graham, which drew a connection between rock music and the ecstatic religious assemblies of the Shakers. Johnny said that whereas Graham's method was merely comparative, his own was properly dialectical. He also claimed that his work dated the origin of rock to a much earlier dissident religious sect than did Graham's *Rock My Religion* — namely the seventeenth-century Baptists rather than the eighteenth- century Shakers. The primal scene of all rock music, said Johnny, was the resistance of Cromwell's Baptist colonels to a mere dictatorship of the bourgeoisie after they had killed the king. It found its summation in the Rolling Stones album *Beggars Banquet*, with its glorification of proletarian revolution on key tracks "Sympathy for the Devil" and "Street Fighting Man."

I thought that seemed like a rather grandiose claim for a stand-up routine. But this was back in the day when alternative comedy still had a militant edge and was open to forms beyond the quick-fire gag, including poetry, cabaret and spoken-word monologue. Johnny gave me his *Jagger's Army* set list years later and I have used this document — as well as the partial tape recording I made on the night — to reconstruct his performance at the Tunnel Club.

As far as I remember, Johnny started by playing a bit from a song that showed, despite all appearances to the contrary, that he understood his audience. It was a moment of pure English surrealism — the chorus from "Can Blue Men Sing The Whites?" by the Bonzo Dog Band. There were a few anticipatory chuckles from the audience. They figured this was the set-up to a punchline. They were mistaken. Johnny stopped the tape. Stared at the audience.

Then he hit them with a few bars of "Sympathy for the Devil", with the "woo-woo" backing vocals echoing Mick Jagger's lead vocal in call-and-response style. Johnny spoke over the cross-rhythms of the samba beat. He was talking about Godard's 1968 agit-prop film *One + One*. The French avant-garde film-maker, he said, had filmed "Sympathy for the Devil" being composed by a band of white guys in the Olympic Sound Studios in London. He had cut the scenes alongside staged footage of a bunch of frizzed-up black guys throwing each other rifles in a scrap-yard as they quoted lines from Amiri Baraka and Eldridge Cleaver. Johnny let the song play for a bit. Jagger calling out the gods of political violence, anarchy and war. Brian Jones responding enthusiastically with the "woo-woo" backing vocals. The Bonzo Dogs' question is posed by Godard in a more precise way, said Johnny. Can the Rolling Stones be taken as seriously as the Black Panthers in the revolutionary moment of 1968?

Johnny dropped his next track. Al Jolson singing "Camptown Races" in a coon accent which could only sound offensive to contemporary ears. "Da Camptown ladies sing dis song, doo-dah, doo-dah." At this point, there was heckling from some brave fellows in the audience, but Johnny simply glared at them and pushed on relentlessly with his theme. Yes, he said. Yes. The same Amiri Baraka, who was quoted in the scrap-yard scene in *One + One*, claimed as far back as 1965 that the Rolling Stones were nothing but a minstrel act. And it's certainly tempting, he said, to see Mick Jagger clapping and squawking in the Olympic Studios as the thin minstrel Brother Tambo and Brian Jones lazing around on the sidelines as the fat minstrel Brother Bones. But is it fair?

Godstar! Godstar! shouted a nutter from the audience. Indeed, said Johnny, with a flash of teeth. Let's condemn Mick Jagger as a phoney for singing the praises of the killing of the Tsar during the Russian Revolution. Let's by all means do that.

But then we should also condemn the black British actors Danny Daniels and Roy Stewart for pretending to be American Black Panthers in *One + One*. Let's not forget, he said, that they both went on to play comical African tribesmen in *Carry On Up the Jungle*. Members of the Nosha tribe, if I remember correctly.

There was sporadic booing at this point and the club compere, a funny little man in big glasses, was becoming restless, walking up and down beside the stage. Johnny managed to keep the mood going his way for a bit. He pressed into his next song.

It was Muddy Waters' 1955 recording of "Mannish Boy". The old Mississippi bluesman chanted about being first a young boy, then the greatest man alive, with the rhythm guitar and the harmonica stepping in each time to play the line back as a stomping one-chord riff. There's the response to the call, said Johnny. Right there! The space that's filled with the "woo-woo" in "Sympathy for the Devil", the "doo dah, doo-dah" in "Camptown Races", the repetition by the Afro-Christian congregation in the Deep South of the short melodic phrases spoken by the church deacon, the whoops of the plantation rebels in Virginia as they responded to the coded whistles of their leader Nat Turner, the, the… Johnny had to duck here as the first empty Pilsener bottle went flying. He pressed on, raising his voice slightly. It all goes back to the Baptist regiments of the New Model Army lifting their voices to repeat the lines of the psalms after they were shouted out by the chaplain on the fields of Naseby and Langport.

The crowd stamped their feet. They shouted "off off off!" Johnny managed to play a snatch of the Rolling Stones song "Street Fighting Man" before the plug was pulled. He took off his hat and threw it to the ground. He said he had many tracks still to play, including a version of "Praise our Lord all ye gentiles" by the Choir of Merton College. The crowd booed and he was ejected from the stage. As he slunk to the bar with his crumpled hat and his boom box, the compere was already introducing the next act, a timid-looking fellow in a paper hat who did comic impressions of fondly remembered kids' TV characters talking dirty. As I remember, he went down quite well.

By the end of the evening, Johnny was quite drunk and foul-tempered. He said that it was a shame I hadn't seen him complete his act, that he hadn't even had the chance to repeat George Melly's famous quip about the British blues boom, the fact that it found its own Mississippi Delta in the Thames Valley. Well, yes, said Watson. More jokes would certainly have helped.

I don't get it, said Minerva, peering over the rims of her flared sunglasses. The Melly joke, I mean. Well, said Johnny, perhaps it's not a joke, more a condensed history lesson. The point being that a lot of the British blues haunts of the early 1960s were on a Thameside belt that stretched south from Ealing down to Richmond and Twickenham. Gerry Potter's record shop, for one. The Marshall brothers' music shop on Uxbridge Road, for another. Shops have always been so important for British youth culture. What about the caffs? said Watson. L'Auberge coffee house, Sid's Café opposite Ealing Art College. He was counting them off on his fingers. The venues were also important, said Johnny. The Crawdaddy at Richmond Station Hotel, the Ealing Club. Don't forget Sandover Hall, said Watson. Points for obscurity, said Johnny. It had become a competition between them, to commemorate the blues shrines of West London. The Eel Pie Island jazz and blues club, said Johnny, with an air of finality. I had a whole riff on that place. I know, said Watson. I know. He clapped his friend on the shoulder.

Johnny later sent me a vintage postcard of Eel Pie Island, featuring a colourised photo of the genteel old hotel which had once been there for many years. By the time George Melly, John Mayall's Bluesbreakers and the Rolling Stones got to gig there, it was damp and dilapidated, mysterious, a world set apart. This was according to the notes Johnny had scrawled on the back of his postcard. He wrote that the Eel Pie Island blues club was a place reachable only by a rickety wooden bridge across the Thames. You bought a ticket to cross in the form of a passport, which granted access to an imaginary nation. "Eelpiland", as it was called. As far as Johnny was concerned, this was a nation as real as the New World to which the radical Baptists of the English Commonwealth had been exiled after the Restoration, as real as the Afro-America of Amiri Baraka, as real as any dream of freedom. It was, he reckoned, a hidden country, a place secreted in the Thames where an emerging generation protested against the constraints of family, work and organised religion by dancing to loud music and getting high on Newcastle Brown and Woodbines. More than that, Eelpiland was a belated response to the original call to arms of English revolutionary forces when they defended the Thames at Turnham Green, a response mediated through the echoes of the gospel and the Mississippi Delta blues. Making Melly's joke a kind of prophecy, in a way.

So said Johnny. He was always a believer in the grand dialectical sweep of history. That became quite clear to me from our conversation in the Tunnel Club all those years ago. He thought a world revolution was an inevitability. It was just a question of when circumstances would allow it to happen. There had been a chance in 1968, he maintained. Watson scoffed at this. He said that Adorno had got it right. The student protests in France, Italy and Germany and the US that year were more regressive than revolutionary. Adolescent tantrums! Johnny disagreed. He said that they mapped present injustice on to past injustice and made it clear that political events like the French Revolution, the American Revolution, were versions of an incomplete project. Watson shook his head. Mysticism! he said.

Minerva wondered what any of this had to do with "Street Fighting Man". I clinked bottles with her in agreement. Johnny said that Jagger's rhetoric in the song, with its acknowledgement of the urgent need for a people's revolution, was as incendiary as anything proposed by the Black Panthers. Making it such a shame that Jagger had missed his own chance to seize the revolutionary moment. Minerva raised an eyebrow. Really? she said. Don't forget, said Johnny, Jagger was part of the big rally against war and injustice in Trafalgar Square in March 1968. All he had to do was leap on-stage with his harmonica, lead the youthful crowd on a round of angry chanting and then march them down Whitehall to storm the Palace of Westminster. Imagine it! he said. The seat of British government turned into a permanent free festival burning with the light of a hundred furious Altamonts. Here would have been a rock'n'roll moment to conjure the ghost of Cromwell and the unfinished business of the English Revolution. Unreal! said Minerva. She placed her hand on Johnny's arm.

But it was not to be, said Johnny. It never is, said Watson. He grinned. Johnny ignored him. Jagger simply followed the crowd, he said, as it was diverted through Mayfair and kettled by mounted police in Grosvenor Square. The revolutionary tendencies of 1968 were blocked in England. People went home for their tea. Johnny drained the last of his lager. Jagger, he said, at least recognised this disillusioning fact. He went home and wrote "Street Fighting Man", with its rebuke to "sleepy London town" for failing to rise to the occasion. And then Godard hit town a few months later, said Watson. To film the Stones recording *Beggars Banquet* at Olympic Studios and preserve for posterity the memory of what could have been. He gave a bright laugh.

You'll have to forgive Watson, Minerva said. He thinks that revolution is a dead concept. Who doesn't nowadays? I said. Isn't Gramsci all the rage? I was thinking of the political influence achieved at that time by the Communist Party magazine *Marxism Today*, which had renounced open conflict with the state in favour of a gradual takeover of the institutions of civil society. Johnny frowned into his empty beer bottle. He seemed to want to disagree with me. Before he could say anything, Watson clapped him on the back and said that I shouldn't worry. Johnny was no politico. Instead he was a poet. Let's face it, said Watson, we're all too young to remember how crushing it must have been for old school communists when Soviet tanks rolled into Prague in 1968. The *New Musical Express*, not the *Morning Star*, has always dictated the party line to us.

It's a long time since anyone took Mick Jagger seriously, I said. He still hasn't clawed his way back from punk opprobrium. Unlike Brian Jones, said Watson. Wasn't he the front-man for the Brian Jonestown Massacre? said Minerva. She was being flirtatious. Ha! said Watson. He was the founder of the Rolling Stones. The man who hired Mick Jagger. Wow! said Minerva. Now she was being sarcastic. Johnny has a whole riff about Brian Jones, said Watson, turning to his friend. What's it called, again? You know what it's called, said Johnny. *Stone Dead*. Maybe you should have done it tonight, said Watson. After all, wasn't it Jones out of all the Stones who made the pilgrimage to see Muddy Waters at the Marquee in London in 1958? Watson grinned. And wasn't it also Jones who organised the Stones' debut gig at the Marquee four years later? Johnny nodded. There was a pause. It was as if the two men were putting on a show.

Look, said Johnny, the whole Jones saga is too pessimistic. You know that. I asked Johnny to explain what he meant. But he stayed silent. In the end, Watson spoke up. Johnny reckons that although Jones got to the blues before Jagger, he failed to recognize it as an implicit call to revolution. Instead, he saw the music as something primitive and fetishistic, a cry from out of darkest Africa. And he submitted to its assumed tradition with all the drowsy eagerness of a cultist.

He was murdered in the end, wasn't he? said Minerva. He died in his own swimming pool, I said. Like the Great Gatsby. He drowned, said Watson. Yeah, said Johnny. Cotchford Farm, I said. That was the name of the place where he died. The memory came out of nowhere. Yeah, said Watson. The rock star in his fifteenth century English manor house. What a cliché. Jones retired there after he was kicked out of the band. Johnny nodded. He packed it to the rafters with antiques and collectables. Like the cabinet of curiosities of some Regency dandy, said Watson. Johnny laughed in agreement. Again, I had the sensation I was witnessing a well-rehearsed routine.

The thing is, Johnny said, Brian Jones was not really equipped to survive outside of the imaginary country of Eelpiland. He crafted a stage persona for himself which was some impossible combination of blond-haired Negro chieftan and eternal Chelsea hipster. He even gave himself a new name. Elmore Lewis. Here was a man who lacked caution. Jones was able to absorb the current of feeling the blues inherited from the dissident religious sects of the English Civil War. But he misinterpreted it. And he was unable to channel it.

He was overcome by it instead, said Minerva. Kind of, said Johnny. He looked at Minerva with a new admiration. The man took drugs, he withdrew, he got fat. And then, said Watson, the Stones turned his death into a carnival at the Hyde Park Festival in London. Those poor butterflies, said Minerva. The ones Jagger released into the crowd. They all died, you know. Whatever, said Johnny. There was certainly no danger of this mob being led down Whitehall to storm the Palace of Westminster, he said. They'd already given up. In fact, they were quite content for the rock scene to settle into becoming a morbid death cult, with Hendrix, Jim Morrison and Lennon following Jones into martyrdom. Like I say, *Stone Dead* is pessimistic.

Minerva broke the awkward silence that followed. Watson is working on a krautrock primer, she said. She beamed at her man. It's true, said Watson, looking a bit embarrassed. Then he gathered himself, as if for a lecture hall address. *Komische Muzik*, as we should call it, is the only original music of the postwar period. Can, Cluster, Kraftwerk, he said… acts like these represent an electronic continuation of the avant-garde compositional techniques of Stockhausen, Boulez and Varese. They made a decisive rejection of both the kitsch romanticism of European pop music and the endless recycling of the blues in Anglo-American rock. Here, he gave Johnny a sly little look.

Hey! said Johnny. I only did this gig to please you. He was shouting at Watson. You said I should get my research out there, the *Rock My Religion II* stuff. So I did. I found a story to tell, a good one, and look what the fuck happened! Watson sighed and gave me a look. He's such a delicate bloom, he said.

Johnny was certainly a bit of a strange case. I got to know his story over the next few months. We went drinking together in the dingy pubs of Deptford and New Cross Gate, where we talked a lot about music, politics and theory and a little about our personal lives. That was how it was in those days among the declasse young men of late Thatcherism. Even so, I was able to piece together some of Johnny's life story. He had been born in Bradford in 1961 as John Hargreaves, his last name coming from his maternal grandfather. His mother had been "knocked up", as he rather savagely put it, by a handsome US airman stationed at Menwith Hill. The man hadn't stuck around for long and had returned to Kentucky. Johnny wanted nothing to do with him.

He excelled at school, finding it a relief from the strain of his mother's chronic mental health problems. He was good at fighting and none of the other boys messed with him. The girls liked to get close to him and touch his skin and he was happy to let them do it. One day he brought his father's old Colt service pistol to school and showed it off in the playground. It was unloaded but he still got the ruler. The only other thing he had from his father was a box of Philips cassette tapes, featuring pre-recorded sermons by Reverend Martin Luther King Jr. He listened to them over and over in his bedroom, absorbing their compelling mix of Shakespearean syntax and Baptist hymn-singing rhythms. He imagined himself a prophet.

It was that box inherited from his father which was the cornerstone of Johnny's tape collection. In his early teenage years, he bought tapes of his favourite hard rock bands – the Stones, Led Zep, Deep Purple – and nodded out to them on headphones. From there, he spiralled off into collecting obscure cassette compilations of blues music, country, gospel and choral music. His interests even then were archaeological. He always wanted to go a stage further back. It was if he were searching for an origin of the rock music that he and his white school-friends loved so much.

Punk put a stop to that. It taught him that pop music was hopelessly compromised by the record industry's need to turn a buck. The Rolling Stones and Elvis offered only reactionary escapism. Their work should be forgotten! What was needed instead were brutal songs designed to open people's eyes to the truth of life under late capitalism – that it was demoralising and rotten and needed to be destroyed. These were the disruptive thoughts that tore through the lower-middle class youth of England in the late 1970s. What also helped Johnny get on-board with the punk movement, it has to be said, was the fact that highly individualistic figures like Poly Styrene, Don Letts and Andy Polaris modelled a new and exciting idea of what it meant to be black and British.

Johnny stopped collecting music tapes and started to write down on index cards his ideas for punk songs. At first, these were fairly conventional odes to fast sex and cheap drugs. But after a while, under the influence of Patti Smith, he began to note down ideas for much more idiosyncratic and surreal songs. Songs that he knew he didn't have the talent to write, but which he thought somebody *should* write, some day. His school-work inevitably suffered. But somehow he scrambled his way through the university applications clearing system to get a place studying history at Leeds. It was here that he first met his inamorato Watson.

The two bumped into each other at the Fenton, a noisy student pub full of cigarette smoke, alcoholic rage and political arguments. Watson accidentally jumped the queue at the bar, took note of Johnny's sullen face and bought him a drink in recompense. Perhaps he thought a black boy like Johnny might deck him one. Watson was dressed in a black V-neck with tapered fawn trousers and Church's brogues. No cheap trainers for him. He looked like Alain Delon. Johnny immediately understood he would have to change his own sartorial game to keep up. He felt this as the first of many painful cuts at his provincial roots.

Watson was a student at the Fine Art Department and, although he never seemed to do any work, he could talk fluently about Art & Language, dialectical materialism and the bracing alienation effect of the Gang of Four's first album. In short, he was a bit of a poseur. The girls loved him, of course. Watson passed on many of his entanglements to Johnny, who soon acquired an intellectual taste for the neurotic complexities of the female mind. Sometimes, their tenure with a girlfriend would overlap and all three might share the same bed.

Johnny's bleak wit, comic monologues about the meaning of Talking Heads songs and unpredictable nature soon gained him an admiring audience among the Fenton crowd. Indeed, Watson was happy to step back and play manager to his protege, massaging Johnny's ego and giving him tips on form. This was when Johnny became known as "Aggro". He denounced Scritti Politti's 1982 turn to New Pop as post-punk deviationism and said that the kids wouldn't be all right until the last *Smash Hits* cover star had been hanged with the guts of the last Radio 1 DJ. His party piece was to play "White Riot" on the banjo ukulele.

It was all pretty exhausting and Johnny barely graduated. When it was time for him to move out of his student digs in Leeds, Watson — who had already made the move to London — turned up to help him. Together, they surveyed Johnny's meagre possessions. A second-hand suit, a tennis racket and all the old shoe-boxes filled with rock and blues music tapes. Johnny said maybe he should throw them out. Watson said no, that would be to fall into the error of what his arts school professors called "non-dialectical thinking." He knelt down and inspected the cassettes, many of them home-made mix-tapes with poetic titles like "Slivers of Brian Jones" and "New Orleans Marching Band Music (Played Backwards)." He also looked kindly on Watson's index-card rack of ideas for political punk songs — a sea shanty set to a reggae beat, a rockabilly version of a Ranter sermon, terrace chants plus Burundi drums. Watson said that Johnny should continue to build on his obsessions. One day — who knows? — he might have a collection to rival Harry Smith's *Anthology of American Folk Music*.

Johnny was grateful to Watson for his encouragement. They drove down to London in a hired van. Watson had managed to talk his way into Goldsmiths to do an MA in Fine Art. He was immensely plausible. He'd also scored a flat in a Peabody Trust block in Southwark, a cheap-rent deal which I expect many poor Londoners probably deserved far more than he did. It was decided that Johnny should move in with Watson until he found his feet. His boxes of tapes naturally moved with him.

It was during this period that Johnny got into the strange and elliptical writings of the rabbinical Marxist Walter Benjamin, particularly his "Theses on the Philosophy of History". Benjamin had been Watson's latest intellectual obsession. He was only now passing his discovery on to Johnny because he could feel himself moving beyond it. Johnny felt an instant affinity for Benjamin's philosophy of history, particularly its claim that revolutionary political zeal was ultimately a form of ecstatic religious experience. This helped Johnny to finally understand that the political inspirations of late '60s rock music were as valid as those of punk. Both owed a debt to the religious furnishings of the blues and gospel. It all went back to the Psalms, as he had long ago intuited.

Johnny was also attracted to Benjamin's advocacy of collecting and curating as revolutionary method. It was an alternative route to the same New Jerusalem as the dialectical supersessions of classical Marxism, a haphazard path rather than a straight path, but a righteous path nonetheless. Benjamin's approach to history made room for expressive, subjective and even entirely speculative chains of association. It justified Johnny's tape collection. Johnny thought of it as a way of linking together events and artefacts which had a similar kind of feel – ecstatic, strange, intense. It represented a weaving passage through the dreamtime of revolutionary history.

It was during this interval that Watson showed Johnny his video copy of *Rock My Religion*, which he had borrowed from someone he knew at Film and Video Umbrella. They watched it together one evening in Johnny's living room. It acted like a key unlocking something in Johnny's mind. He experienced a sudden flash of illumination. He kissed Watson on the forehead. He said that he now understood that his tape cassettes of obscure hymns and rocks songs and his index-cards of ideas for political pop songs were part of the same project. Of course they were! *Rock My Religion II?*, said Watson, with a faint smile. Exactly! said Johnny. Notes towards a sound-track for an imaginary film. Or a spoken-word monologue, said Watson. The two men grabbed their cigarettes. They went out to Upper Marsh and found a tiny pub they knew had a lock-in. They were on a mission.

That night, they figured out the theory behind *Rock My Religion II*. Watson said that Benjamin was a collector of visual impressions. He had strolled through the old Paris arcades and assembled in his mind a diorama of revolutionary images. This was well known. It would take Johnny Aggro, said Watson, pointing at his friend, to wander the folkways of the North Atlantic and compile an anthology of revolutionary sounds. Johnny accepted the compliment. The two men nonetheless figured that this presented a certain difficulty. The audio archive didn't go as far back in history as the visual archive. We have pictures of how the Iroquois people looked in the seventeenth century, said Watson. And that gives us a visual context for Marx's praise of the Indians as models of primitive communism. But the Smithsonian didn't record their medicine songs until the 1930s. Same with the blues, said Johnny. In fact, the very earliest blues recordings have all been lost.

There's a lag, said Watson. Perhaps even a void. One which I intend to fill, said Johnny, triumphantly. He searched his pockets and showed Watson some of his latest index-cards. They featured ideas not for songs, but for the raw sonics of revolutionary history. Sounds which should have been recorded but which weren't. Sounds which could never have ever been recorded except by a time-traveller with a tape-deck. Sounds of the old weird Atlantic. "War cries of the Chowan River", "Slave dancing his chains on deck to a sea shanty", "General Lambert's call to arms at Daventry." Watson gave a long low whistle. He said he could only imagine what a Conny Plank or a Holger Czukay, one of his beloved tape-edit composers, might have done with access to such sounds. He shook his head. Did Johnny know what he was doing? In entering upon this new field of study, a purely hypothetical field of study, he was setting himself up for an intellectual career which would exceed any one man's lifetime. Was he willing to risk it? Especially when the only reward was the dubious distinction of being called a prophet.

So began a long period of indigence for Johnny. He survived by doing odd bits of clerical work — proof-reading for the *South London Press*, temping at the GPO in St Martin's Le Grand — while grimly hanging on to the Peabody chambers after Watson had departed. During his spare hours, Johnny wrote out ideas at a furious pace. These were mainly ideas for time-traveller field-recordings: "The scratching of Colonel Okey's quill on the king's death-warrant in 1649", "The splash of the water over the head of Muddy Waters when he was baptised in Deer Creek",

"An escaped slave whistling on the Underground Railroad". But there were also ideas for completely imaginary sounds: "Mob singing 'woo-woo' at the burning of Parliament in 1968", "Brian Jones elegy on mandolin for the hanging of Colonel Axtell at Tyburn." And there were even ideas for impossible, joke sounds: "Hinges creaking on Davy Jones' Locker."

By the late 1980s, Johnny had over 10,000 index-cards. They filled scores of shoe-boxes which were piled up in the nooks and crannies of his flat. One day, Watson paid him a surprise visit. Accompanying him was Minerva, a medical student. He suggested Johnny needed a filing system, some way of organising his material. Otherwise, he was at risk of simply compiling a shopping list of magic moments from Marxist historiography. Watson said it was something Adorno had warned Benjamin about, the danger of being spellbound by mere facts at the crossroads of history. Johnny frowned. He was aware that Watson was now working in advertising. He told his friend he didn't get it. His collection was nowhere near complete. He had to keep going. Watson tried again. He asked what Johnny was expecting. Some kind of miracle? Johnny nodded. He felt like he was on the verge of a breakthrough. Watson gave it one last try. He said that Johnny's father would never return to him through the dusty magic of his shoe-boxes. It was a cheap shot. But it worked.

Johnny paused his collecting, he re-surfaced from the detritus of his shoe-boxes. He surveyed the world around him, like a man disturbed from an opium dream. Let's get to work, he said. Watson nodded. He dropped the needle on the 12-inch of Model 500's "Interference", hoping the rush of Kraftwerk-style synth riffs and squelchy bass lines would get them both into the right kind of mood. Johnny immediately began plucking a series of index cards from his archive. As he handed them to his friend, Watson stuck them to the wall with adhesive, trying to get them to line up, to form some approximate dialectical progression.

Gradually, the outline of a narrative emerged. It was the first incarnation of *Stone Dead*, a surrealist treatment of Brian Jones considered as an idea. Johnny's starting point was to take seriously Jones's alter ego Elmore Lewis, casting him as a historically novel cultural figure, the Anglo-African bluesman, whose lineage could be traced back far beyond the Baptist ministers of the Afro-Christian church to the riverine shamans of the Yoruba people. In this conception, Jones was shaping up to be a kind of Ubu Roi figure, complete with cruel temperament, insatiable appetite for drugs and women, and fascination with ritual violence. Watson became obsessed with Jones's visit to North Africa in August 1968 to record the Master Musicians of Joujouka. They were playing at the sacrificial feast of the G'nou tribe. Johnny saw the whole ceremony as an occult reckoning. The black men wanted to dress their honoured guest in the skin of a slaughtered goat, but Jones backed off from the initiation. Less than a year later, he was dead. Johnny shook his head. In the end, he spiked this treatment, worried that it was a form of racist mystification. Watson wasn't sure if he agreed. Nevertheless, he suggested that Johnny might do better to focus his Rolling Stones research on Jagger rather than Jones. Jagger, he said, was a more legibly dialectical figure.

A few weeks later, Johnny got his slot at the Tunnel Club. The fact that he bombed with the audience obviously depressed him. By the end of the evening, I had joined Watson and Minerva in their efforts to console him. Minerva punched his Puritan hat back into shape. Watson slapped him on the back and said he was ahead of his time. I bought him a cigar and said I'd be glad to interview him about his work. He perked up a bit.

Outside, it was cold and damp. The tall iron frame of the gasometer presided over our good-byes. Johnny said he would send me a tape. I walked home in silence.

After that night, Johnny and I met up a few times. That was when we went out on our epic pub crawls of south-east London. Johnny was trying to make a go of his life at this point. He thought he could be a rock critic for the music press and submitted a review of a Throwing Muses gig to the *NME*. But they said it was "too academic" for them. He had a brief fling with Minerva. But she soon left him, complaining of his "dark moods". He drifted back into his Brian Jones obsession, talking of the call-and-response horn patterns of the Master Musicians of Joujouka. I could see he was sinking into depression. Abruptly, he stopped returning my calls.

The only reliable news I had of Johnny after that came from Watson. I bumped into him quite unexpectedly at the Clock House in East Dulwich one night. He said that Johnny's stand-up career, such as it was, had stalled after he had discharged a firearm at the bar of the Royal College of Art. I expressed my shock and disbelief. Watson said that he was there. He had witnessed it. Johnny was doing a version of *Stone Dead*, a new version, a version of alternative history, in fact, which saw Brian Jones reimagined as a Shango Baptist. It was good! said Watson. Very good. But, of course, Johnny being Johnny, he had to go and sabotage any possibility of success. Watson and I drank in silence for a time. The small pub had a convivial atmosphere.

How the fuck does Brian Jones, in anyone's wildest dream, get to become a Shango Baptist? I said at last. Watson smiled. He was kitted out in a large check suit. Johnny took liberties with Brian Jones's life story, he said. Johnny figured that Jones should have gone to the Caribbean rather than Africa in 1968, that he should have recorded the hymn-singing and bell-ringing of the Shouter churches in Trinidad rather than the pipe-playing of the Master Musicians of Joujouka, that he should have allowed himself to be baptised into their faith. This would have saved him, Johnny was convinced, from drowning in the pool at his country house in East Sussex. How? I asked. Watson said that for Jones to have been ceremonially immersed in running fresh water rather than stagnant chlorinated water, to have cleansed himself of his resentments and rages, to have tamed his *orisha* and taken a holy sign from the Psalms, as the Shango Baptists did... all this, according to Johnny, would have enabled him to succeed where Jagger had failed in leading the revolutionary mob of London in 1968. Really? I said. Watson nodded. That was the moment in his performance, he said, when Johnny had removed his Colt from his jacket and fired a round into the ceiling.

Crikey! I said. Indeed, said Watson. He sipped his vodka and tonic. Desperate, really, he said. Maybe Johnny is an embittered revolutionary who has ended up falsifying history in order to maintain his lost illusions. That's a bit harsh, I said. Watson shrugged. Okay then, maybe Johnny is just mad! It was clear Watson was suffering, in his own way. Maybe, I said, Johnny imagines himself a second Adam renaming a world redeemed by Karl Marx the Messiah. Jones's miserable drowning, in his eschatology, is transformed into a righteous baptism. I laughed, despite myself. And all the sinners saints, said Watson, quoting the Jagger lyric from "Sympathy for the Devil."

We decided to get drunk together. Johnny Fucking Aggro, Watson said, after a long interval. Maybe Johnny was on to something. The English bluesman as Shango Baptist does rather make sense of the oddities of Jones's early life. I raised an eyebrow. Oh, said Watson, the fact that he was always attracted to bodies of moving water. The mineral springs of his home town of Cheltenham. The flow of the Thames at Eel Pie Island and, then, at Barnes, where the Olympic Studios were based. The fact that Jones was a good little church-goer in his youth — a member of the choir, in fact — and knew all the old hymns by heart. The fact that he could go into a trance-state as easily as succumbing to one of his asthma attacks. Watson leaned in confidentially. He used to say that he could hear the dead talking to him from the water-pipes of his Courtfield Road flat in South Ken. Imagine!

That was the last item of reliable news I had about Johnny. Minerva, when she drifted more into my orbit, with her scented skin and silky underarm hair, said that he had moved out of his Peabody flat. She thought he'd put his collection of "bits and bobs", as she called his musical treasures, in a self-storage unit in Vauxhall. This must have been in the early 1990s. I wondered if Johnny had effectively made himself homeless, preferring as he might to have his sealed boxes of tapes and jottings rather than his own shivering limbs protected from the elements. It was a haunting thought.

I tried to track down Watson, but he too had disappeared, as if his fate were tied in some mysterious way to Johnny's own. Minerva flashed her eyes at me and said I should watch out. I might be next.

At odd moments, especially after Minerva left me, I had fantasies about waiting under the arches at Vauxhall for Johnny to turn up. I was sure he must be secretly adding to his collection, one way or another. By this time, Mrs Thatcher's "B Team", as she called them, were in power. They were no friends to the dispossessed. They criminalised unlicensed rock festivals. They even forced the closure of gypsy camp sites. It became very hard after this to imagine Jagger, or any figure from the entertainment business – including those alternative comedians who had joined the rock stars of old in performing at huge arenas in London – leading an angry mob down Whitehall. In the 1990s the prospect of any kind of revolution on the 1968 model seemed, well, laughable.

It didn't escape my attention that Johnny's method of stand-up commentary, with its juggling of memories from the archive of popular culture, went on to have some minor success with the more intellectually-inclined British comedians of the early noughties. Dave Gorman stood on stage with his PowerPoint slides projected behind him and riffed in stream-of-consciousness fashion on the connection between, say, *Twelfth Night* and powdered chicken beak. Stewart Lee, similarly, was able to prowl the stage with a mike and squeeze sparks from the collision of sundry items – an Edward Lear nonsense poem and a broken toilet, a reality TV show and a Martin Luther King sermon. Even Russell Brand got in on the act for a bit.

Johnny, like Watson always said, was ahead of his time. What made him inimitable, though, was that he was piling up cultural fragments in the hope they would be transvalued by collective political action. He was indeed a prophet. Figures like Gorman and Lee, by contrast, were baroque artists whose virtuoso compilations could only be redeemed as tributes to their own solitary genius.

Did Johnny ever return to his silo of scribbled notes, index cards and reels of audiotape? Or do they moulder even now in a damp nook of the Thames Embankment on a steadily expiring lease? It's a mystery.

One thing I do know is that the ancient pre-Socratic philosophers believed that all things decay and return to the watery abyss from which they emerged. And certainly when Brian Jones drowned under the spot-lights at his swimming pool, his precious collection of treasures at Cotchford Farm was looted immediately, some say by the very guests attending the party he had hosted that night. The cavernous bedrooms and apartments and waiting rooms of the rotting pile were emptied out. Everything disappeared – the woven rugs and brocade cushions bought from Christopher Gibbs's Chelsea antique shop, the kaftans and Berber jewellery found in Morocco, the rare vinyl cuts by Snooks Eaglin, Champion Jack Dupree and Lightning Hopkins, the stacks of Gibsons and Firebirds, the sitars, dulcimers, harpsichords, marimbas, tambouras and mellotrons picked up over a career of effortless musicianship, the flutes, trombones and saxophones, the pan pipes of the Joujouka, the plated bottles of brandy and fine wine, the wardrobe of velvet jackets, striped trousers, cravats, silk ties, high-collar shirts and white shoes gleaned from Carnaby Street, the Ascot hats, fur capes and scarves plucked from women's department stores – all the accoutrements of a gilded youth. Gone!

And that is how I think of Johnny Aggro and his fabulous collection of revolutionary sounds. Gone, all gone.

YOUNG MR KRAUS

Writer of an Alternative History of Ian Curtis

IT SEEMS FAINTLY LUDICROUS to insist on using the name Derek Cross to identify the author of *City of Dolls*, when the man himself put so much effort into inventing an alter ego for himself. Indeed, you might say that Dieter Kraus killed off Derek Cross. In place of the working-class boy born in Manchester at the shabby terminus of its 300-year-long industrial period, there emerged... something else. Dieter Kraus was a strange amalgam of petty clerk and savage *Ubermensch*, a blond beast with polished shoes, a weird figure of fantasy transplanted from the Bavarian Alps to a twilight corner of England. He railed against the traditions of laissez-faire capitalism which had brought Manchester to ruin and argued instead for a *Nationalsozialismus* of the left. He was first identified in a few marginal poems and nightclubs before colliding with the image of a national rock star, flaming out in the pages of a novel, and falling to the ground in Berlin.

Despite all this, it was indeed the 21-year-old Derek Cross who shut himself away in 1981 to write the novel just mentioned, an exercise in alternative history as astonishing in its own way as Philip K Dick's *The Man in the High Castle*. *City of Dolls* imagined what it would have been like to have lived in Manchester during the 1970s if the Germans had won the war and occupied much of England. Taking a more everyday view of a similar topic than the film *It Happened Here*, the novel paints a convincing picture of a dismal province of empire in which the local middle-classes have made a Devil's bargain with their imperial overlords — submission in exchange for a modicum of peace. Of course, some of the civic dignitaries in Cross's vision of a Nazi England are keener on the bargain than others. Among them is Dieter Kraus, a temperamental young civil servant who swings between moods of wild elation and bitter depression as he embraces the banality of evil.

Kraus, as many clues and in-jokes in the novel indicate, is a thinly disguised reference to Ian Curtis. Cross was an early fan of the band which Curtis fronted. His take on Joy Division was that they had maintained a defiant post-punk stance in the shadows of Manchester's industrial decline, one that was unafraid to lean into the darkness and square off against old phantoms of discipline, self-punishment and submission. He thought that Curtis had deliberately reinvented himself as a messiah figure. It meant he was better placed to absorb the desperate feeling of abandonment seeping out of Manchester and, indeed, England in the late 1970s. Joy Division's bleak songs of personal betrayal and dystopian salvation were a far cry from the usual escapist pop chart fodder. That was why Cross and a generation of young men like him had loved them.

It was also why he took it so badly when Curtis killed himself at the age of 23. He was angry. He thought that, at best, the man had been weak. At worst, he had been incompetent. Either way, he had failed to control the artistic persona he had created for himself. Cross didn't want to hear any of the stories about his hero's epilepsy, his depression, his marriage break-up, his struggles with Factory Records over the prospect of an American tour.

These things were mere excuses. Curtis had failed the test of history.

Cross wrote his novel as an act of revenge – on Curtis, on himself, on 1970s Manchester. It killed his literary career before it had really begun. The puritan left called *City of Dolls* a "fascist apologia". His publisher withdrew the book only a few weeks after its initial print run in 1982. And he was chased down and beaten up by an Anti-Nazi League squad in the Arndale Centre. Things came to a head on the opening night of the Hacienda, when Cross turned up to the nightclub with his personal Factory Records invite, only to be turned away at the door. He quit Manchester for good just a few weeks later, protesting that the city was finished. He singled out for contempt the release of a synth-pop single by New Order, the band which had formed from the ashes of Joy Division. "Temptation" was nothing more than gay disco music, he said. The band were dancing on the grave of Ian Curtis. Factory was over. Manchester was over. England was over. From now on, he would live in Berlin.

Of course, Cross couldn't have got it more wrong with his various proclamations of death. New Order became a huge commercial success. They bank-rolled the 15-year run of the Hacienda. And the Hacienda, as a hub of cultural activity, attracted investment capital to selected parts of Manchester's inner city. It all amounted to a text-book example of Richard Florida's thesis about the urban regeneration which could be achieved by a new creative class. Cross missed out on joining this class and moving up in the world. But he had no regrets. He was proud of having written nothing after *City of Dolls*. It contained everything he ever wanted to say about an alternative path of development for

Manchester in particular and England in general. In fact, he said to me when I interviewed him, his novel became bigger with every passing year. Its vision of a fascist England threw down a challenge to the neoliberal England of selective gentrification, benign neglect and spiralling inequality. What, after all, was so funny about an English *Volksgemeinschaft*?

Cross was saying all this in 1999, two years into Tony Blair's first term as Prime Minister, when the glossy young politician was still riding high in the polls and his Department for Culture, Media and Sport was pushing Florida's creative-class thesis under the banner of "Cool Britannia". So that's five years before the demand for semi-skilled labour in England's regenerating cities resulted in Blair importing hundreds of thousands of low-wage migrant workers from the beaten countries of Eastern Europe. And that's 17 years before the consequences of that decision — which amounted to a refusal to spread newly-acquired wealth beyond the creative class — showed up in the disintegration of his rebranded one-nation Toryism and the emergence of a lumpen class of Brexit-voting social rejects howling betrayal.

I remember well the night I spoke to Cross. It was late, well past pub closing time, and I had my feet up in the office. Basement Jaxx were on the turntable, the sirens, synth riffs and dirty female vocals of "Red Alert" forming an unlikely counterpoint to Cross's one-note prophecies. His voice was scratchy on the line, as if coming in from way off. He said he was enjoying life in Berlin. He couldn't take England. He would never go back. In fact, he wouldn't speak English. In the end, we agreed on French and were on the phone for many hours.

Cross was born in 1959. He was raised for the first decade or so of his life in a semi-detached council house with a tiled roof and an overgrown back garden. He had the run of the Wythenshawe estate on his bike as a boy. But he kept himself to himself. He found the other lads too predictable to satisfy the needs of his restless and curious nature. He used to watch them from a distance, marking boundaries in the park with their cast-off jerseys, scraping knees in cul-de-sacs. Then he would ride on. He preferred to play in the woods at the side of the motorway, imagining this to be a place where deer still roamed and he could become a hunter, like Hiawatha.

Cross's father Bill took the bus every day to work as a maintenance engineer at Ringway Airport. His mother Vera did piece-work from home on her Singer sewing machine. Cross was an only child but he was far from lonely. He examined the progress of red ants across the pavement with his magnifying glass and observed the flight of swallows in the cold weather. He knew the names of the neighbourhood dogs, whose innocent play touched his heart like nothing else. He lost himself in tales of ancient warriors by Rosemary Sutcliff and Henry Treece. His female teachers coddled him at school. He was the master of his little universe.

Then he passed his 11 Plus and everything changed. Accepted into Manchester Grammar School, he found his father suddenly interested in what he self-satisfyingly assumed would be his progress towards joining one of the professions. Would he become a doctor or would he become a lawyer? Neither prospect appealed to Cross. He didn't want to sit at a desk doling out papers. It seemed too much like an adult version of the same miserable tasks the cranky old teachers had him doing at school. Would he be forced to compete with the boys in his class forever? Already, the little kings of the playground had managed to put him in his place. They made cutting remarks about his ill-fitting suit, his coarse manners, his instinctive patriotism. He bled inwardly. But he realised their cruelty was only a reflection of the confidence they had in their ignorance. He really didn't want to become like them. So he coasted during lessons and kept his own counsel.

Inevitably, he became depressed. School placed an invisible filter between himself and his home, himself and his family. When his mother told him he could be anything he wanted to be when he grew up, he couldn't help but wince at her common way of speaking. And when he cycled back to his house from school, having to run a gauntlet of derision from the local comprehensive schoolboys, he found it hard not to see them as dangerous beasts, reared on a diet of class resentment. As for the Wythenshawe estate, it seemed no longer a universe of boyhood adventure but a holding pen for the shambling men discharged from the closed factories of Manchester.

He became morbid. By the time he was 14 and taking the bus into the city to troll round the shops, he obsessed about the signs of industrial decline he observed through the window. The "For Lease" placards on the tattered streets, the crumbling warehouses, the rotting hulk of Manchester Central station. He began to think of it in terms of the theory of Darwinism he had been taught in biology class. Manchester was a social organism rotting from the inner core outwards, he thought. The most florid symptom of this decay for him was the empty shell of the Royal Exchange in St Ann's Square. Five years after cotton trading had ceased on it floors, the grand stone-clad building, with its neo-classical columns, domes and stately turret, was still unoccupied.

His father eventually earned enough money to buy his own home, a new build in Barlow Moor, getting towards the "nice bits" of Sale as his mother put it. But this was not enough to console Cross. On some deep level, he dreaded being infected by what he saw as Manchester's horrible degeneration. He worried that he would end up joining the ranks of the useless old men he saw loitering outside betting shops. Would he become part of a surplus human population abandoned by history? An unemployed non-person who drifted into the dank recesses of the city, sleeping on newspapers and eating out of rubbish bins. Would he become a homeless person with a squashed nose, like one of the ape-like troglodytes in the H G Wells novel? Better to throw himself into the canal. Thoughts like these made him sick. It never occurred to him that he might move to Aberdeen and get a well-paid job in the booming North Sea oil industry.

Cross considered himself far too good for what England in the mid-1970s had to offer a lower-middle-class boy with a taste for adventure. In a previous age, he might have made a satisfactory colonial officer somewhere on the rim of the British Empire — Shanghai perhaps, or Rangoon. Even better, he might have gone native and submitted himself to the fanatical urgings of some Mahdi or sultan, helping to dash the British Army to pieces in the desert. He imagined himself a Kipling hero, like the fateful swashbuckler played by Sean Connery in *The Man Who Would Be King*. But his fantasies did him no good. His gloom persisted. He resigned himself to a life of diminishing social returns.

There was nothing in the culture that expressed the destructive thoughts he had about his situation. Nothing contemporary, anyway. He snuck into the Sale Folk Club at the Railway one Wednesday night. It was a disaster. Although he responded to the despondent mood of the murder ballads, he was put off by the old men's jokes and the warm pints of ale, the suffocating talk of an organic community of England stretching back into the ancient forests of time. It made him want to puke.

As for films set in Manchester, the ones advertised on TV as kitchen-sink dramas, they made him feel teeth-grindingly sentimental. Watching *A Taste of Honey* and *A Kind of Loving*, he was struck by the beauty of the old canals, railway viaducts and brick warehouses, shot in a time before the industrial decay of his hometown had become advanced. But the depiction of the frustrations of factory work and pub life failed to move him. Orwell's stupid proles in *Nineteen Eighty-four*, he thought, remembering the novel they had made him read at school. Interested only in working, breeding, fighting and gambling. What had changed since Orwell's day? Not much, he thought. The proles were still breeding in Wythenshawe and fighting on the terraces. But they were no longer working. What was the point of them?

Cross unburdened himself of painful thoughts by keeping a record of his dreams in a school exercise book. The dark tides of desolation which swept over him were shot through with a longing for human fellowship. He imagined himself a young Rimbaud or a Keats and tried to marshal his emotions into lines of verse.

And then Mackenzie came into his life. A private tutor hired by his mother to get his grades up after his disappointing O-Level results, Mackenzie was a graphic design student at Manchester Polytechnic. He was only four years older than Cross, but the difference between 16 and 20 is always immense. Mackenzie was a decisive influence on Cross's intellectual development, a culture bringer and a forbidding authority figure. He had dark swept-back hair and a vague aristocratic contempt for all forms of lower-middle class *aspiration*. The tutoring was merely his attempt to fund a dope habit.

Mackenzie introduced Cross to Patti Smith, the Stooges and the New York Dolls, standard proto-punk fare for 1975. But he also lent him heavy prog rock albums by King Crimson and Jethro Tull. Cross felt a connection with the phantasmagorical milieu explored by these artists, with their varied combinations of cynicism and sophistication, defensiveness and aggression, nihilism and transcendence. He felt purged after listening to them on his headphones.

Mackenzie also did something else. He fed Cross photocopied pages of the recent English translation of Guy Debord's *La société du spectacle*. They struggled to decipher the arcane text together. Mackenzie was impressed with the prophetic sweep of Debord's rhetoric, his warning that the industrial future of the developed world lay in the manufacture of media and culture, in ever more stupefying and nullifying forms. Mackenzie took the theory to heart. One day, he said, the empty mills and warehouses of Manchester would be full once again, only this time with film companies, recording studios and advertising agencies. They will, he said, one drunken night out on the bare cobbles, cram people's heads with shite which will make *The Towering Inferno* and "Bang-A-Boomerang" – and the fucking Cadbury's Smash jingle – seem like works of genius by comparison. Cross shook his head in disbelief. It's already happening! said Mackenzie. He pointed to the fact that the Royal Exchange was now occupied by a theatre company. Culture is taking over from cotton, he said. And culture is a con.

Is it though? said Cross. The message he took away from Debord was hopeful. Yes, he accepted that the mass of people had been drugged into a stupor by standard entertainment formats – the TV soap opera, the Tin Pan Alley pop song. Cross thought guiltily about his parents when he said this. But didn't Debord see an emancipatory role for culture as a spontaneous effusion rather than a mass media production? Something provoked into being by the deliberate construction of poetic situations, pranks, experimental behaviours? Wasn't that what Debord intended when he set up the Situationist International? Cross mentioned the alter egos created by the likes of Patti Smith on *Horses* and Tull's Ian Anderson on *Aqualung*. Weren't these ground-breaking cultural interventions? Patti Smith had modelled herself on the gutter poet Baudelaire to explore an idea of America saturated with grief and visionary defiance. Anderson had found a way to externalise his alienation and sexual guilt by imagining himself a broken-down homeless person tramping up and down the Thames Embankment. Even Debord had imagined himself as someone else, a troubadour, when he wandered the streets of Paris.

Cross kicked around Piccadilly Gardens. He dipped into the House on the Borderland and picked up NEL horror anthologies, books on the occult by Colin Wilson and lurid paperbacks about Hitler and the Nazis. It was here that he first came across

The Man in the High Castle. He also bought a copy of *House of Dolls*, a gruesome novel about Nazi concentration camp brothels which was either memoir or fiction, he couldn't tell. Its catalogue of atrocities seemed too close for comfort to the sensationalism of banned Nazisploitation films like *Isla, She Wolf of the SS*. As an index of totalitarian degradation, though, it felt right at home in the blighted Manchester of the time. Cross certainly found it quite the objective correlative to his own anxiety, guilt and distress.

It was at this moment that Dieter Kraus first crept into Cross's mind. Imagining himself as an *Ahnenerbe* researcher transported from mid-twentieth century Auschwitz to late-twentieth century Manchester, Cross wandered the streets, notebook in hand. He surveyed the dead bingo halls of Salford and Hulme, he listed the names of shuttered working men's clubs and closed-down factories, he identified weed-grown alleys with their rows of crumbling terraced houses. There were many new uses to which these old social spaces could be put, in the mind of Dieter Kraus. But their successful transformation would depend upon a revolutionary purification of memory. Forget the gnome-like housewives who used to empty their tea-pots in the gutter, forget the pale little savages who shouted at each other in the streets, forget the stunted old men who tramped their rounds from the betting shop to the pub. Let them go, let them all go, to the peaceful land of the dead, beneath the evening star. So thought Kraus, who was a kind of romantic poet.

These situationist musings gave Cross relief from the anxieties that plagued him, his fear that the city of his birth would claim him for one of its own as its death spiral intensified. Could he ever escape? The poetry in his bedside notebook began to take on a more fantastical edge. Here was Dieter Kraus, complicit witness to a historical episode of urban destruction and large-scale social death. How could he save himself? He didn't know. There was no future in the dreams offered to him by England.

The Sex Pistols hit Manchester in the summer of 1976. They lit a long fuse. The city's emergent punk scene would metamorphose over the course of a generation into the milieu of the new creative class. Cross was having absolutely none of it. Still under the influence of the dour Mackenzie, he persuaded himself that the Pistols were a manufactured band like the Monkees before them. All they offered was the warmed-up residue of '50s rock and roll. Even so, Cross read the punk fanzine *Ghast Up*. He even sent it one of his poems, "Faith Test". They rejected it. Maybe it had something to do with his pseudonym.

One place Cross used to take his alter ego out to play was Rafters in the Oxford Road, a disco cellar beneath the cabaret club Fagins. Here, Dieter Kraus was let off the leash. He cut a striking figure on the dancefloor, with his peroxide crew-cut and punk armband. The girls flocked to him, intrigued, but he was cold and dismissive towards them. Sex was a distraction for Dieter Kraus. He was saving himself for higher things. He used to do a self-protective little hand-jive — all bent arms and open palms held at shoulder height — as he skanked along to the reggae tunes. He passed little notes to the DJ, a staunch fellow with a long face and heavy glasses, Rob was a Wythenshawe-raised grammar school lad, like Cross. The notes contained his latest poems, terse hymns to the grinding violence of psychological deadlock and despair.

Cross left school with good A-Levels. Mackenzie graduated and moved to West Berlin for work. Cross was even more irritable and moody than usual. His mother made him apply for a temporary job with the local council. Much to his consternation, he got it. A period of confusion followed. He knew he was just a lowly clerk in the housing department of a provincial English city, but the daily transit in and out of the grand neo-gothic edifice of Manchester Town Hall in St Peter's Square made him feel important. He took to wearing a cravat and began to prepare for his Civil Service entrance exam. He resigned himself to becoming one of those unlucky chaps burdened with the responsibility of managing England's steady decline. The only alternative to a strong state, he thought, was sudden social collapse and generalised barbarism. Sometimes, late at night, when the barbiturates took hold, he comforted himself with the thought that the town hall was a defensible space, with its tall arched windows ideal for nesting machine guns.

Living with his parents was becoming impossible, what with his mother's endless fussing and his father's strange, unexplained absences. He rented a grotty flat in Whalley Range, which he told himself was Manchester's bohemian quarter, like the Left Bank in Paris. Here, he thought, was where all the artists and the intellectuals would inevitably gather to bear witness to the death of the city. He continued to write his poems. The casual brutalities visited upon Manchester by industrial decline was a constant theme. He still shared his poems with Rob, the DJ from Rafters, who had become a nodding acquaintance. There was one titled "Kings of Misuse" and another which imagined what it would have been like to work for the *Judenrat* in the Warsaw ghetto, deciding who would live and who would die.

Cross bought the first Joy Division record when it came out in June 1978. He was intrigued by *An Ideal for Living*'s Nazi-themed packaging. The cover sleeve featured a drawing of a Hitler Youth boy pounding on a drum. The fold-out artwork included a black and white photo of a Jewish boy surrendering to a German soldier after the failure of the Warsaw uprising.

The music at this early stage in the band's career was still influenced by punk rock. It didn't interest Cross much. But he became obsessed by the lyrics spat out by Curtis in the raw din of the production. There were snatched mentions of "holy wars", the "total man" with his "new strength", talk of "some other race" and "the house of dolls". Here were powerful ideas about the longing for mass salvation, suspended violence and the emptiness that attracts messiahs. Cross couldn't believe it. Here was a man articulating his own feelings, repeating his own thoughts, down to the references to the camps and the Nazi subjugation of the Jews. What was going on? Cross knew that his old Rafters associate Rob had blagged his way into becoming Joy Division's manager. Had he passed on the poems Cross had handed him? Was that possible? It was a wild thought.

Cross studied the black-and-white photos of the band members included in the EP's fold-out. He saw youths barely out of their teens, much like himself, casually posed with arms crossed or hands in pockets. Ian Curtis, unsmiling, stick-thin in a greatcoat with collar turned-up, leaning away, looked guarded and uncooperative. Cross saw something of himself in the portrait

— young man at bay. Was he somehow looking at an image of Dieter Kraus?

Cross felt bonded with Curtis. He imagined the man understood him. Manchester was an urban ghetto, just like Warsaw had been under Nazi occupation, an intense zone of absences and hauntings, with fewer and fewer people on the streets and the foreboding sense of a dark future closing in. The temptation to identify with the forces assembling to crush the city was overwhelming.

The only escape, thought Cross, with a frisson of self-recrimination, was to submit to the fanatical zeal of some saviour figure who could turn things around. Could that saviour be Ian Curtis? Or at least the persona he had invented for himself? How serious was he? Were Joy Division planning some beer-hall putsch from the depths of the Russell Club in Hulme, where Cross knew they played? Were they looking for a hooligan *Kampfbund* to help them storm Manchester Town Hall? And would they set up concentration camps for the Tory politicians, the lords and ladies, the bankers and newspaper owners who seemed to control everything? Was there such a thing as a fascism of the left? More fantastically, was it time for North-West England to declare independence from the colonial powers still haunting the corridors of power in Whitehall? Might Curtis play the role of a white Mugabe, an English Mandela? And might Dieter Kraus become his right-hand man? Such were Cross's late-night, drug-baffled thoughts.

When the news broke that Ian Curtis had killed himself, Cross was devastated. He felt sick. His first thought was that death by hanging was an ugly way to go, a death reserved for criminals and fools. He should have shot himself, like Hitler. That would have been dignified, a death befitting a world-historic individual. His second thought was of the final telegram sent by Hitler to Speer from his Berlin bunker, demanding the destruction of Germany now the war was lost. Germany had failed Hitler like Manchester had failed Curtis. The city deserved to be burned down, he thought.

Cross, he didn't mind admitting to me, considered the suicide of Curtis a personal betrayal. His grief and anger turned to outrage when the surviving members of Joy Division reformed as New Order. The first single they released was a re-recording of an old Joy Division song, with someone else singing the lyrics written by Curtis. Cross immediately composed a letter of protest to the *NME*, saying that the remnants of Joy Division should have followed their lead singer into silence after his suicide. Voluntary self-cancellation, wrote Cross, was the only honourable form of sub-cultural resistance left after the ending of Joy Division. The paper published his letter under a mocking headline. Within weeks, he had quit his job at the town hall and left Manchester in disgust.

Cross's first period of self-imposed exile from his home city lasted about a year. He travelled to the Channel Islands to "tour the Nazi monuments," as he put it. He wanted to sharpen up his Dieter Kraus persona and reflect on what life must have been like in the only part of Britain to be occupied by the Germans during the war. The experience had a profound effect on his thoughts about an alternative Nazi England. He wrote *City of Dolls* at speed, during October and November, before returning to Manchester with his manuscript.

Cross's Channel Islands tour took in the *Hohlgangsanlagen*, the tunnel-based fortifications built into the hillsides of Jersey's west coast by occupying German forces. He learned from the tourist centre at *Hohlgangsanlage 8*, an old artillery depot, that the tunnels had been designed to protect German troops and munitions from aerial bombardment as they prepared to invade England. Of course, Operation Sea Lion never happened in the end. And as the tide of the war turned, *Hohlgangsanlage 8* was turned into an emergency hospital.

One thing that really struck Cross about the *Hohlgangsanlage 8* tourist centre was its exhibition of historic documents. Old newspaper photos, identity cards and transcribed interviews gave a haunting sense of what a full-scale Nazi occupation of England might have looked and felt like. He saw a photo of Jersey government flunkies taking tea with uniformed officers of the *Wehrmacht*, posing for the picture with china cups raised, smiles all round. He read about local people going to the same cinemas as the German forces, the same dancehalls, the same parades, the same rallies. It would have been easy to have slipped into that life, under the circumstances, thinking that it was both acceptable and inevitable. Why let war get in the way of *la société du spectacle*?

Cross understood too well the mentality of the petty bureaucrat who felt he had to go along with the Nazis. A small number of resistance members needed to be shipped to prisoner-of-war camps in Eastern Europe. Would he rubber-stamp that decision? Of course! Nobody likes troublemakers. Three people need to be sent to a transit camp in France? Yes, all right. It's only three people, after all. Three Jewish people. We all know how funny

the *Schutzstaffel* can be about Jews, there's no point in antagonis-
ing them... Cross imagined the servile thoughts that would have
run through his mind if he had been a Nazi collaborator in Jersey
during the 1940s. Or a Nazi collaborator in Manchester during
the 1970s, for that matter. The idea of Dieter Kraus took shape
in his mind as a literary character.

Most appalling for Cross's surviving attachment to the still-
echoing Churchillian rhetoric of his childhood, with its talk of
fighting the invading Germans on the beaches, was the news that
Hitler had claimed Guernsey by flying a single *Luftwaffe* platoon
into the airport. He concluded that his lingering devotion to an
idea of the British bulldog spirit was perhaps only the legacy of
wartime propaganda. Now, in this tiny sliver of not-quite England, he would turn his face against the future, put *An Ideal for
Living* on the record-player for one last time and imagine himself the guilt-ridden citizen of an occupied country from an imaginary past. As Dieter Kraus came into focus, so Derek Cross
slipped out of view.

The man went to Alderney, the northernmost of the Channel
Islands, known as the "island of silence." It was here he learned
about Organisation Todt, the German military engineering company which had built the fortifications, bunkers and tunnels on
Jersey and Guernsey. The organisation had imported a slave
labour force from Eastern Europe to do the work and housed
them in four concentration camps on Alderney. The camp at
Sylt was run by the *Schutzstaffel* and its inmates were routinely
starved, beaten and hanged. The *Kommandant* had given orders
for it to be burned to the ground and its records destroyed before surrender to Allied forces. Cross took photographs of the

three solitary gateposts, which granted access only to an empty field, overgrown with vegetation.

Was he bearing witness to the wasted lives of captive Eastern Europeans? His guidebook told him that hundreds of Russians were buried on the common. Or was he worshipping at the shrine of an archaic death cult, with its stirring neo-pagan legends of purity, brutality and loyalty-unto-death? Cross didn't know. But he was no fool. He understood the psychological enchantment of the SS's refusal of conscience. It was intoxicating.

Cross wrote his novel in the breaks from his work as a porter at the general hospital in St Helier. In his version of history, Manchester is a beleaguered outpost of Nazi-occupied Europe. Operation Sea Lion had been a success back in 1940. German invasion forces took the South-East of England in a matter of days. However, their push northwards had been permanently stalled by the rough uplands of the Yorkshire Dales, the Lakes, the Pennines. It's now 1978. Manchester has settled into its history as a Nazi frontier town, with all the unrest, intrigue and uncertainty that implies. Every corner holds a secret police informer and the appeal courts of the Reich are hundreds of miles away in Berlin.

City of Dolls does not avoid the obvious poetic gratifications of situationist estrangement. Why should it? Selected details of everyday English life are subverted by the spectre of Nazism. There are the small boys in Manchester United strip playing bugle and drums in a Hitler Youth parade, the cigarette cards with their illustrations of the Aryan World of the Celtic Tribes, the red collection boxes for *Britische Freikorps* veterans in the post offices, the separate seating for *Deutschen* and *Britischen* in cinemas and theatres, the Bavarian brass bands playing Vaughan Williams and

Brian Eno in the parks, the informal ID checkpoints in St Peter's Square, staffed by the polite constables of the *Feldgendarmerie*. It all attests to a collective English yearning for stability and hierarchy able to merge seamlessly with the dream of an eternal Reich.

Just as telling are the absences in the novel. No jazz, rock'n'roll or any kind of *Neger* pop music is played in public. Smuggled American records are only ever played clandestinely in private rooms. Trades union officials are nowhere to be seen. The heavy clink of pennies and shillings is replaced with the soft rustle of *Deutsche Marks*. People in clubs and offices are tight-lipped. There are no jokes, no banter, just in case a stray word gets tangled up in the dreaded and fiendishly complex *Gleichschaltung* laws. Most devastatingly of all, there is no trace of traditional English working-class culture on the streets. The filthy old bingo halls, betting shops and working men's clubs have been closed down. In their place are hygienic swimming pools, airy concert halls and indoor tennis clubs. Even the football terraces have been cleaned-up and made family-friendly. They are now part of all-seater stadiums filled with the off-duty members of a sanitised Reich labour force, one detached from the *Untermenschen* of old and schooled in the ethics of "strength through joy."

The particular genius of *City of Dolls* is to make its protagonist an enthusiastic rather than reluctant Nazi collaborator. Dieter Kraus is a lower-middle-class official more than willing to adopt the role of political commissar in his dealings with an English mandarin caste whose claims to superiority he has always despised. The Nazi occupation regime has created an opening for young men on the make to settle old scores with traditional class enemies. And Kraus does this with great relish. It's a witty move by Cross to play back the notes of kitchen-sink realism in an off-key, positioning Kraus as an angry young man using Nazi doctrine as a stick to beat down the class system of Old England. Kraus imagines himself a conscientious revolutionary. Cross makes it clear he's merely a clever functionary, an Eichmann with an eye on the glittering prizes.

The events of the novel don't stray too far beyond the public heart of Manchester. Kraus is employed as a town planner for Organisation Todt in Manchester Town Hall. Much of his work is secret. The diary entries which make up the text of the novel don't give much away. Kraus is a mystery even to himself. He spends a lot of time studying maps and schedules in a tiny office under one of the ceremonial staircases. It seems he is working on the final stages of an urban renewal project in Greater Manchester, involving plans for the renovation of the central station, the rehousing of slum dwellers and the construction of grand avenues, parade grounds and war memorials. Occasionally, he attends a meeting in the Council Chamber. Here he views aerial photographs of the internment camps and ghettos of Eastern Europe, blueprints for gates, fencing and blockhouses, kitchens, concert halls and crematoria. He listens to the talk of improving rail links to the Lancashire Coast, converting Blackpool from a seaside resort to a transit port and shipping building materials to the Isle of Man.

In the course of his duties, Kraus finds himself hopping backwards and forwards across St Peter's Square. He is frequently called upon to service the bureaucratic whims of a Nazi high command who have ensconced themselves in the Edwardian baroque splendour of the Midland Hotel. Here, he waits nervously in the lobby close to lounging SS officers who wear the death's head insignia on their collars. They drink vegetable juice and debate the origins of the English folklore of faeries and goblins. The little people, one claims, refers to a sinister prehistoric race of albino dwarves cleared from the British Isles by the Celts. Another says that it looks like some have nevertheless managed to survive in the slums of Manchester. Laughter all round. Kraus avoids eye contact. He gets his papers stamped and his dockets signed. Sometimes, after that, he might have to dart across to the imposing neo-classical rotunda of the Central Library. Checking the files is delicate work. He might have to locate a questionable ethnic registration form, an anonymous letter of denunciation, or assess the transcript of a monitored phone call.

Dieter Kraus knows things. He is always washing his hands and wiping his feet. He traffics in the dirty secrets of the city. At the end of the day, he waits for the bus home to Oldham outside the Royal Exchange, its neo-classical columns draped with a gigantic red swastika banner. It is only then that he takes off his armband.

Cross returned to Manchester in December, just after New Order released their third single, "Everything's Gone Green". This was the last record where the lugubrious influence of Joy Division on New Order's sound was still tangible. Cross ignored it. He tapped up his old pal Rob at Factory Records and persuaded him to publish his novel, saying it was the final word on the Ian Curtis cult. Factory Records, inspired by the same situationist *jeux d'esprit* as Cross had been in his younger days, was quite willing to experiment with the items in its catalogue. Publishing a book was hardly a big step for a record company that had already assigned a catalogue number to the idea of the Hacienda night-club.

City of Dolls was published in a limited edition of 100 copies in March 1982. The fact that its catalogue number was FAC 61a, an interstitial designation, probably indicated that Factory didn't take it very seriously. They had already assigned the catalogue number FAC 61 to a lawsuit brought against them by one of their founding partners. They probably figured that FAC 61a could only refer to another type of document which had a similar nuisance value for their idea of themselves. As it was, they failed to secure the rights to the book's cover photo, found themselves faced with the prospect of another lawsuit, and so pulped the entire run of *City of Dolls*. Only a few review copies survived, one of which I was lucky enough to stumble across in 1989.

Recalling the cover in my mind's eye, I can see another reason why Factory might have lost its nerve. The photo in question is a 1933 press shot of the England football team doing Hitler salutes at the *Olympiastadion*. The book designer had placed the image over an abstract grid to make it clear that here was a formal black-and-white composition abstracted from history. Even so, it was provocative, raising memories of England's pre-war flirtation with certain aspects of Nazism. Cross, when I spoke to him, was sanguine about it all. He thought that Factory had always planned to destroy his novel right from the start. It was the kind of situationist prank they excelled at, like when they'd made a cover sleeve for *The Return of the Durutti Column* out of coarse sandpaper, to put off casual buyers. I could almost hear him shrugging down the phone.

In April 1982, Factory released "Temptation", the first New Order record to definitively break with Joy Division's legacy and move into synth-pop. Factory forgot all about *City of Dolls*. They were focused on opening the Hacienda. Cross got his invite to the launch from Rob. He told me he didn't know why he was turned away on the night. But it cemented his decision to leave Manchester for good. What he had envisioned as a triumphant homecoming had turned into a bitter reckoning with the past, which had lasted less than six months. He caught a taxi to the airport. His mother wept at the gate.

My copy of *City of Dolls* arrived in the post as a job-lot of review materials from the Manchester publishing house Savoy Books. Set up in 1976 by a duo which included the same man who had managed the House on the Borderland bookshop, Savoy by 1989 had run into trouble with the police for publishing their own brand of Nazisploitation – a surreal and inflammatory horror novel set in Auschwitz. They were desperate for any good press they could get. I didn't know if the inclusion of *City of Dolls* in their review package was a mistake or an inducement. I even wondered if they were negotiating with Factory to republish the novel. Anyway, I read it in one sitting. I was particularly struck by the author photo on the back cover, a moody black-and-white shot of a gaunt young man with bug eyes. It was obvious that Cross had modelled his look on Ian Curtis.

The exact nature of the relationship between Cross and Curtis eludes me to this day. Did Cross have any of the mean, resentful, stalkerish tendencies associated with the obsessive fan? He had raised the outrageous possibility with me that Curtis had stolen ideas from his poems. I no longer have the tape of the conversation we had, so can't be certain whether he was joking or not. My notes from that long-ago night in 1999 range hazily over many topics – the gentrification of Manchester, Mark Reeder, Cross's reunion with Mackenzie at the Love Parade in Berlin, Ralph Rumney's expulsion from the Situationist International, the naming strategy behind the post-punk group the March Violets, Speer's theory of architectural "ruin value" and Arthur Machen's weird fiction. It's difficult for me to recover the contextual thread of these remarks after so many years.

One thing I do remember, though, is the meaning of one particularly cryptic word in my notes – "pseudocide". This was the idea that Curtis had faked his own death. Cross admitted this was all speculation on his part. But he had certainly done his research. He said that the note left on the mantlepiece in Curtis's home on the night of his death was no suicide note. Instead, it was a letter to his wife about Joy Division's upcoming American tour. Curtis had never really wanted to die, said Cross. He had attempted suicide a month before, and found he couldn't go through with it. But he did want to disappear from his own life, which was causing him too many problems. When he confided his feelings to his manager, Factory saw an opportunity for the ultimate situationist prank. They would produce Curtis's death as a spectacle, a classic rock'n'roll suicide, in order to provoke the public expressions of grief and anger which Manchester's industrial termination properly merited. The hope was for mass insurrection. Curtis himself, meanwhile, was spirited away to Factory's office in West Berlin.

I can still remember Cross breathing noisily down the phone when I challenged this whole ridiculous idea. People had viewed

Curtis's body in his coffin, for Christ's sake! How did he explain that? Cross said that Curtis was quite capable of playing dead, the way stick insects did to repel predators. He had done it many times on-stage, when faced with the bared teeth of a hostile audience. The epileptic fits were part of it. I continued to argue with Cross, distressed beyond reason by his sacrilegious theory. He finally said I could believe what I liked. All he knew was that when he was on his way to Potsdamer Platz one day, a solitary man in grey had passed him by, head bent, arms crossed over his chest, in another world. It was Ian Curtis, he swore. The man turned the corner and was gone.

What should anyone make of that? I don't know. I lost Cross's phone number. He disappeared from the scene in Berlin. And I gave away my copy of *City of Dolls* to a beautiful Jewish girl I was trying to seduce in Notting Hill. Sometimes I think I must have dreamed the whole unlikely episode of Factory Records publishing a novel inspired by Ian Curtis's death. Other times, I wonder if I've been the victim of an elaborate prank. Does Derek Cross even exist? Or is he, in actual fact, a false identity, created by a man who only ever wanted to create one perfect recording career and one perfect novel, before retiring into obscurity? If that is indeed the case, then all I can do is raise a toast to Ian Curtis on his trek to the evening lands.

SAMMI REDFOOT

Witness to the Hendrix Assassination Theory

THE LAST TIME I SAW SAMMI REDFOOT was on her canal boat at
Camden Lock in 1993. She was throwing handfuls of stinking
kitchen rubbish at Bradley, her on-again off-again boyfriend. He
made no attempt to fend off the barrage of tins and cartons and
just stood there, in the narrow quarters of their floating home,
with a goofy smile on his face. He was high again. Sammi said
he was a no-good pathetic loser. He laughed. She pulled down
her moleskin combat trousers, squatted on the floor, and rum-
maged between her legs. Seconds later, a used tampon hit Bradley squarely in the face. He smeared the blood on to his lips.
Tasty, he said. Sammi sprang at him, screaming. She knocked him
down, kneeled over his supine body and began to choke him, her
bare arse raised above him in a lewd victory salute. I had to separate the two of them, like a referee at a wrestling match.

I had got used to their fights over the preceding weeks. It was
all part of their Sid and Nancy routine, the final act in their self-
created rock'n'roll psychodrama, the one whose first act had
opened with such high hopes, even if those hopes were restrict-
ed to being London's answer to Kurt and Courtney. Honestly,
I think they would have settled at any time for being king-and-
queen-for-a-day of any rock circus going. By the time they got to
me, they were running low on audiences. I certainly hit my limit
that night. I never went back for more of their abject brand of

entertainment, concerned that I was being drawn into a spiral of mutually reinforcing self-loathing.

I suppose that night must also have been the final curtain for them, because they split up soon afterwards. Bradley went back to Washington DC and got a job in the State Department. And Sammi, free at last from her boyfriend's draining influence, wrote her one brilliant song, her punk rock testament, "The Ballad of Monika D". To my knowledge she never got round to playing it live and I have one of only a few cassette tape copies of the original demo. But, lord, what a song! Sammi's gut-punching vocals are delivered over a clatter of choppy guitar chords in syncopated style as she raps about "M-M-Monika", the "skater queen fucked the war machine, glam-ass bitch killed the rock star snitch."

This was Sammi's take on the death of '60s guitar legend Jimi Hendrix, which she boldly reimagined as the righteous killing of a powerful and corrupt rock star by one of his abused ex-girlfriends. It was a devastating and very funny attack on the male sexual ego. It was also a complete fantasy, of course. One that, more than anything else, was a dagger aimed at the heart of the despised Bradley, who was a devoted Hendrix fan. In his time on the DC punk scene he used to pose with a Fender Stratocaster and talk in breathless tones about how much sheer noise his cultural hero could wrestle from the instrument. A Hendrix slap of the humming strings could produce a whistling crack as loud as a gunshot, said Bradley, while his vibrato drone resembled the whine of a Phantom jet at 30,000 feet. Bradley himself, of course, was incapable of such feats. But he liked to pontificate about them in front of Sammi, whom he expected to be admiring and respectful, like a good student in college.

Sammi's put-down of Hendrix in song form was one indication of how she would never back down in any contest with a man. In fact, her particular brand of third wave feminism dictated that she should always find the biggest alpha male in the room, pick a fight with him and put him down in front of his buddies with a savage barb. It was all part of her mission, she said, to reclaim public space from the boring artifice of male domination and open it up for girls and young women to express themselves and connect with each other. It was why she started her fanzine *I Love Myra*.

Sammi had always been an angry girl, despite coming from a relatively privileged background. She was born Samantha Radford in 1969 and raised as an only child in Holland Park, an affluent pocket of London just a stone's throw from the immigrant enclave of Notting Hill, whose African-Caribbean population was at that time only just over a decade old. Sammi's father Frank was a Ministry of Defence consultant who was often stationed abroad, first in Africa and then in the Middle East. Sammi hardly ever saw him as a child. She gave her mother Beryl much trouble with her tantrums and petulant behaviour. Things only got worse for poor Beryl when her husband left her for an American cultural attaché and moved to Washington DC in 1976. She and her daughter had to move to Royal Tunbridge Wells in a kind of social disgrace. Beryl packed her daughter off to prep school in Hampshire and settled down to conducting a string of leisurely affairs with entirely unsuitable men.

Sammi was withdrawn and truculent at school. She defied her teachers and refused all their liberal indulgences. When she turned 13 and moved into Bedales, she suddenly discovered the power she had over older boys. Sex in the toilets soon followed as did smoking dope in the dorms. At the age of 14, she developed an elaborate system of deception that enabled her to flit in and out of London during the holidays and even, sometimes, term time. Her father didn't know and her mother, she thought, didn't care.

This was how she came to be drifting around the North London squat scene in 1983 under an assumed name. Sammi Redfoot, as she called herself, hung out with scruffy hippie-punks at Mollys Café, a derelict night-club in Upper Street, and St Ives House, a Greater London Council property in Rosebery Avenue known as the "Peace Centre". They were a pretty mild-mannered lot in general, drinking tea, knitting and growing their own vegetables. But when riled by a sense of injustice, they could turn belligerent. They might climb on-stage at the disused Bingo Hall in Highbury & Islington to rant about the dehumanising effects of corporate capitalism. Or they might venture out into the street to protest against the deployment of US Air Force cruise missiles at RAF Greenham Common in the Thames Valley. At moments like these, the repressed fury came tumbling out of them, in a rush of anti-authoritarian invective and bold sloganeering.

Sammi was most impressed by the fact that these ratty-haired anarcho-punks practised what they preached. They were not like her father, who talked about making the world safe for democracy, while collaborating, she was sure, with CIA war criminals in Zaire and Iran. Instead, they applied their radical beliefs to their personal lives in an effort to propagate a culture of disobedience and direct action. They formed co-operatives, occupied empty dwellings, practised communal living, recycled old materials and made music without any expectation of making a profit. They also made their own fanzines to spread the news about anarcho-punk culture.

Sammi devoured the punk zines, especially *Kill Your Pet Puppy*, *Chainsaw* and *No Cure*. They were produced on photocopiers in short runs of a hundred or so and were quite hard to find. Sammi picked them up at independent record shops and gigs held at youth clubs and community halls. She found them lying around in squats. What she loved about them was not just the angry content but also the cut-and-paste collage form, the stencil design aesthetic. It all communicated a powerful sense of how anyone could get their views out there, free from the strictures of publishing houses and taste-makers.

Best of all about the anarcho-punk scene for Sammi was the ideological emphasis on gender equality. It brought out a puritanical streak in the boys, who competed to see who could behave in the most servile way towards the girls. They willingly desexualized themselves and that, in turn, gave young women the space to be free of being defined by their power of sexual attraction. Sammi stopped wearing make-up, started to wear baggy Army Surplus clothes, chopped her hair and dyed the tufty remnants orange. In fact, she stopped thinking about the men around her at all. What she actually wanted to do was expand her domain of authority by taking on the real enemy, which she dimly imagined to be some monolithic entity known as the "patriarchy".

She soon got her chance. On the night of September 28th, the Special Patrol Group came crashing through the doors of the Peace Centre brandishing clubs and riot shields. The raid took place just hours before a Stop the City demo was due to kick off at St Paul's Cathedral at 6am the next day. The Metropolitan Police had very little intelligence on the protest and had wrongly concluded there was a bomb factory in the basement of St Ives House. That was why they had sent in their elite force of thugs to make arrests and crack heads.

In the noise and confusion of grappling bodies and shouted commands, Sammi was a real spitfire, biting the fingers and kicking the shins of offending officers. It took two giant men to drag her out of the building into the street. She squirmed and wriggled and finally slipped free from their grip. The coppers were left holding her empty jacket as she hopped on a passing 73 bus. They were glad to see the back of her. She flicked Vs at them as she sped away. They grabbed their crotches and jeered her.

Sammi spent the night shivering on the steps of St Paul's Ca-thedral. A Greenpeace activist arrived in the small hours and sat down next to her. He said they were expecting a good turn-out and that if there were any trouble she could find first aid points at Finsbury Square and Tower Hill. Sammi said she was looking for trouble. The man from Greenpeace tittered. He reminded her they wanted a peaceful demonstration.

By 10am there were hundreds of punks milling about at St Paul's, chanting and drumming. A group of young women were staging a lie-down at the top of Ludgate Hill, blocking traffic. Sammi handed out leaflets in Cannon Street to curious stock-brokers going to work. The leaflets explained that the City of

London had been targeted for occupation because it was the financial district where the world's arms trade was funded. Sammi had designed the leaflets herself, using asymmetrical layouts and a broken typeface to give them a rebarbative feel. She was very proud of the way they looked.

Sammi ran with the crowd as it surged along Queen Victoria Street towards the Royal Exchange. She was one of the reconnaissance scouts who dodged mounted police cordons, leading small mobile units of rioters up and down side-streets on lightning hit-and-run assignments. They smashed the windows of brokerage houses, lobbed stink bombs at the chichi restaurants and spray-painted graffiti on the facades of the big banks. A favourite anarchist stencil which popped up all over the place was the Crass logo, a stylised version, at least to Sammi's mind, of the anti-fascist clenched fist sign.

Crass were an anarcho-punk band who had been releasing records on their own label for years. Their members and supporters were active in the streets that day. Sammi knew quite a few of them by sight and clapped them on their leather-jacketed backs as she ran past. A young man with a spiked Mohican helped her over the barricade formed by an overturned car and she made it to the Royal Exchange. Here was the heart of the City, a crossroads where the stone fortress of the Bank of England met the glass tower of the London Stock Exchange. It was thronged with marching protestors, waving banners and shouting anti-war slogans. "One, two, three four; we don't want your fucking war!" Yellow smoke drifting across the open space from jettisoned flares. Sammi ran past police and climbed on top of the plinth supporting the statue of the Duke of Wellington, whose military exploits had secured British dominance of world trade. She un-furled her black flag and waved it above the whistling and dancing crowd. She wondered what her father would make of her now and hoped, quite bitterly, that he would see her picture in the paper and be appalled. Then, she lost her footing. The flag dropped and she fell into the crowd. Two policemen pounced on her, two others came running and together the four of them lifted her up and carried her away.

Sammi was disappointed she wasn't charged with a public order offence when she got to Wood Street. But her school had filed a missing person report on her and the police had no interest in the prosecution of a minor, especially one with such a well-connected family. She was released into the embarrassed custody of her mother.

Back at Bedales, Sammi continued to struggle with her ontological crisis. Her teachers encouraged her to develop her graphic design skills. In spring 1984, she produced the first issue of *I Love Myra* on the photocopier in the bursar's office at night. It was mainly a hymn of praise to Eve Libertine. She had been the moving force on the Crass album *Penis Envy* and had put an aggressively feminist stamp on the band's anarchist social critique. She sang songs about marriage as enslavement, romance as oppression, sexual intercourse as gladiatorial combat. It had all sounded very overwrought to the ears of male music critics when the album was released in 1981. And that's still the case with me, I'm afraid. But Sammi put Eve up there with punk icons like Slits-frontwoman Ari Up and Poly Styrene, defiant young women who sang their own way, in their own voices, and who didn't care what men thought about them. Unlike Siouxsie

Sioux, wrote Sammi in her fanzine, who while undoubtedly a great vocal stylist, always conceded too much to the male gaze with her retro notions of female glamour. Siouxsie, in that sense, was for Sammi the Great Satan.

It was to be many years until Sammi produced the second issue of her discerning little zine. The miner's strike of 1984 split the anarcho-punk scene, with many of its original members getting caught up in the geo-politics of class war, while others, the more artistically inclined perhaps, disappeared into the voyaging of camper vans and buses around England's free festival circuit. Crass stopped performing soon after the Battle of Orgreave, when striking miners fought with police in Sheffield. They bunkered down in their little cottage on the outskirts of North Weald in Essex. At the same time Sammi was getting her O-Level results through and choosing her A-Level options.

In 1986 Sammi had a brief fling with her private tutor, got pregnant and had an abortion. A year later, she was packed off, still a bit shell-shocked, to America in a vain attempt to reconcile with her father. She enrolled in Georgetown University, where she majored in politics and economics, while living a parallel life – like a select few of her fellow students – on the DC punk scene. It was here that she adopted her old alias Redfoot and started wearing thrift-store dresses teamed with white socks and sneakers. She was also introduced to a reinvigorated punk zine culture with a decidedly contemporary feminist slant. *Jigsaw*, *Bikini Girl* and *Girl Germs* were all zines which came out of the radicalised college culture of the Pacific Northwest and ended up in DC as part of the baggage of touring riot grrrl bands. Sammi couldn't get enough of them. The scrappy Xerox aesthetic was like the face of an old friend while the anarcho-feminist political content, with its raw confessional urgency, connected with her on a deep level.

There were stories on the way sexism was enforced through covert acts of male violence, through street harassment, incest and rape. There were arguments that derogatory labels like "slut" and "bitch" could be reclaimed as terms of self-empowerment, as the gays had done with "queer" and the blacks with "nigga". Sammi was especially drawn to the exercises in alternative canon formation, which promoted the importance of British female post-punk bands such as the Slits, the Raincoats and Delta 5. She was disappointed, though, by the room given to Chrissie Hynde, who she felt was too much like Siouxsie Sioux, another daddy's girl who loved looking good on camera a little too much.

Sammi would have preferred an emphasis on Marianne Faithfull, the Swinging London it girl who had walked out on Mick Jagger to live as a heroin addict on the streets of Soho. She had destroyed her beauty through an over-indulgence in sex and drugs, ruined her melodic girly singing voice, and then gone on to make one of the most caustic rock albums of all time, *Broken English*. Marianne Faithfull went from rock groupie to rock artist in the course of a gruelling decade. Now that, thought Sammi, was a career worth celebrating.

She produced the "Marianne" issue of her zine, the second issue of *I Love Myra*, in 1990. It brought her to the attention of Bradley, who cornered her one night in the old 9:30 Club and said he liked the chaotic feel of its design, with its almost illegible hand-written screeds and its arbitrary red, blue and black backgrounds. He said it was a fine example of "ecriture feminine" and Sammi, despite herself, was flattered. In fact, she was so flattered she let him lead her outside the club to an alley near the cavernous J Edgar Hoover FBI Building, where she got on her knees and took his big beautiful cock in her mouth.

Sammi later confided in me that she had fallen hard for Bradley. She was secretly pleased that he managed to make a good impression on her father, who – with the affected Southern gentility of his later years – insisted on calling him her "beau". Sammi loved Bradley's long eyelashes and his shy smile, his intensity and introversion, his grand flashes of temper. She was also attracted to his vulnerability. He used to write these really sappy ballads on his amplified electric guitar, songs about true love and failed romance, the kind of thing Crass had satirised with their trashy give-away song "Our Wedding". When it was time to audition, he gave his songs big political titles like "Gulf War Blues" and "Jesus Was An Oil Man Too". He was surprised that he kept failing to get into grunge bands. But the punks didn't know what to make of him. Looking back, said Sammi in one of our long late-night phone calls, what was so compelling about him in the early days was that he was his own particular kind of mess. Of course, that in itself was what later repulsed her about him.

Like Sammi, Bradley was a child of divorce. His father Bill worked for the CIA as a film technician. Together, Sammi and Bradley would lie awake at night on the futon, smoke pot and make up wild tales about their fathers working together as a secret team for the American military-industrial complex. First, Frank was organising weapons sales to Iran while Bill was channelling funds to the Contras in Nicaragua. Then, Frank and Bill were together in Panama, as part of the op that blasted ear-splitting rock music at Noriega to force him out of his bolt-hole. The elaboration of this particular fantasy was the trigger for their first break-up.

Bradley said he reckoned the Clash were on the "Get Noriega" playlist. The "Frank and Bill" playlist, said Sammi. Right, right, said Bradley. They should definitely have featured Bad Brains and Minor Threat on it. What about Nirvana? asked Sammi. Or is the chronology not right? She was feeling a bit foolish. Technically feasible, said Bradley, in lordly fashion. But I don't see Frank and Bill being that hip, do you? They were probably playing Rick fucking Astley, let's face it. Of course, he said, they should have been playing Hendrix. He was suddenly quite solemn. Like the black US Marines did at the siege of Khe Sanh in Vietnam. They stacked their tape-decks up on the trench walls and bombarded the attacking gooks with those heavy, heavy guitar solos from "Purple Haze". Don't say gooks, said Sammi. It's dehumanising.

I know, said Bradley. He started to talk about the genius of Hendrix's sound engineers, men like Roger Mayer, who invent-ed the Octavia, an effects pedal which reproduced the guitar input signal one octave higher, and then mixed the two sounds together with added fuzz. Hendrix called the Octavia the secret of his sound and used the effect extensively on "Purple Haze".

Sammi yawned. Somehow, they had got on to Hendrix again, always the favourite subject for one of Bradley's rock music lec-tures. Hendrix's sound engineers, said Bradley, had enabled the rock guitarist to make a real breakthrough by placing an empha-sis on the musical possibilities of noise rather than melody. He went on to talk of "musique concrete" – Sammi was beginning to find out how much Bradley loved his little French phrases – and Fluxus. He was in full flow.

Sammi lit a cigarette as Bradley droned on about how the 100-watt Marshall amplifier was a technological invention essential for the evolution of Hendrix's sound. It was high-volume and high-gain, he said, which enabled Hendrix to modulate the feedback from his guitar and master its use as a sound effect. Hendrix's drummer had personally introduced him to Jim Marshall when he first came to London from America and formed the Jimi Hendrix Experience. It was one of the great rock encounters, said Bradley, up there with Bowie meeting Ronson or Strummer meeting Jones.

Sammi said that if Bradley were interested in the avant-garde use of noise in rock music, then he should check out the first side of *Yoko Ono / Plastic Ono Band*, where Yoko really got into the whole primal scream thing. That album should have been top of the "Get Noriega" playlist, she said. Bradley laughed. He said that 20 minutes of Yoko Ono would be enough to make any man crack.

At that point, Sammi dug her nails into Bradley's nipples. Hard. He howled. Sammi sat up and straddled him. She said that Yoko was the first girl punk rocker, that she had saved John Lennon from a life of mind-numbing complacency in the corporate rock world. These thoughts weren't original to Sammi. She was quoting from a Tobi Vail article in an old issue of *Bikini Kill*. Furthermore, she had never actually listened to *Yoko Ono / Plastic Ono Band*. But Bradley wasn't to know that. And, besides, the Yoko Ono article expressed how she felt about girls being sidelined in the music scene by male rock bores. Bradley said there was nothing wrong with being a rock star. It was a way of connecting with people. He was busy thrusting up inside of her. Sammi ground down on him with the full weight of her hips. She said that he would never be a rock star. He was too much of a little prick. Bradley threw her off the futon. She landed awkwardly and hurt her elbow. Bradley picked up his flannel shirt and stormed out of the bedroom.

When Sammi graduated from Georgetown, she applied for jobs in journalism. Then, her father died of a pulmonary embolism. She refused to go to the funeral. She was too upset. She ignored her mother's phone calls. She clung to Bradley. They started doing crack cocaine together. He'd score at the Strip and bring back the little bag to their rented room in DC. She'd fashion a pipe from a Bic biro and smoke the little rocks from a plastic soda bottle. Bradley used to strum his guitar and watch while his girlfriend got high.

Sammi called 1992 her lost year. She didn't go out very much and relied on her boyfriend to make sure the rent was paid out of the small legacy her father had left her. Bradley was now talking about writing a biography of Hendrix, or at least a history of the circumstances surrounding the singer's unexpected death in London in 1970. Scotland Yard had been prompted to consider reopening the case by Kathy Etchingham, one of Hendrix's first English girlfriends, a decent sort by most accounts. The coroner had originally returned an open verdict based on a post-mortem which found the musician had choked on his own vomit after over-dosing on barbiturates. But since the declassification of Hendrix's old FBI file in 1984, rumours had spread that Bureau boss Hoover had subjected him to surveillance for fear of his association with the Black Panther Party, who were Public Enemy Number One in the old man's book. Bradley picked all this up from his drug buddies standing in line at the Strip. One old junky told him that the CIA had put out a contract on Hendrix as part of their covert assassination programme. It was, apparently, well known.

Bradley wasn't quite sure if he believed the rumours. But he did think that the riddle of Hendrix's death could be solved if the police spoke to the last person to see him alive. This was Monika Dannemann, one of his many London girlfriends, the moonstruck Monika, as Bradley called her. He ranted on about Monika as Sammi hit the crack pipe. Hendrix had been approached by the pretty ex-ice skater on tour in Dusseldorf. They went to bed together and she followed him home to London. Is that right? said Sammi. Monika, said Bradley, was a jealous girl, a needy girl, a liar, a stalker and a Vesparax addict. She had driven Hendrix to a party in Great Cumberland Place in London's West End on the night of his death. He made her wait outside while he went in to spend time with Devon Wilson, his long-time on-again off-again girlfriend from New York. Classy dude!, said Sammi. Anyway, said Bradley, Monika kicked up such a fuss in the street outside that Hendrix had to leave the party to calm her down. She ended up dragging him back to her grey little basement flat at the Samarkand Hotel in Notting Hill. This would have been at 3 o'clock in the morning. Sammi inhaled the smoke and nodded. How rude of Monika, she said.

Yeah? said Bradley. Anyway, they crashed out together fully-clothed. Then later that day at 11.18am, Monika phoned for an ambulance, saying her boyfriend was lying in bed, unconscious and unresponsive. She said that ten minutes later she was helping a groggy Hendrix into the back of the ambulance. But that's contradicted by statements from the ambulance crew, Bradley went on. They arrived in Lansdowne Crescent to find themselves confronted by the two decaying multi-storey buildings of the Samarkand Hotel and no Monika. The door to her basement flat was open and the gas fire was still lit. But Hendrix's body was cold and covered in dried vomit. He had been dead for many hours. So what really happened that day? asked Bradley. The bitch killed him, said Sammi. It's obvious. She was mumbling.

Maybe, maybe, said Bradley. There are stories that before she phoned for an ambulance, like hours before, closer to dawn, she had phoned Hendrix's management. They sent round a clean-up crew to get rid of the hard drugs and other incriminating evidence before any police arrived. Sammi nodded off. So, yeah, maybe.

Bradley developed his Hendrix assassination theory over the succeeding months. It all hinged on Hendrix's business manager, Michael Jeffrey, the shady British character who handled his money. Bradley found a clipping in the Library of Congress which had a photo of Jeffrey. It showed a mysterious fellow in a suit and regimental tie, his face obscured by dark glasses, an operator, a spiv. He had apparently worked with MI6 in Western Europe during the 1950s and boasted to business rivals of his CIA contacts, his mafia connections. Bradley discovered that Jeffrey had taken most of Hendrix's money and laundered it through the same banking system in the Bahamas used by the CIA. Soon he convinced himself that Jeffrey had picked up the CIA hit job on Hendrix, the one which his dubious buddy on the Strip had told him about. Sammi remembered that Bradley used to pace the room as he theorised, shambling around in ever-decreasing circles. Hendrix had got wise to his manager's corrupt dealings, said Bradley, and by April 1970 was talking about breaking his contract with him. The contract was due to last until 1972 and so Jeffrey was looking at a two-year loss of earnings from his 20% share in Hendrix's royalties and publishing rights.

The over-dose was no accident, said Sammi, one eye still open. Right, right, said Bradley. Monika was probably an old CIA honey-trap asset from West Germany, first hired by Jeffrey to spy on Hendrix and keep him dosed up on drugs, then directed by him to poison Hendrix and make it look like an accident.

Hey, that's my theory!, said Sammi. Except maybe, you know, Monika didn't need a man to tell her to do the job, some fucking CIA clown. She did it herself, okay. Maybe, said Sammi, Hendrix was such a pain-in-the-ass boyfriend, such a dick, that she just decided to off him on general principle, to make a point. Like when Valerie Solanas shot Warhol. Maybe Hendrix was stealing Monika's ideas, huh? Sammi asked Bradley if he'd ever thought of that!

Sammi told me that was when the idea came to her for an issue of *I Love Myra* dedicated to the girls in Hendrix's life. The "Hendrix Girl Band" issue of *I Love Myra*. She knew from Bradley's background chatter that Hendrix, like Mick Jagger and Jimmy Page, was almost constantly in the company of groupies throughout his career peak. Sammi wanted to reclaim the term "groupie" and turn it into a badge of respect, an honorific, in recognition of the vital and undervalued role these women had played in the 1960s rock revolution. She also wanted to give

Hendrix groupies like Monika and Kathy the chance to do a Marianne Faithfull, to reinvent themselves as rock stars in their own right. And the only way that could happen was in "what if?"-style fantasy. So Sammi made up hypothetical biographies for Monika and Kathy as members of a fictitious girl group who in her mind represented the feminist alternative to the cock-rock of the Jimi Hendrix Experience.

What if Monika had played drums for the Hendrix Girl Band and Kathy had played bass? thought Sammi. And what if they backed not Jimi Hendrix, but his old New York flame Devon Wilson, who by all accounts was glamorous, aggressive and a little bit crazy. Now, how cool would that have been? Sammi wrote a whole story about it. She also, in passing, lamented the actual fate of Devon, a Milwaukee runaway who flitted between Jagger and Hendrix and gave inspiration to both, before getting hooked on junk and occultism and dying a lonely death in New York in 1971. Sammi noted that Devon was reputedly a member of the Black Panthers and mounted fierce guard over who came and went when Hendrix was jamming in the studio. Sammi speculated that it was Devon who had radicalised Hendrix, pushing him to oppose the Vietnam War and get more involved with black musicians and funk music after the break-up of the Experience.

The final scenario Sammi conjured in her *I Love Myra* zine involved Linda Keith, the London model and Rolling Stones scenester who first talent-spotted Hendrix at the Cheetah club in New York in May 1966. It was Linda who introduced Hendrix to the powerful men who would jump-start his rock music career in London. And it was Linda who suggested Hendrix should cover "Hey Joe", which became his first hit. Shouldn't Linda have been given a shot at management? What if she had become the manager of the Hendrix Girl Band? They would have been the most influential all-female rock group in the world. So Sammi thought in her angry feminist rewriting of rock'n'roll history.

Sammi really let it rip with her design of the "Hendrix Girl Band" issue. She printed layers of graphic imagery over the text and pixelated all the archive photos. She included hand-drawn maps, diagrams and cartoons. The result was an almost abstract expressionist map of dark feelings and extreme thoughts. Sammi didn't care that the whole affair was at times almost illegible. That was the point, she told herself. The information contained in her little zine was so special and important that people should be made to struggle to access it. It wasn't for everyone. It certainly wasn't for boy rockers like Bradley.

Sammi slapped a bold picture of Devon Wilson in a kinky afro on the front cover of her zine and took a stack of copies along to the Riot Grrrl Convention in DC that summer. She arrived at Dupont Circle on the Sunday in an excited state. It was the first time she had been out in months. But the reaction to her zine was not what she had hoped. One snooty Heavens To Betsy fan told her that she was merely appropriating black culture to make herself look good. Another white girl berated her for not including in her zine the Black Panther Party Ten-Point Program, with its demand that the US government compensate black people for their years of enslavement and persecution. Sammi felt guilty and depressed. She stuffed her zines into the hands of a group of slightly baffled African American punk girls and left in tears.

When she got home and told Bradley, he became angry. He said it didn't matter because the whole riot grrrl scene was over, anyway. He said it had sold out to corporate rock interests with female grunge bands like Hole and L7 and all that remained was the factionalism and in-fighting of losers. He used the phrase "political correctness gone mad." Sammi couldn't help thinking that Bradley would have been quite happy to have signed up with a commercial grunge band like Stone Temple Pilots, but she let the point slide.

It was at the back end of 1992 that Sammi started to recover from her bleak period. She stopped smoking, packed up her things and decided on a move back to England. Bikini Kill had toured the UK and seemed in Sammi's eyes to have passed on the riot grrrl torch to a receptive new audience of misfit teen-age girls. It was exciting. Bradley said he would join her. He had been thinking that London was the place for him to launch his international rock career, just as it had been for Hendrix. Sammi couldn't find the courage to say no to him. So now she was stuck with Bradley the tag-along

They went to Camden and Sammi rented a house-boat on a year-long lease. They drifted up and down the Regent's Canal to dodge mooring charges. Bradley strapped his guitar to his back and went out to auditions. Sammi stayed in and planned the next issue of her zine. They were almost a suburban couple and Sammi hoped they would reach some kind of contentment.

Except they had chosen a bad time to make it in London. The shoe-gazing scene was winding down. Bradley was miffed to find he had just missed the indie rock hey-day of Syndrome in Oxford Street. At the same time, he was unwelcome at the nascent Brit-pop scene at the Laurel Tree in Camden, where he was branded a "grunge twat" and "so American". This was all despite Bradley sporting eyeliner and bracelets and doing what he thought was a pretty nice cover of Bowie's "Running Gun Blues". Meanwhile, Sammi was finding that record shops and tour venues thought that fanzines were a sad joke. They were more into glossy magazines and celebrity culture. The practice of selling out, which she had been taught to despise in her Crass days, was now something that British pop kids openly courted.

It was all very depressing for both of them. Sammi was now 24 years old, no longer a teen rebel. She felt lost. Bradley was now smoking heroin to make himself feel better and Sammi kept finding little pieces of tin foil all over the house-boat. He gave up on auditioning and got back into his Hendrix assassination theories, whose elaboration had entered an acute phase. There was no talk of a book now. Instead, Bradley was working on a wall chart and mapping out florid connections between Hendrix, his sound engineers, his thuggish manager Michael Jeffrey, the CIA, Project Pandora, the British Admiralty and sonic weaponry.

Sammi didn't even want to remember Bradley's crazy wall-chart. The trigger for its composition had been his accidental discovery of Paul Virilio's 1983 book *Pure War* in Compendium on Camden High Street. One of those little black books on French theory published by the New York avant-garde publishing house Semiotext(e), it argued that contemporary politics was the continuation of war by other means. This reversal of the Clausewitzian formula was, according to Virilio, the strategic norm rather than the exception in America. This was eye-opening for Bradley. The American military-industrial complex, he thought, had been waging covert war against its own domestic population as a matter of routine. Suddenly, Bradley felt he had found the Rosetta Stone to deciphering the mystery of Hendrix's death.

His researches during the summer of 1993 hit a feverish intensity. He discovered many facts, wrote them on Post-it Notes and assembled them on a timeline. Fact: in the late 1950s Russian/French physicist Vladimir Gavreau developed the prototype of a low-frequency sonic cannon at his Marseilles plant. His team experimented on themselves and induced effects ranging from disorientation, nausea and vomiting to unconsciousness and, reportedly, death. Fact: in 1961 Hendrix trained as a paratrooper in the elite 101st Airborne Division at Fort Campbell in Kentucky. Fact: in 1965 the CIA gained partial oversight of a top-secret DARPA project to study the effects of microwaves on the central nervous system of rhesus monkeys. Fact: in 1966 DARPA recommended weaponisation of its Project Pandora research. Fact: Roger Mayer met Hendrix back-stage at the Bag O'Nails and introduced him to his Octavia fuzz-box, having finished working as an acoustic engineer at the British Admiralty Research Lab on underwater research projects. Fact: in 1967 the MI6-connected Jeffery encouraged Hendrix's sonic experimentation on his recording of "Purple Haze".

What did it all mean? Sammi didn't know. She didn't really care. What she did know was that Bradley had done a full one-eighty on Hendrix, now speaking of him contemptuously as a CIA stooge and public enemy of the counter-culture. She also couldn't help noticing that there was no room for Monika or Devon or Kathy or Linda on Bradley's wall-chart. In fact, there were no women there at all. When she pointed this out, he assaulted her. They both went flying across the quarters of the house-boat and she landed on her back with his hands around her throat. She hit him in the head with a kettle, twice. Bradley released his grip, curled up in a ball and went to sleep.

Autumn came. The Scotland Yard line of inquiry into Hendrix's death was running into the sand and by the end of the year would be terminated. But Bradley's wall-chart continued to grow, like a giant and insidious mould. Another fact: in 1967 Hendrix was quoted as being in favour of the Vietnam War. Fact: in 1969 the Pandora scientific committee planned to move forward with human testing. Key fact: in 1970 Hendrix performed at the Isle of Wight Festival during a set notorious for what were euphemistically labelled technical sound difficulties. He did a 22-minute version of "Machine Gun" where he cranked the Uni-Vibe pedal to produce guitar effects which mimicked the sounds of rockets, bombs, and diving planes. Mixed in with it all was amplified interference from security guard walkie-talkies and wind-whipped taxi radios. The crowd went wild. They threw mud at the stage and shouted obscenities at Hendrix. They tore down the festival's walls, destroyed concession stands and burned their own tents. Fact: in 1970 DARPA became suddenly doubtful about human testing and shut down Project Pandora. Last fact: in 1970 Hendrix died in mysterious circumstances after choking on his own vomit.

As he worked, Bradley kept on click, click, clicking his lighter under his precious little vessels of tin-foil, until the powdered heroin squirmed and released its magic cargo of fumes. The final ostentatious touch to his chart was the addition of a Post-it Note bearing the name of Monika Dannemann.

It was November 1993 when I first met Sammi. She was standing outside the Rocket in the Holloway Road selling copies of her fanzine at a Megadog club night. The crusty kids filing inside were a mass of rainbow hair extensions, nose-rings, petticoats and 12-hole Doc Martens. Sammi, in her fake fur jacket, her gamine hair-cut and her silver pendant ear-rings, her flat court shoes, looked rather out of place. I bought a copy of *I Love Myra*, the "Marianne Faithfull" issue, and we got talking. She kept smoothing the hair at the side of her head to shield the fact she had a lazy eye. I confess I was smitten.

She said she was working on a new issue of her zine, the "Sunset Strip Groupies" issue. Would I like to see how it was going? I immediately said yes. And that's how I ended up on the canal-side at Camden Lock, just next to the railway bridge. As we stepped aboard, Sammi rather grandly referred to her house-boat as a "temporary autonomous zone." Inside, asleep on the bunk bed, much to my dismay, was a young man in a ragged mohair cardigan and jeans. Bradley. Sammi said I should ignore him. The wall-chart above his bed was coming loose from the wall. The Monika Dannemann Post-it Note was barely hanging on. Little foil wraps littered the floor, like so many broken promises.

Sammi made me a cup of mint tea and we sat cross-legged on a rug. She took me through the designs for the next issue of her zine. It focused on the teen groupie scene which flourished under the hot lights of the Sunset Strip clubs in Los Angeles during the early 1970s. There were pictures of young girls in feather boas, garters and clown make-up, mugging to the camera, their small breasts barely concealed by loose halter-tops. Girls with invented glam names like Lori Lightning, Sable Starr and Bebe

Buell. Sexually exploited girls, according to Sammi. Underage girls who were pursued by the likes of Lennon, Bowie and Hendrix.

As if summoned by the name of his ruling passion, Bradley awoke. He yawned and ran his fingers through the clumps of his dirty blonde punk cut. There was a rattling of bangles. His face was a mess of eye-liner. He squinted at me in surprise, then caught himself. Fucked her yet? he asked.

Play nice, said Sammi. I could see that our quiet time was over. Bradley started needling Sammi, calling her a hypocrite, a born-again virgin, saying that the Sunset Strip girls were no different from Sammi in her school days. They were bored teenage sluts looking for excitement and empowerment. And what was wrong with that? Face it, said Sammi, her gaze a blank. Hendrix was an abuser of women. He was worse than that, said Bradley, suddenly quite gloomy.

Bradley started to take me through his Hendrix conspiracy theory, in a half-hearted way. He spoke of the clandestine operation of microwave weapons. They can put voices in a target's head, he said. A targeted individual. Sammi had picked up his guitar and was strumming away in the background. M-M-Monika, she sang. Shut up, Sammi, said Bradley.

And so they got into an argument, and then a fight. I had to step in and try to calm them down. It was useless, of course. And it was only after many such visits that I realised I was at risk of becoming part of the show. An enabler, I think they call it.

As I walked back to Camden tube station on the night of that last visit, I heard Leftfield's "Open Up" playing from the open doorway of a pub. You lied, you faked, you cheated, sang John

Lydon. I saw a faded slogan stencilled on the Chalk Farm Road. "Burn It All Down". I felt a deep emotion I couldn't name.

I never saw Sammi again although I did phone her a few times. That's how I learned that she'd finished her Monika song. I persuaded her to send me a tape cassette version of it in the post. "The Ballad of Monika D". I loved it at once. But the lyrics were hard to decipher. Cryptic phrases like "sonic lie detector" and "killing him with silence" seemed to allude to Monika's troubled relationship with Hendrix, although the rock star's name was never mentioned. When I challenged Sammi about the meaning of the song, she said it was a rape revenge fantasy about an abused groupie who kills a predatory rock star with one of his own infrasonic gizmos. She had written the song mostly to annoy Bradley. He had told her in one of his interminable monologues that "Purple Haze" was inspired by a science-fiction story Hendrix had found in an old pulp mag lying around at Fort Campbell, a story about a death-ray. I asked Sammi what she thought had really happened at the Samarkand Hotel that desperate night in 1970. She laughed and said I was asking the wrong person.

Sammi's phone got disconnected soon afterwards and I lost touch with her. I didn't really think of her again until three years later when I read in the newspaper that Monika Dannemann had been found dead in a fume-filled Mercedes Benz close to her home in Seaford, East Sussex. Her death was ruled a suicide, but those close to her muttered about foul play. It was certainly a strange death. I was reminded of the other strange deaths that had happened soon after Hendrix was buried. Devon Wilson falling from the 8th floor window of the Chelsea Hotel in New York in 1971. Michael Jeffery dying in a freakish mid-air plane collision over France in 1973. Coincidence or conspiracy? I wondered what Bradley would make of it all. I wondered how Sammi would react. But they were both long gone from my life.

And then, one day, quite by chance, I saw Sammi in the Waitrose supermarket car park in Hove. She was busy lifting a young child out of a buggy into the back of one of those heavily-armoured SUVs. A man was at the wheel, waiting for her. He looked nothing like Bradley. I waved, but she didn't recognise me. She was too happy.

TOMMY LOVE

Author of the Jim Morrison Conspiracy Novel

I FIRST MET TOMMY LOVE in a little court off the High Street in Edinburgh. It was 1991. The gloss was starting to come off Glasgow's European City of Culture award and Scotland's capital city was reasserting its old cultural dominance. I was at Canongate Books to arrange an interview with Jim Kelman. Tommy had crashed the office in the hopes of giving a copy of his manuscript to Alasdair Gray. Both authors were featured in the Scottish short story anthology *The Devil and the Giro*, which was just about to be published by Canongate. Neither author was in the building.

Tommy and I retired to the pub. Tommy grabbed the pints of lager from the bar, after a spot of banter with the tapster. When he got to our table, he said that he used to work as a bar-tender in Paris. He touched his quiff and smiled. Tommy had a boyish face which suited a smile. He was dressed in a check shirt, beige chinos and deck shoes. The look would have been discreet if it hadn't been for his chunky mustard cardigan.

We got talking about Scottish literature. I praised Kelman's stories for their abrasive social realism and faithfulness to working-class Glaswegian idiom. I said if there was one thing punk had taught us, it was that we should speak in our own voices. Tommy snorted. He quoted Deleuze and Guattari on minor literature. He said the Scottish working-class owed it to themselves to speak English better than their colonial masters. That was why he was a fan of Alasdair Gray. The author of *Lanark: A Life in Four Books*, he said, wasn't afraid to write down his prophetic visions in the most public voice he could find. Like William Blake. Tommy slapped down his manuscript between us.

Get a load of this! he said. *Night on Fire*. A punk update on *The Illuminatus! Trilogy*. There must have been about 500 loose leaves inside the black binder. I picked it up and read the first line… "It was the night when Jim Morrison finally immanentised the Eschaton." I laughed. It was a good line. Tommy raised his finger and made an "O" shape with his mouth. The KLF's acid house anthem "3AM Eternal" had dropped on the juke-box. "Synchronicity!" said Tommy, as if he were used to counting out the meaningful coincidences in his life. He chanted along with the chorus. "Ancients of Mu!" He had a lovely singing voice.

I had skimmed at least one of the three pop conspiracy novels published by Robert Shea and Robert Anton Wilson in 1975. Their semi-satirical take on the occult workings of the Illuminati secret society ranged far and wide, from its historic struggle with the beatnik Discordians to its creation of a cult rock band designed to, well, "immanentise the Eschaton" – that is, destroy the world and create a new one in its place. I knew that Bill Drummond had been influenced by a lot of these ideas when he put together the KLF. I vaguely remembered the band capering around on *Top of the Pops* dressed in hooded jackets and monkish cowls.

I flicked through Tommy's manuscript. It was mostly composed of a stream-of-consciousness narrative written from the point of view of rock star Jim Morrison on the night of his death in 1971. He was 27, in exile from North America after making a disastrously obscene exhibition of himself at a concert in Miami, and expiring in the bath of an apartment in Paris. Morrison's mind took him back to his 1960s past. The dying star remembered his jolting performances as the Doors front-man in Los Angeles, acting out the myth of the sexually potent bluesman for screaming white girls, while singing about snakes and lizards and other totems of South American shamanism. He remembered his talks to bearded Jewish freaks about how he was inspired by the celebrated madman Antonin Artaud. He remembered his peyote trips in the desert. So far, I thought, so true to the facts.

Where Tommy veered wildly off-course from history — as I discovered when I read the manuscript on the train back to London — was with the demented fantasies he attributed to his fading rock god. His deviant sex life, his recruitment into the ranks of the Surrealists by the ghost of Artaud in Southern California, his final self-destructive drift into the heroin trafficking rings of the Corsican mafia in Paris. Of course, it is this level of invention which makes *Night on Fire* so beguiling. Who wouldn't want to think of Jim Morrison as the last of the Surrealists, involved in a psychic struggle with an esoteric neo-Nazi group, known simply as the Initiates? Tommy's novel describes how the Initiates penetrated the CIA and were running Operation Chaos for its chief Richard Ober. They were using occult means to crack down on American dissidents abroad. One of their favourite tricks was to chase them with the Nazi flying saucers they had launched from an underground base in Antarctica. Morrison was the man tapped to call up the ancient gods of the Americas in revenge. His lewd antics on-stage were explicitly designed to incite Dionysian frenzy among the teens while disabling the older generation with various moral panics.

In sum, the history of the postwar period in *Night on Fire* was the history of the struggle between two occult groups to "immanentise the Eschaton", each in their different ways. On one side were the Initiates with their secret CIA wars and covert operations around the world, their worship of the god of death in the basement of the Langley building in Virginia. They wanted to build a Hell on Earth. And on the other side were the Surrealists, who with their sex cults and omens of mad love, their devotion to the pagan gods of desire, wanted to build a Heaven on Earth. Who would emerge victorious? Tommy told me his novel dealt seriously with the last religious mythology of the Western world, the one elaborated by Freud and his disciples, which re-envisioned Judaeo-Christian eschatology as a conflict between Thanatos and Eros.

Night on Fire dramatises this cosmic struggle as a battle for possession of the Baculus Jesu, the staff Christ used to beat back the Devil when he fasted in the Judean desert for forty days and forty nights. Tommy imagines the occult Christian relic passing through various hands — Pontius Pilate, Charlemagne, the Duke of Savoy, Joshua Janavel — before reaching Antonin Artaud on the streets of 1930s Paris. From here, it made its way to Adolf Hitler in 1940s Berlin, Richard Ober in 1950s Marseille and the Count de Breteuil in 1960s Tangier. The Count sold the Baculus Jesu to Jim Morrison in Paris in 1971. Quite a tale!

I remember how excited Tommy was when talking to me about his novel in the pub. He thought he had a hit on his hands. The Oliver Stone movie about the Doors had been released earlier in the year and Tommy figured there was a new audience for Jim Morrison's self-made recusant mythology. We talked about the story Morrison liked to tell about himself, how his mana as a performer was the gift of a powerful Native American shaman, whose spirit had possessed him as a child. It was a story Stone took seriously in *The Doors*. He shows the four-year old Jim in the back of the saloon on a family road trip in the desert of New Mexico. The car passes the scene of a traffic accident, involving a truckload of Native Americans. Storm clouds gather overhead as the young Jimmy locks his gaze with that of a dying old man. The dead Indian is later seen on-stage at a Doors concert, chanting with the rock star, as the crowd metamorphoses into an archaic tribe of celebrants at a ghost dance.

Of course, said Tommy, Morrison's tutelary spirit abandoned him in the end. It's why he had a sudden heart attack in the bath in Paris. I shook my head. I said the tale about the dead Indian was so corny, it was like something out of a barker's mouth at a P.T. Barnum carnival. Tommy disagreed. He said Morrison's voluntary shamanism was in the tradition of Artaud, who had travelled to Mexico to take part in a peyote ceremony in the 1930s. In the tradition too, he said, of the CIA, who had investigated various tribal practices as part of their mind control research in the 1950s. They had funded the trip of a J P Morgan man to investigate magic mushroom rituals in 1951. It wasn't just Morrison who had wanted to break on through to the other side.

I liked Tommy and, over time, I got to know his story. He was born in the rough part of Edinburgh in 1960, the youngest of four brothers. His father worked at Robb's Yard in the Leith docks and his mother was a barmaid. His grandfather on his father's side, Old Billy Love, was a disgraced minister for the Church of Scotland. He lived with them, now and again. He was a brooding presence on his stool in the kitchen, methodically packing his pipe and working his way through the Johnnie Walker Red Label. He seemed to have it in for young Tommy. He used to give him the eye over the rim of his shot glass, before downing the whisky. He said to his daughter that unless her "wee dobber" joined the Young Communist League and helped to build the New Jerusalem, there was no hope for him. He'd end up being thrown into the bottomless pit of Gehenna.

Old Billy lived in the past, in a time before his own ghostly vessel of a life hove into view. He talked with great enthusiasm about how his father had taken part in the land raids on the Isle of Lewis, digging up the fields of "Lord fucking Leverhulme" to create a smallholding for his family. Four acres of land, Lloyd George promised! said Billy, as if the grant had been made to him personally. At this point, he would look scornfully round the kitchen. How has it come to this? If his eye landed on Tommy, he would quote the old Highland Land League slogan: IS TREASA TUATH NA TIGHEARN! It scared the devil out of the boy.

There wasn't much room in the family council flat and Tommy spent a lot of his childhood outside. Most of the boys on the housing scheme were diehard Hearts supporters, but Tommy wasn't much of a football fan. Instead, he used to parade around with a prized record sleeve under his arm. When glam rock hit the charts, Tommy was defiant in his support for the Osmonds' "Crazy Horses". The other boys snickered, saying this was music for teeny-boppers. They were more impressed by his devotion to Alice Cooper. The band's "School's Out" video was banned by the BBC in 1972 and a petition was raised to stop them performing. Their exercises in Grand Guignol – killing chickens, staging a mock-hanging on a gallows, chopping up bloodied baby dolls – were certainly disturbing. "School's Out" hit the top of the charts.

When Alice Cooper came to Glasgow in November, Tommy's brother Caleb hitch-hiked to see them play at Green's Playhouse. Tommy wasn't allowed to go. He was too young and impressionable, said his mother. She felt vindicated when Caleb came home with a cut lip. He said the concert had been so exciting there'd been a wee bit of a rammy. The local neds had wrecked three rows of seats. Nothing to do with me, said Caleb, winking at young Tommy. Their mother tutted. Caleb handed his little brother a torn poster of the band's lead singer, himself named Alice Cooper, cavorting on-stage in black leather and drizzled eye make-up. Tommy taped the picture above his bed.

Punk rock didn't really get going in Scotland until 1977. Tommy took Caleb, who was into the rehashed R&B of the Valves, to see the Rezillos, Siouxsie and the Banshees and the Mekons at Clouds in West Tollcross. Caleb had to admit they all showed wit and invention.

Tommy's favourite punk band was the Scars. He and Caleb saw them twice at Transport Halls on Annandale Street. He appreciated their glam make-up and moody poses, their arty lyrics. He was intrigued by the talk among Caleb's pals at the bar of how punk was an avant-garde movement, like Dada and Surrealism before it. The whole point of a punk gig, he learned, was to break down barriers between the performers and the audience. If that took the form of pogoing fans spitting at the band or a front-man stopping the music to have a go at the crowd, so be it. Nothing wrong with a bit of aggro.

Caleb talked knowledgeably about Artaud's "theatre of cruelty". He had picked up the phrase from a back-issue of the rock mag *Creem*, which had been posted to him by his pen pal in Schenectady, New York. Artaud, said Caleb, had argued that the quickest way to break down the barrier between art and life was through the impact of violence. Not random violence, he added. Not like the old Glasgow razor gangs. But violence perfected on-stage. Violence as production design. Like Alice Cooper? said Tommy. Caleb laughed. More like Cooper's old Detroit buddy Iggy Pop, he said. Iggy liked to slice open his chest with a sharpened drum-stick and spatter the audience with his blood. He would dive into a hostile crowd and get beaten up. Wow! said Tommy. Yeah, said Caleb. Iggy was the real deal. He wanted everyone to live a life as intense as his own.

Iggy liked to rub his cock on-stage, didn't he? said one of Caleb's pals. Underneath his tight, leather breeks. Caleb nodded. Iggy got that from Jim Morrison, he said. The Doors frontman was famous for shocking the wee lassies in the audience by touching himself down there. He even got his cock out on-stage in Miami in 1969, didn't he? The cops came down on him like a ton of bricks and he got done for indecent exposure. It finished him, said Caleb, mournfully. He lost his nerve after that.

Tommy became disenchanted with punk when it swapped pop for abstraction. Suddenly, rhythm was more important than melody. Guitar riffs were crowded out by drumbeats and basslines. Where there had once been the Sex Pistols, Warsaw and the Buzzcocks, there was now Public Image Ltd, Joy Division and

Magazine. Caleb was intrigued by the new post-punk bands. But Tommy felt betrayed by their withdrawal into a cloistered space of airless experimentation. He switched his allegiance to the second wave of punk bands which were starting to attract a skinhead following. At least bands like Sham 69, Cock Sparrer and the Angelic Upstarts, for all their lack of originality, were still committed to the idea of breaking down barriers between artists and audience.

Tommy was secretly thrilled whenever he read in the music papers about another Sham 69 gig disrupted by skinhead violence. It tickled him how lead singer Jimmy Pursey would stop the music and try to reason with the rioting audience. The bloody fool! He should have carried on belting out "If the Kids Are United" until the crowd had stormed the stage, stripped him naked and beaten him black and blue. That's what Iggy Pop would have done! That's what Jim Morrison would have done! They would have made the bloodlust into a thing of beauty…

Tommy's introduction to the music of the Doors came soon after Caleb's impromptu lecture on the theatre of cruelty. He went to see the Vietnam war flick *Apocalypse Now* at the local ABC and was blown away by the Doors song "The End". Its pulsating fusion of exotic keyboards and droning guitars overlaid the climactic scene in the film where a troubled young assassin slaughters the old and washed-up leader of a tribe of outcasts in the jungle. As the light glints off the killer's machete, Morrison is heard growling "Come on, yeah!" Tommy later learned that "The End" was written by Morrison as a Freudian love song. It was all about the Oedipal complex discharging itself in a hallucinatory dramatic outburst of patricide and incest. In the film, the song took on new meaning. To Tommy's mind, it offered a sardonic and horrific take on the 1960s hippy dream of exiting family life to find enlightenment in alternative social structures.

Screenwriter John Milius said he came up with the title for the film when he saw a Southern Californian flower kid wearing a badge which read "Paradise Now". Tommy thought Milius must have figured if a bunch of 1960s social misfits got together in isolated country, the result would not be a festival of brotherly love, but a gala of fratricidal violence. The only thing that could prevent this, as Freud suggested in *Moses and Monotheism*, would be a guilt-bonding ritual of collectively authored violence against a designated victim. The killing of the king. Such was the message Tommy took out of the film.

In the summer of 1980, Tommy went Interrailing in Western Europe. It was then that he read *The Illuminatus! Trilogy* and came across the idea of a rock band being part of a cosmic power play between different occult groups.

In Paris, he visited Jim Morrison's grave in Pere Lachaise cemetery. The stones around the grave were scrawled with lines from the rock star's songs and poems. Some were famous: "I am the Lizard King", "Break on through to the other side". Others were inscrutable: "Words resemble walking sticks". Morrison's own tombstone was a roughly-hewn, squat affair heading up a dwarf-sized plot. The grave was strewn with wilted flowers, bottle caps, postcards, messages scribbled on metro tickets, odd trinkets and souvenirs. Four scruffy young back-packers stood around the grave, smoking. Tommy joined the vigil.

Inevitably, the kids were talking about Morrison's mysteriously premature death. He didn't die of heart failure, said a young man from Texas. He over-dosed on his girlfriend's smack in their Paris apartment and his management covered it up. A fellow from Germany said it was worse than that. Morrison had gone to a night-club on the Left Bank to buy some heroin from the Corsican mafia. He had tasted some of the China White in the toilet and it was so pure that he OD'd and went into a coma. His dealer – a mysterious figure known as the Count – had arranged for him to be taken back to his apartment and dunked in a cold bath to revive him. It hadn't worked. The CIA must have been involved, said a French girl. They wanted him dead because they thought he was a revolutionary, like Che Guevara. He knew it was coming, said the Texan kid. He said he'd be the next rock star to die young after Brian Jones and Janis Joplin. He came to Paris to get away from his enemies, said the French girl, but they got him in the end. They gouged out his eyes, said an English boy. Why would they do that? said Tommy, shocked. To release his demon, his tutelary spirit, said the boy. Really? said the French girl, wide-eyed. The English boy nodded. Morrison's death was an occult rite. I doubt that, said the German fellow, suddenly all matter-of-fact. The English boy protested. How do you explain the fact, he said, that when the apartment on rue Beautreillis was cleaned out, a bloody dagger was discovered under the bath?

There was silence around the headstone. I'm amazed they got a six-foot man into such a small plot, said Tommy at last. Maybe he's not there, said the French girl. What do you mean? said Tommy. She shrugged. He faked his own death. This comment came from a tall young man, another American, from California. Just like he said he would when the Doors performed at the Fillmore in 1967. He'd had enough of the pressures of the music business and wanted to stage a disappearing trick. Really? said the French girl. The Californian man showed his teeth as he dragged on his joint. Yeah! He said. My friend's brother saw him last year hanging out in a gay leather bar in LA. God's truth! He must have survived his heroin overdose, said the German boy, with an air of solemnity.

Cemetery officials arrived to move the group on. As they were leaving the grave, the English boy commented on Tommy's accent. He said that Morrison's family were originally from Scotland. They'd emigrated to America back in the eighteenth century. Maybe Tommy was related?

Before leaving Paris, Tommy bought a copy of *American Prayer*, the last Doors album. It featured spoken-word recordings made by Morrison of his poems in 1969 and 1970, set to music by the band in 1978. The last track on side one was titled "Curses, Invocations". Here, Tommy found the full version of the lyric which had baffled him at Pere Lachaise: "Words resemble walking sticks, plant them they will grow."

In September 1980, Tommy went to the Glasgow School of Art to study for a BA in Graphic Design and Illustration. The low meanness of Glasgow came as a shock after a childhood spent in the easy pomp of Edinburgh. The city still bore the scars of the slum clearance projects of a generation before. The tenements had been partially torn down or evacuated and the old working-class population decanted to new housing estates on the edge of the city. People came into the city centre to work, but in the mornings and evenings, the streets were empty. Tommy walked for miles at night looking for signs of cultural life. He went past block after block of wasteland, bordered by plywood walls coated in fliers for local post-punk bands – Orange Juice, Josef K. There were few cars parked in the streets. The only welcoming light came from the Victorian bingo halls and corner pubs.

Tommy decided to do a mixed-media project on Surrealism and the city, using Glasgow as a stand-in for the Paris of the interwar period. Andre Breton in *Nadja* had wandered the Paris flea-market at Saint-Ouen, looking for signs of his heart's desire in broken and useless, almost incomprehensible, lost objects. In *Mad Love* he had drifted through Les Halles at night, elevating chance encounters into fateful interventions. So Tommy toured the desolate streets of Glasgow in 1980, notebook in hand. It was only later he realised he had been a prospector for marvels as gimlet-eyed as any property developer hoping to renovate the sooty old tenements on the Saltmarket.

Tommy found much inspiration at Paddy's Market on Shipbank Lane. The cries of the street traders hawking second-hand clothes and furniture, the chatter of the guys unboxing counterfeit perfumes under the railway arches, the mutterings of the addicts waiting for the latest heroin shipment from Iran. They touched him like the emanations of an ancient love. Tommy wasn't the only trendy young aesthete at Paddy's Market. He recognised familiar faces from the Vic Bar, the student union watering-hole opposite the art school's Mackintosh building. There was Jill Bryson, whose punk approach to glamour saw her sorting through great piles of old clothes on the street in her quest for discarded ballgowns and gloves. There was Peter McArthur, with his camera. There was Edwyn Collins, the lead-singer of Orange Juice, and his record-label boss Alan Horne, who together formed an experimental unit dedicated to breaking down the barriers between what was available on the street and what was wanted in the heart.

For Horne, tartan kitsch inspired the image of Postcard Records and its ambition to be for Scotland what Motown Records had been for America — the sound of a nation renewing itself. For Collins, the soul and disco music found on second-hand compilation albums like *Black Explosion* and *Souled Out* signalled a way out of post-punk's creative exhaustion. He had even found a way to incorporate the twang of the Country & Western tapes played at Paddy's Market into the band's last single, "Blue Boy". Orange Juice turned the meanness of everyday life into the conditions for epic romance. When the band messed around in their second-hand tweed jackets, silk ties and suede boots, they acted for all the world as if they were Scottish lairds. The pantomime of class defiance was infectious.

Tommy understood all this instinctively. His interest in bands like Sham 69 had waned as the SWP and the BNP had squabbled over the meaning of the music and loaded it up with political ideology. The music had become thin and evasive. He was actively turned off by the resentful prole gestures of *Oi! The Album*. Tommy wanted to be a dandy. With his vintage satin bowling jacket and check shirt, his floppy fringe, he fitted right into the rather camp entourage which had formed around Postcard Records. When girls asked him if he were gay, he quoted Oscar Wilde and said he was more perverse than that — he was celibate.

Tommy never met Alan Horne, but he knew all the stories about him. They circulated among the art students, intellectuals and musicians-on-the-dole who hung out at the Vic Bar. Alan Horne was an angry dreamer like Malcolm McLaren, they said, a damaged genius like Joe Meek. Alan Horne expected Postcard Records to challenge the major record labels for chart success, even though he was running it from a shabby tenement bedsit on West Princes Street. Alan Horne hated the self-regarding elitism of the post-punk underground and loved the possibilities offered by the pop mainstream. Alan Horne knew that pop music could be life-changing and he wanted the bands on his label to re-enchant the world.

In December, Tommy went to see Orange Juice play at Tiffany's on Sauchiehall Street. The band were supporting the Undertones and promoting their third single, "Simply Thrilled Honey". Tommy was transfixed by their chiming guitar-based sound. He was accompanied by his new best friend, a stony-faced postgrad who always carried with him a copy of Deleuze and Guattari's *Anti-Oedipus*. MacLeish pointed out Alan Horne at the bar. A belligerent little man sporting transparently-framed spectacles, Horne was scanning the crowd around him as if looking for enemies.

At the end of the year, the *New Musical Express* published a manifesto which rejected post-punk in favour of radio play and chart singles. So the dialectical turn of punk was made into what became known as "New Pop". Horne's vision had effectively been packaged into a record industry slogan.

Tommy told me that Horne was a year ahead of the *NME*, a year ahead of New Pop, a year ahead of his time. Everyone in the Vic expected 1981 to be the break-out year for Postcard Records. Some were even talking about the sound of young Scotland becoming the sound of young Britain, America and the world. Why not? Hits by the Human League, Adam and the Ants and Scritti Politti – all ex-punk bands like Orange Juice – came and went. Even Glasgow's own little Clare Grogan became a pop star with Altered Images. But Orange Juice and Josef K failed to chart.

The truth was, said Tommy, that Horne didn't have the promotional heft to drive his pop acts into the mainstream. His response was typically obstinate. On the one hand, he continued to advance the idea of an independent music scene in Glasgow, signing the 16-year-old Roddy Frame to his label and attracting the Pastels and the Bluebells into his orbit. He also inspired Jill Bryson to form her own band, Strawberry Switchblade. On the other hand, he lobbied London-based radio stations with sensational and largely untrue stories about Postcard Records. He said he had signed Sheena Easton and David Bowie's son, that he had turned down Altered Images before they became famous, that he had recruited Barry White to produce Roddy Frame's band Aztec Camera, that he had cut a flexi-disc with The Associates' Billy Mackenzie singing a cover version of the Cadbury's Flake jingle.

People at the Vic made up their own promotional stories about Postcard, some of which got back to West Princes Street and ended up being used in press releases. Alan Horne had signed a chimpanzee, dressed up in a suit like the monkey in Alice Cooper's "Elected" video. Alan Horne had formed a band with a gang of schoolboys and named it Oscar Wild – without the "e". Alan Horne had come into the possession of Jim Morrison's legendary lost Paris tapes, featuring the singer performing with a couple of buskers he'd discovered in Les Halles. That last one was invented by Tommy, who had just finished reading the Morrison biography *No One Here Gets Out Alive*.

It all came to nothing, said Tommy. Orange Juice concluded that to fulfil Alan Horne's dream of taking the charts by storm, they would have to ditch Postcard Records and sign with a major UK label. They duly moved to London in the summer and bagged a deal with Polydor. Their first chart hit "L.O.V.E… love" followed in October. Tommy observed this with great disillusionment from his spot at the Vic. The band which had emerged from the fabulous street market of Glasgow had accepted its revaluation as a commodity on the corporate music market of London. *Que sera*, said Tommy. By the end of 1981, Alan Horne was a year behind his time. Postcard Records collapsed.

As New Pop continued to dominate national radio over the next three years, the young Scottish bands from the Postcard scene followed in the footsteps of Orange Juice. They signed with London-based record labels and took their place in the charts alongside English bands like ABC, Haircut One Hundred, Spandau Ballet and Frankie Goes to Hollywood. Tommy felt like they were each taking a little piece of his heart with them. Roddy Frame wrote his first chart single "Oblivious" on the bus down to London to meet with Rough Trade. Cunt! The Pastels got a deal with Rough Trade in October 1983 when they literally offered themselves up as "the next big thing out of Scotland". Double cunt!

By the time the Bluebells released their debut album on London Records in July 1984, Tommy had graduated. No more grant money from the Department of Education and Science. He got a job behind the bar at the Vic and learned to mix cocktails. When

Strawberry Switchblade got signed to WEA and debuted their goth glam look on the cover of *Smash Hits* in December, he felt like vomiting. He told MacLeish he finally understood some of the bitterness experienced by his grandfather at the failure of the Scottish devolution referendum in 1979. MacLeish laughed.

Tommy was serious. Why should London get to decide the terms of failure and success in Scotland? he said. MacLeish laughed again. He said that Tommy was suffering from an Oedipal neurosis. Fuck Scotland, he said. Fuck grandpa. Fuck Postcard Records. Get over yourself, man. Deterritorialise! he said, quoting one of Deleuze and Guattari's pet phrases. Let loose. Go a bit mad.

Tommy's grandfather died in January 1985. Billy went home to Edinburgh for the funeral. It was a spartan affair. Old Billy had always said that when he died, they should throw his body in the earth at the kirk. His family saw no reason to demur.

Tommy felt the need for ritual. Back in Glasgow, he got roaring drunk with MacLeish and made a banner out of an old bedsheet. He then performed the time-honoured Scottish trick of disrespecting the English by placing an orange traffic cone on the head of the statue of the Duke of Wellington in Royal Exchange Square. The cone was festooned with his banner, which carried the English version of Old Billy's favourite slogan: "THE PEOPLE ARE MIGHTIER THAN A LORD." MacLeish stood below in his winter greatcoat, clapping.

After that, Tommy decided to write a porno novel in the spirit of Alexander Trocchi, the Scottish literary outsider who had been profiled in a recent issue of the *Edinburgh Review*, just a year after his death. MacLeish said that was a great idea, but didn't it mean Tommy should get out there and start having, like, sex? Tommy waved away the objection. He said he wanted to take the sex out of pornography. He wanted to focus on the body in a state of extremity, beyond pleasure and pain.

MacLeish nodded. The body-without-organs, he said. Tommy seized on the phrase. What the hell was that? MacLeish said it was Antonin Artaud's second great idea, after the theatre of cruelty. Frustrated by the limitations of French theatre, Artaud had fled to Mexico in 1936. He had met with the Indians in the mountains and taken part in a traditional peyote ceremony. An old shaman, said MacLeish, had introduced Artaud to the mysteries of his craft. Upon his initiation, the old man said, he had travelled to the spirit world, where his body was torn apart and he was remade with the bones of his ancestors. Artaud was enthralled with the idea, said Tommy. He referred to it as the creation of a body-without-organs.

Tommy nodded. He said he had heard that Jim Morrison had visited a shaman when the Doors toured Mexico in 1969. His poems mentioned Aztec rituals.

MacLeish ignored the interruption. He said that when Artaud returned to Paris, he tried to convince himself that he too was a shaman. He became fixated on an old rustic walking stick and was seen leaping and dancing with it through Les Halles. The stick had been given to him by a friend, who told him that it used to belong to a Waldensian sect leader in the Western Alps. Artaud used to study the stick's various knots and cut branches, as if they encoded some great secret. And then one night, said MacLeish, the night Artaud broke through to the other side, the stick spoke to him. It told him it had a provenance older than the Waldensians, that it was the magic staff of Jesus itself, the Baculus Jesu, and that it would have a great role to play in the apocalyptic war which was about to unfold.

What happened next? said Tommy. They locked him up, of course, said MacLeish. Artaud was interned in various Paris asylums from 1937 to 1946 — the duration of the Second World War, in fact — and was given electro-shock treatment. They sparked him up over fifty times, said MacLeish.

Poor bastard! said Tommy. Aye, said MacLeish. Though it finally gave him the chance to live out his fantasy of being a shaman, eh? Really? said Tommy. Oh aye! said MacLeish. Artaud called insane asylums "repositories of black magic". Each day the doctors would drug him. Placing the electrodes on his skull and inducing a seizure, they attempted to break his body and destroy his mind. The asylums in which he was confined during the German occupation of Paris were starved of rations and little better than concentration camps, said MacLeish. Artaud was convinced he was in Hell. But he fought back against what he called the Devil's Initiates. Each night, he would rebuild himself in his mind. He imagined his body stronger, more powerful, even better than God had designed it. It was a form of counter-sorcery, an occult means of collapsing the distinction between art and life.

Christ! said Tommy. Indeed, said MacLeish. Artaud felt there was a design solution for the human body capable of resisting old age and death. Something to do with removing the sex and digestive organs, he said, stripping away the skin, leaving only the skeleton, the lungs and the face intact. A blueprint for immortality.

Crazy! said Tommy. Of course! said MacLeish. Artaud was a madman who believed that the Devil had risen in Europe and the world was about to end in a holocaust of air and fire. A lot of his time in the asylums was spent in a furious letter-writing campaign, said MacLeish. He sent out manically-written "sorts" or spells to curse his enemies and bless his friends. They were ritually torn, stained and burned. He even sent a letter to Hitler.

Really? said Tommy. Sure! Said MacLeish. He picked up his copy of *Mille plateaux*, Deleuze and Guattari's follow-up volume to *Anti-Oedipus*, which he was struggling to read in the original French. He turned to the essay on Artaud, whose title he translated for Tommy as "How Do You Make Yourself a Body Without Organs?". He found the page which quoted Artaud's letter to Hitler. It was sent in September 1939, at the start of the Second World War, and seemed to anticipate the Nazi occupation of Paris. Tommy was fascinated. Artaud spoke to Hitler as an equal. He reminded him of the quarrel they had once had when they were wild young bohemians in the Ider Café in Berlin.

This was when Tommy had his moment of inspiration. What if World War II had been fought not just on land and sea, not just in the air — but also in the spirit world? What if Artaud and Hitler had been twin magicians fighting a cosmic battle for possession of the tutelary spirits of the Western world? He told MacLeish his idea. In the final six months of the war, he said, there was Artaud in his asylum and Hitler in his bunker, equal and opposite forces, each raining down their mad spells on the remains of Europe. How about it?

MacLeish nodded. He said that Artaud claimed to have cast his spirit body into the *Führerbunker* at the end of the war. He had been there when Hitler shot himself.

Tommy pressed his friend for more detail. But MacLeish shrugged. He said information on Artaud's life was sparse. That was when Tommy knew he would have to go to Paris to conduct the research for his novel.

His stay in Paris lasted from the summer of 1985 to the end of 1990. It was here that he changed his look. He swapped his satin bowling jacket for an MA-1 flying jacket, his penny loafers for Doc Martens. He lost the fringe and got a clipper-grade Number 2 crop. He kept the button-down check shirt. The suburban boys in the night-clubs of Les Halles called him *le skinhead anglais*, which he didn't mind too much. They appreciated his knowledge of New Pop and rare groove. He found himself in demand as a bartender and occasional DJ. He flitted between Le Club on rue Saint Denis, Le BH on rue du Roule and the Broad on rue de la Ferronerie.

It was a time of bomb threats and police raids in the emerging gay district of Paris. Clubs could find themselves closed down for refusing to light their small back-rooms, where many irregular sexual practices took place. Tommy soon discovered his own particular kink. He liked to watch. He spent many long hours seeing how far bodily orifices could be stretched or filled, body parts dilated or squashed, taut skin whipped and loose skin cut. He supplied the razor blades and the anaesthetic drugs. He washed up the semen and the blood. He wondered what his grandfather would make of the holes he frequented. Pit-stops on the road to Gehenna, no doubt.

The Arab heroin dealers who hung around outside the gates of Châtelet–Les Halles told him that the area actually used to be known as *le trou*, the hole. This was back in the early part of the previous decade, before the metro junction had been built and the gay clubs and the restaurants and the antique dealers had moved in. It was before even the opening of the Pompidou Centre. The origin of le trou lay back in July 1971, when the historic wrought-iron pavilions of the old medieval food market had been torn down. Tommy met an old boy from Algiers in an exposed concrete plaza above Châtelet–Les Halles. He quoted Zola and said, approvingly, that bulldozing the Paris food market had been like ripping out the belly of the city. It had created a space for dissolute experimentation and play – *les agissements*. Tommy couldn't help but think of Artaud and the body-without-organs.

One thing his disreputable research taught him was that wherever he looked in Paris for Artaud, he found Jim Morrison had gone before. It was if he were the explorer Lidenbrock, whose journey to the centre of the Earth in Jules Verne's novel had been waymarked by the passage of an earlier pioneer. What arcane secret of existence had Morrison been chasing? And what would it mean to Tommy, if he found it? He told me the story of his tour of Paris.

He had gone to the famed Café de Flore on the boulevard Saint-Germain, where Artaud had drunk with his bohemian pals in the 1920s, when he was head of the Bureau of Surrealist Research. On the surface of an old wooden table Tommy found etched the initials "AA". Beneath these were the initials "MR", which he took to be a reference to Jim Morrison's alias, "Mojo

Risin." He imagined Morrison sitting at the table with a small knife, listening to the French philosophy students talk about Deleuze and his recently published take on the body-without-organs.

Tommy went to the Odeon national theatre on the Left Bank. Here, the cultural influence of Artaud had reached a high-water mark in May 1968, when it was occupied by radical members of the Living Theatre. In the spirit of Artaud, these American activists proclaimed that theatre should become an "art of combat". Tommy was aware that only a few blocks away, on the rue de Seine, was the site of the Rock'n'roll Circus, the club where Morrison had supposedly received his lethal freight of heroin, on the night he died.

What really astonished Tommy, though, was to discover that the Living Theatre had gone on to perform in 1969 at the University of Southern California, and that Morrison was in the audience. Morrison witnessed their most notorious piece, *Paradise Now*, in which the performers recited a long list of all the social taboos they wished to break. On the list was nudity. Usually, the actors would disrobe on-stage at this point. But the prospect of another arrest for indecent exposure led them to hold back at the USC show. Even so, Morrison got the idea. It was only a few days later that he faced his own charge of indecent exposure when performing at Miami.

Tommy idly wondered if John Milius, a budding screen-writer active in Southern California at the time, had got the idea for *Apocalypse Now* from a Doors fan exiting the USC theatre on the night of *Paradise Now*.

Certainly, Tommy told me, his strangest experience in Les Halles was being introduced by one of his black-market colleagues to *le Chinois*, a dealer in tainted artworks and collectables. In the hive of vaulted cellars in the basement of the Broad, *le Chinois* spread out his wares with long supple fingers. On large sheets of paper were vivid crayon sketches of the human body split and broken and reformed into grotesque new forms. *Le Chinois* said these were among the thousands of drawings produced by Artaud in the last few years of his life, after his release from the asylums. Not everything, said *le Chinois*, had made it into the Artaud exhibition at the Pompidou Centre in 1987. He snickered. Tommy was also shown works purported to be by other Surrealists. Drawings by Zurn, said *le Chinois*. Occult daubings by Masson, nihilistic poems by Bataille. But perhaps Tommy would prefer something of more recent vintage?

At this point, *le Chinois* pulled out a bundle of half-burned letters and soiled hardcover notebooks. He put his finger to his lips. These rare items had been looted from Morrison's apartment on the rue Beautreillis in the confused period between his death in the early hours of July 3rd and his burial four days later. His girlfriend was keeping his body on ice, said *le Chinois*. She was throwing papers into the burning fireplace. He showed me pages of lost poems, composed in a large and loping hand, full of violent and darkly sexual imagery. They spoke of abortion and rebirth, the plucking out of the eyes, the amputation of the member, the genesis of weird new gods. Tommy traded a packet of Persian smack for one of the folios.

He had the opening scene to his novel. Tommy wrote it up at the bar in the Broad's ground-floor disco. Jim Morrison lowered semi-conscious into the indoor pool in his apartment, after the botched attempt on his life by les Initiates in the night-club. *Le Chinois* handing the Count the ceremonial flint knife. And the Count surveying the prospect for a successful act of counter-sorcery. Morrison's girlfriend leans in to paint his eyes a delicate shade of blue. She places Artaud's walking stick in his hand. *Le Totem*. Later, it will be buried in place of his body in the plot at Pere Lachaise cemetery. The Count gets busy with his blade, nicking the earlobes, removing the tongue, the penis. Slicing open the calves and peeling back the skin. He works for many hours.

The rest of Tommy's novel came quickly. He finished it in a matter of weeks. *Night on Fire*. I could never understand why Canongate hadn't picked it up. Maybe they didn't think it was literary enough. I wondered if Tommy had tried Rebel Inc. after it started up in Edinburgh in 1992. Its motto was "Fuck the Mainstream!" and it had published Irvine Welsh's early short stories.

Whatever. Alasdair Gray and James Kelman stayed in Scotland and won the great English literary prizes. The Postcard Records acts moved to London, where they were chewed up and spat out by the music industry machine. Orange Juice folded after a string of chart failures. Roddy Frame broke up Aztec Camera and retreated into his Notting Hill flat, to smoke dope and add to his guitar collection. Strawberry Switchblade were one-hit wonders. Jill Bryson settled in Islington and became a mother.

As for Alan Horne, he remained in Glasgow, where he gained a reputation for being a bit of a recluse. He spent many years curating his past and nursing his grudges.

Paddy's Market was closed down by Glasgow City Council in 2009. They said it was a "crime-ridden midden."

I don't know what happened to Tommy Love. His whereabouts are unknown. Although I like to think he has returned to Paris, where he perhaps haunts the Châtelet-les-Halles metro junction, chasing after the rumor of an elusive and ancient figure who moves through the sickly fluorescent light of sunken concourses, deep beneath an underground shopping mall, his bone-white fingers tapping out a rhythm on his chest cavity, his skin pulled taut over his eyes, as he sings about making the earth stop in its tracks and gropes his way towards other worlds.

SHEIKH EDDIE K

Developer of the John Lennon Multiverse

WHENEVER MOST PEOPLE HEAR "FREE AS A BIRD", I'm sure they think of John Lennon's ghost, conjured from an old demo tape to resume its place at the front of the Beatles, in a digital reformation of the band that split too soon. Whenever I hear the song, though, I think of Idrak Kahn, the Pakistani-British kid who cast his own digital spell on the leader of the Beatles.

I never met Idrak — or "Eddie" as he was also known — face-to-face. He was a reclusive young man from Bury. He was also, in my judgement, one of the most imaginative British writers of the 1990s. More ambitious than Rushdie, more erudite than Amis, more elegant than Barnes, he went completely ignored by the likes of *Granta* magazine and the Book Marketing Council. And that wasn't because he was a Muslim. It was because he wrote in computer code.

It's a different story today. Owing to the efforts of software studies professors such as Matt Fuller and Lev Manovich, a canon of cyber-texts is beginning to emerge. The uninitiated might think of a cyber-text as a species of literature which makes use of webpages, text messages or other forms of digital media. How naïve they would be! A cyber-text, to those who are computer-literate, is a sequence of instructions for a digital machine, written in any one of a thousand or so different formal languages, each with their own varied approach to syntax and semantics.

The works of "Sheikh Eddie K", as he styled himself, surely deserve a place in any reckoning of computational aesthetics. His infamous CD-ROM, *Cyber-Fatwa*, was especially ground-breaking. Unfortunately for the retro-gamers and the new media art curators, though, Eddie K has renounced his old creations, retired from the digital media scene and gone back to being plain old Idrak.

I corresponded with Idrak for a while, back when he was still going by "Eddie". This was when I was writing a book proposal on the "Madchester" indie-rave scene of the late '80s. For a period in 1987, Sheikh Eddie K was a club kid who produced trippy ambient videos for off-Hacienda clubs like Bugsy's in Ashton-under-Lyme and the Osbourne in Miles Platting. These simple films were looped screenshots of a home computer playing the 8-bit video games he had designed as a teenager — the isometrically-projected rooms of *The Seven Layers of Hell*, the explosive kicks and punches of *Yajuj versus Majuj*, the flips and somersaults of the cute little cartoon demon in *Flying Carpet*. All shared the same blocky, pixelated aesthetic of the old cassette games, but had a distinctive geometry of interlocking tiles that was all Eddie's own.

His father had bought young Idrak a copy of *The Complete Spectrum ROM Disassembly* manual, the Bible of do-it-yourself video game design, when he was in his teens. He had seen for himself how much time his young son spent hogging the family TV set to play *Jet Set Willy*. In truth, Mr Khan didn't quite understand how the game was loaded on to Idrak's ZX Spectrum. All he could hear, if he stuck his ear close to the little black computer, was a stream of sinister squeaks and pulses. What he did get was that the audio cassette unspooling on the tape deck was where the magic was stored. This was the source of the primitive glyphs that popped up, herky-jerky, on the TV screen when his young son played the game at his keyboard. This was the *software*, the commodity, the packaged item. This was where the money was. And so long as the Nintendo and Sega products were flying off the stalls of Bury Market, Mr Khan thought that his son Idrak would be better off making and selling his own games rather than buying someone else's.

Mr Khan was an entrepreneur. His philosophy of life was built on the axiom that time was money. He had moved from Pakistan to England in 1959 because he thought his days would be better spent labouring in the textile mills of Lancashire rather than looking for work in the Punjab. He saved money and opened a clothing stall in Bury Market. It wasn't until 1962 and the passage of the Commonwealth Immigrants Act that he finally brought his wife and two young children over to England. Idrak was born seven years later. Mr Kahn made sure that the boy attended mosque regularly enough to be respectable. But he was secretly pleased when he picked up the nickname "Eddie" at primary school. He always thought of his youngest, quite proudly, as a "proper little Englishman". It was only in later years, when Eddie dressed in outrageously flared jeans and brightly-coloured shirts, when he affected a nonchalant Mancunian accent and ran with a pack of rough boys to the local nightclubs, when he smoked hash and dallied with promiscuous white girls, that Mr Kahn began to worry that Idrak was being led astray from traditional Pakistani habits of thrift and hard work.

No such anxieties attached themselves to Mr Kahn's eldest son. Sajid had been identified by his teachers as an exceptional academic talent from an early age. As a result, the boy had effectively been removed from his father's care and entrusted to the watchful supervision of the imams at Darul Uloom Bury. The regime was a strict one – Koran readings in the mornings, O-Level studies in the afternoons. The boy's mother quite approved.

Sajid graduated near the top of the class and stayed on at the seminary as a teacher of Islamic law. He grew a beard, spent time in Karachi topping up his studies and dithered about finding a suitable wife. At the age of 27, he was still living in the family's small terraced house in Bury, rather swanning about the place as if he owned it, to his father's way of thinking. Mr Khan deferred to Sajid in most things, generally to keep the peace with his wife, but he was not greatly in the mood for hitting the carpet five times a day. His years alone in England had helped him develop a rather distant attitude towards Allah, whom he vaguely thought of as a wealthy silent partner in the affairs of Khan family life.

All of this I have surmised from later conversations I had with Eddie. One thing I know for sure, though, is that the rising tensions in the Khan family household hit a flashpoint on December 2nd 1988. This was the Friday when Sajid travelled to Bolton to join a group of his colleagues at the central mosque. He marched with thousands of Deobandi Muslims to the town centre and watched with approval as the elders burned a copy of Salman Rushdie's recently published novel *The Satanic Verses*. When he returned home in jubilant mood, Mr Khan was waiting for him at the gate. He said that the Khans were not the kind of Muslims who burned books. Sajid responded that Rushdie's novel was blasphemous. It had insulted the Prophet, peace be upon him, his wives and also the patriarch Abraham. It was a deliberate provocation of the Muslim population by the British cultural elite. They had to stand up for themselves.

This was when Eddie laughed in his brother's face. He hooted that the great scholar, top of his class and all that, had not even read the novel. Sajid became indignant. He said that he was not a liberal "kafir" — he actually used that word — like Eddie. He did not have to make his own mind up about every single issue. That was the job of Sharia law. Eddie said that the old men of the local mosques were still living in the medieval period. They were a national embarrassment who gave British Pakistani youth a bad name. Sajid said he wouldn't be lectured to by a young heathen who drank beer, the European peasant brew, and muddled his mind with profane rock music. Eddie said the Happy Mondays weren't rock, they were, if anything, a late variant of Northern Soul. The hipster reference was completely lost on Sajid, to Eddie's solitary and bitter satisfaction. By this time, Mrs Khan was ostentatiously weeping and wailing, her daughter was watching the argument between her brothers with appalled fascination and Mr Khan was sat in his arm-chair with a depressed look on his face.

Six weeks later, there was another book-burning stunt, this time in Bradford, and the religious controversy about *The Satanic Verses* hit the national headlines. Sajid strutted around town with a new-found confidence. Mr Khan worried that trouble was coming to his family. On February 14th, one of the most learned and fanatical Muslim clerics in the world issued a fatwa against Rushdie, calling for his death. Sajid was elated. Mr Khan shook his head. And Eddie got a nasty surprise. He found that his old mates on the rave scene in Manchester were pointing fingers at him, asking him to decide whether he was English or Muslim, Eddie or Idrak. The Pakistani-British lad was shocked. He had been quite used to having it both ways up until then. Had his sense of freedom been nothing more than an illusion?

Sajid sneered at his brother's discomfort and said that it was about time he grew up. He said that English culture was licentious and destructive, that it was fuelled by a nihilistic rage that would trample all religions to dust unless god-fearing men stood up to it. He pointed to the example of the Anglican faith. The Archbishop of Canterbury, he said, had let John Lennon and the "Beatles band" get away with blaspheming against the prophet Jesus and now the Church of England was nothing more than a hollow shell.

Eddie laughed in disbelief. He asked whether Sajid was really willing to defend the evangelical Christians — he called them "nutters" — who had held public burnings of Beatles records in America. Sajid said they should have gone further. They should have made a public example of Lennon himself. And isn't that what happened in the end? said Sajid, his eyes glittering. Wasn't the man shot down and killed in the street like a dog? At this point, Mr Khan rose from his chair. Enough! he said. No more! Nobody has the right to kill a man just for something he has said.

The next day Sajid moved out of the family home. Mrs Khan was inconsolable. A week later, Mr Kahn was admitted to Fairfield General with chest pains. He died of cardiac arrest under the paddles. Eddie was not invited by his brother to the washing and wrapping of his father's body. And when Mr Kahn was lowered into the ground at Bury Cemetery, the two brothers avoided each other. Soon afterwards, Eddie told his mother he was going to live in London. She begged him not to go. But Sajid, with ruthless efficiency, used his connections at the Union of Muslim Organisations to find Eddie a flat in Tower Hamlets. And so Eddie moved to the Bigland Estate.

This was the beginning of an indeterminate phase in Eddie's life, when he stripped away as much of his identity as he could. He dropped out of family life and, in an act of negligence verging on cruelty, let the machine pick up messages from his mother. He refused to set foot inside the East London Mosque, despite being within broadcasting range of its call to prayer. He also stopped going clubbing, stopped drinking, stopped smoking. The one thing he permitted himself as a lonely consolation for these losses was a string of girlfriends, most of them very well brought up second-generation Bangladeshi girls, whom he treated with amused contempt. They loved him for it, of course.

He bought a Macintosh Classic and got back into the 8-bit gaming industry. He worked long hours as a freelance coder for the Bitmap Brothers up the road in Wapping. And in his spare hours, he got into god games like *SimEarth* and *Populous*. Playing the role of a powerful creator god appealed to his narcissism. But it also allowed him to invent artificial worlds that took him far away from England, from Pakistan, from the tribulations of his youth. The only constraint on his imagination were the rules of Darwinian evolution, which were embedded in the source code of the god games just as much as they were in the free markets of Thatcherism. Before he knew it, Eddie had become a neoliberal in the mould of Hayek, just as much of an ideological purist, in his own way, as his brother. It didn't matter whether he was British or Pakistani, Muslim or *kafir*, gentleman or scally. All that mattered was that he could write code better than the next man and that the code — based as it was on the unalterable axioms of mathematics — would never let him down.

As Eddie's grim satisfaction with his own life grew, so did his bank balance. He rented a small office in the West End, a basement room in one of the scuzzy grey blocks north of Oxford Street, bought a filing cabinet and installed internet dial-up from Demon. He diversified his business, finding work as a CD-ROM programmer for ed tech publishers like Microsoft and Dorling Kindersley. He worked punishing hours, often till three or four in the morning. When he found himself stuck on a problem, he would go outside and wander up and down Oxford Street, hawking up phlegm and spitting on the pavement, making his mark on it, so he thought. This was the capital's high street, "town" as he understood it with his fiercely provincial mind-set. He refused to be impressed. The shops in the Plaza were no better and no worse than those in Mill Gate at home. He could flick through the top-shelf mags in W H Smith just the same.

Some part of him must have been rankled by London's superior airs, however. Otherwise there's no explaining why he signed up to do a part-time master's degree in what was then called "new media" at the University of Westminster's School of Design & Media. Eddie's teachers were baffled by him. They couldn't really teach him anything when it came to coding. He seemed to respond better to the theoretical components of the course, with its rather dilettantish exploration of anthropological concepts borrowed from Marcel Mauss, Marshall McLuhan and Jean Baudrillard. It seemed that what Eddie was really looking for was some way of framing his life that went beyond the philistine reductionism of neoliberalism while stopping short of any rapprochement with Allah.

He found it in "The Extermination of the Name of God", Baudrillard's essay on Saussure, which had just been published in the English translation of his book *Symbolic Exchange and Death*. Saussure's concept of structural linguistics stripped language of any cultural or ethnic markers and considered it instead as a self-contained abstract system of inter-related units. These units were not even words, but subdivisions of words, phonemes. The comparison of the phoneme with the smallest addressable unit of computer code, the 8-bit sequence, was irresistible for Eddie. Suddenly, he understood the whole of the English language — which had once so bedeviled him in the guise of elocution lessons paid for by his mother, Shakespeare soliloquies stuffed down his throat at senior school, viciously changing street slang and nit-picking lectures on translations of the Koran by his brother — as nothing more than a computer programme executable from source code. This source code, according to Saussure, was nothing more fearsome than a general idea of grammar.

Eddie laughed when he read that. He was sat by himself in a big half-empty pub on Berners Street, sparkling mineral water to hand. The other solitary drinkers ignored him. They were lost in their own thoughts. Eddie put his book down. Fanned out on the table before him were representative documents from his father's life. One of those big brutal blue British passports, containing a flurry of stamps from the late '50s. A couple of airmail letters from Mr Khan to his wife, the tiny script creeping to the very edges of the fragile blue paper. Eddie couldn't bring himself to read them. And a creased photo of his father as a shy young man in Karachi, squinting into the light, standing tall in his RAF uniform. Could such fragments of a life ever be properly reassembled? That would depend on there being a general grammar of a life well lived. Eddie bit his lip. He went back to his book.

Baudrillard was berating Saussure for not taking his structuralist approach to language far enough. The rules of grammar stretched to their absolute limit — which was the substitution of one phoneme for another — permitted the expression of nonsense poetry as much as they did the sense-making propositions of law and religion. This was something which had been intuited by Saussure in earlier drafts of his theory, but he had abandoned what Baudrillard called his "anagrammatic hypothesis" because it seemed to offer linguistic justification for the effusions of the insane. Actually, according to Baudrillard, it was more like an anticipation of the nihilistic playfulness of post-structuralism, the "pleasures of the text" as enumerated by Barthes. This was Baudrillard operating at his most provocative and arguably sophistical, but it was a thought that appealed to Eddie, the game-playing side of him at any rate, the kid they called Sheikh Eddie K, the 8-bit coding king.

He thought that the old imams at the Union of Muslim Organisations had made a mistake when they appealed to the British government to ban *The Satanic Verses*. Banning an offensive book was an archaic method of censorship, something which belonged to McLuhan's "Gutenberg galaxy". In the new digital universe of copy-and-paste software and the World Wide Web, a banned text could be instantaneously reproduced and globally distributed at the click of a mouse. So much so that a new method of censor-ship was required. The obvious solution, to Eddie's mind, was "anagrammatic". It was a matter of exhausting the sense-making properties of a banned text by producing the maximum number of variations of itself permitted by the recombination of its pho-nemes. A thousand – or even a million – unique versions of *The Satanic Verses* among which the original blasphemous text would be hidden. Now there was an act of truly digital censorship!

Eddie imagined the different titles he might find on the inter-net under such a system of disappearance. Some might promise slight variations on the censored text, such as *The Verses of Satan.* Or *Satan's Lyric Poems*, perhaps. Others might be more antitheti-cal in meaning. *The Holy Word of Allah.* Or *Secrets of the Koran.* Yet others might offer to tackle barely related subjects. *Vatican Se-crets. Eastern Cravats.* There would always be room for the many nonsense versions of the text, of course. *Very Tiny Seances. Thirsty Velocipedes.* As there would be for obscure titles. *Seven Sick Thetans.* And even for titles marked by unintelligibility. *Het Savak Nurses. Insate Thevistan.* Ha ha! Eddie scooped up his bits and pieces and left the pub.

It was time to propose an end-of-year project to his tutors at Westminster. They were eager for him to do a digital media piece in the realm of identity politics – his take on the British Muslim experience, perhaps? – and he found himself only too willing to oblige. He said that he wanted to create a *Cyber-Fatwa* on CD-ROM. His tutors blinked. This wasn't quite what they had in mind. But they didn't have the nerve to talk him out of it. Instead they hemmed and hawed and asked him what he meant. Eddie said that sentencing a man to death for blasphemy was an archaic method of condemnation, something which belonged to McLuhan's "Gutenberg galaxy". His tutors nodded, warily. In a digital universe, where every miscreant had the chance to become a martyr for nailing their 95 theses to the door of an internet chat room, a new kind of death sentence was required. A digital death sentence. A cancellation! His tutors breathed a sigh of relief. Then they again asked him what he meant, exactly.

Eddie said he would write a programme capable of destroying the reputation of a condemned man by creating a thousand – if not a million! – false accounts of his life, each one different from the last. Many of them, of course, would be scurrilous and defamatory. Others would track in the opposite direction and eulogise their subject to a ridiculous degree. Still more would tell the story of an unremarkable life full of entirely conventional achievements. While other narratives would be distinguished by spectacular actions and hidden motivations. Inevitably, there would be some versions of the man's life which made no sense at all. But what each one of these fake biographies would have would be a degree of plausibility. And that would be because they had all been generated by the principle of anagrammatic substitution from an authorised version of the targeted man's life.

His tutors nodded, enthusiastically. They saw parallels with the digital remixing techniques used to produce different versions of a dance music track. They signed off on the project. And Eddie went to work.

It was clear to him that the development of his *Cyber-Fatwa* programme would depend upon a structural analysis of the genre of biography as comprehensive as anything conducted by the

Russian Formalists on the folk tale. He would need to isolate the smallest abstract units of biography – the "biographemes", as he called them – before he was in a position to write the code capable of producing their maximal recombination. And so he began to haunt the biography section of W H Smith, flicking through the books about Winston Churchill, Oscar Wilde, Adolf Hitler, John Lennon – the secular saints of Western pop culture, as he thought of them.

The name of the subject, that was the first and most obvious biographeme. He put it at the top of his list. Then there was the subject's date of birth, their date of death. The names of friends and family, of mentors. Also to be considered were the subject's formative Oedipal experiences, whether of love, rivalry or abandonment. He ran through the index of Gilbert's *In Search of Churchill*. Ah, yes! The tribulations of youth, the early setbacks. Marriage and children. Places of interest. The deaths of loved ones. Eddie was scanning Hugo Young's biography of Margaret Thatcher at this point. The moments of glory. The decline and fall. Had he missed anything out of his list? His eye fell on the cover of a display copy of Goldman's *The Lives of John Lennon*. The rock star's chalky face stared out of the darkness like a defeated ghost. Eddie picked it up. Homosexual tendencies, he mustn't forget that. Addictions. Scandalous public statements, obviously. Eddie thought back to the argument he had had with Sajid about Lennon's blasphemous comments about Christianity. And then, at the end, the retreat from fame. The public assassination. All the dark stuff. Eddie had quite a long list of biographemes at the end of his researches.

Now he needed proof of concept. Who deserved to be the first subject of his *Cyber-Fatwa* software? Salman Rushdie was too close to home. Lennon seemed a preferable target. Eddie was indifferent to the man. So that was good. Plus, he was dead. The facts of his life comprised a closed data set ideal for anagrammatic recombination. And his legal right to privacy had died along with him. Besides, thought Eddie, it was one advantage of a digital cancellation that it could be applied just as well to a dead man as to a man still alive.

Eddie went to the shop counter with his copy of *The Lives of John Lennon*. He didn't know massive amounts about Lennon. He knew he was world famous and had got shot by a crazed Beatles fan outside the Dakota building in New York. But the title of Goldman's biography suddenly seemed like a promising omen. It appeared Lennon was such an excessive figure that even the one life he had been given was not enough for him. He had possessed many lives. Well, thought, Eddie, by the time the Sheikh had finished with him, he would have possessed many lives more. Many, many lives more.

Eddie shipped his new book off to a copy shop in Holborn and got the whole of its contents typed up into a Microsoft Word file. He hadn't read the biography and wasn't really that interested in what it had to say. He certainly didn't know of the controversies it had generated among Beatles fans, who had objected to its depiction of their hero as a closet case manipulated first by fellow Beatle Paul McCartney and then by second wife Yoko Ono. When he got the Word doc back, he went through it patiently, chunking out the text into a series of manageable narrative units which he then tagged with relevant biographemes. A data chunk would typically have more than one tag. Anything involving Paul McCartney, for example, he tagged not just with "McCartney" but also with "friend", "rival" and "musician" – and even "proper name". This permitted McCartney's place in Lennon's life story to be exchanged not just, say, with Lennon's drinking buddy Harry Nilsson, his art school peer Stu Sutcliffe or guitarist Eric Clapton – but also with Yoko Ono or, absurdly, his own father. Eddie permitted the user to hand-pick the tags through which the exchanges took place. But he also built a random selector to add to the fun.

All of Eddie's code was like that – simple and precise, alert to the possibilities of elegant variation. Original. When it came to developing the swap sequencer which would execute the remix commands, he used many Java scripts of his own invention. He also wrote a manual for his software. He recommended that *Cyber-Fatwa* should be run at least five times on any input file. And he insisted that when the various output files were exported to Word, they should each be given a rigorous copy edit. All good! The final touch was to get a CD-ROM cover sleeve designed. Eddie briefed Buggy G Riphead, whose psychedelic cover art for the Future Sound of London he had admired. Soon enough, everything was done. His project was ready for submission to his tutors.

It seems almost churlish at this point to go back and examine the tests run on the Lennon biography. Eddie's artistic focus was always on the code. However, I would argue that the playability of *Cyber-Fatwa* – considered as a game – constitutes a significant part of its aesthetic appeal. And that one way to judge that particular characteristic is by evaluating the quality of the texts that the game produced. For that reason, I asked Eddie to send me his exported Lennon files a few weeks after we had first made email contact. There were nine in total. They plopped into my inbox, one by one.

The titles of these scrambled Lennon biographies were nothing to write home about, although they did contain a sly nod to the Goldman source. There was *Life of Lennon #1*, *Life of Lennon #2* and so on… all the way up to *Life of Lennon #9*.

I note here some of the variant Lennon riffs across the spectrum of the texts. His retirement after the break-up of the Beatles is one recurring theme. In *Life #4*, he retreats with second wife Linda Eastman to his sheep farm on the Mull of Kintyre and doesn't re-emerge into public life until 1980. In *Life #6*, the alternative Lennon tracks his received history more closely when he shacks up with Yoko Ono in Manhattan. However, their application to live at the Dakota on the toney Upper West Side is turned down and they end up moving into the Sheraton Hotel in scuzzy Times Square. In *Life #5*, the events of Lennon's later life take a bizarre turn. He holes up with Yoko not in New York, but on the island of Dorinish, off the west coast of Ireland. Here, they form a religious retreat for Jesus freaks.

Another recurring theme was sudden death. There were all the tragic early deaths which feature in the received history – the death of Lennon's mother in a car crash when he was a boy, the death of his pal Stu Sutcliffe from a brain aneurysm during the Beatles' early days in Hamburg, the death of Beatles manager Brian Epstein from a barbiturate overdose. But then there were the new variations on the theme produced by the software – the death of McCartney in a car crash in *Life #4*, the death of Yoko

Ono at the hands of deranged gunman Mark Chapman in *Life #6*, Lennon's own bath-tub suicide at his Surrey country house in *Life #7*.

In only one of Eddie's nine texts did Lennon suffer a non-violent death. The rest of the time, either he gets shot by a fanatic or he kills himself. In *Life #1*, he is assassinated by Mark Chapman, just like in real life. But it happens a day later. Chapman had missed his shot at Lennon outside the Dakota and so the next night turns up at the Booth Theater on Broadway to finish the job. Lennon has a front-row seat to see his friend David Bowie starring in *The Elephant Man*. He gets shot by Chapman in the back of the head. In *Life #2*, he is again shot in the head, this time by the lunatic John Hinckley Jr after his meeting with President Reagan at the White House. In *Life #3*, he gets shot on-stage in Memphis during the Beatles' last American tour. The assassin is an outraged Klu Klux Klansman who objected to Lennon's blasphemous remarks about the Christian religion. I imagine Eddie appreciated that one. And in *Life #9*, which has always intrigued me, Lennon gets shot outside the Dakota by his old buddy Sutcliffe, who had dodged death in Hamburg and gone on to become a political revolutionary. This death could have been a staged suicide, though, because the text hints that Lennon was given advance warning of the hit but deliberately ignored it.

The Dakota was a brooding presence in many of these texts. Its strange, hybrid, almost Gothic Revival architecture, with its narrow pitched roofs and high gables, its profusion of ornamental details — its terracotta spandrels, its panels, niches, balconies, and balustrades — seemed to hint at coiled metaphysical secrets which lay beyond the scope of any simple church or mosque.

I was invited to the launch of *Cyber-Fatwa*, but couldn't make it until the end of the *soiree*, by which time Eddie had already left. It took place in Cyberia, London's first internet café, whose very existence was a testament to the Habermasian idea underpinning digital media in those days — the idea of a public sphere open to entrepreneurs, activists and dissidents, just like the coffee-houses of old. It was 1996 and the talk that night among the Westminster Hypermedia Research Centre students and cyber-*cognoscenti* was of the internet browser wars, Nasdaq, William Gibson and the latest issue of *Mediamatic*. 2Pac's "California Love" featuring Dr Dre played over the sound system, the album version, that is, with the computer-voice effects.

I picked up a press copy of *Cyber-Fatwa*. The cover featured a digitally streaked photo of a beach landscape with the shadow of a human figure cast on the rocks. Enigmatic, certainly. I left the party. Outside, on Whitfield Street, it was sheeting with rain.

Eddie's tutors put me in touch with him so I could do an interview about *Cyber-Fatwa*. My story about him never did get published. The "f-word" was still a controversial subject in the late 1990s. In fact, Rushdie didn't stop living with security guards until 2002. By that time, Eddie had disappeared. Someone at Westminster said, in a hushed voice, that Idrak had gone to Afghanistan to join an Al-Qaeda training camp as their IT guy. Someone else said, no, he had moved to Karachi and made a fortune from computerised spread-betting on the cricket. His family in Bury refused to talk. So I still don't know what happened to Eddie.

What I do know is that one of the texts produced by Eddie's *Cyber-Fatwa* — his *Life of Lennon #9* — is a literary masterpiece of the digital age. In actual fact, that may be under-valuing it, because I'm not at all sure that it was produced entirely by computer from the claimed source. The sinister feel of Goldman's take on Lennon is certainly in evidence. But there are bits of story that could only have come from a book on the Beatles and other items of general knowledge that were perhaps filched from Encarta. Whatever. Perhaps Eddie just had a highly creative copywriter working for him in Holborn.

At any rate, *Life #9* is worth spending a bit of time on. I remember the first time I read it, sitting on a roof in Chapel Market with a beer. I was captivated. The first thing to say about *Life #9* is that it's the version of Lennon's life where his friend Stu Sutcliffe features most prominently, rivalling both McCartney and Yoko Ono for his influence on the man. The two men bond in the strip clubs of the Reeperbahn. And then Sutcliffe quits the Beatles to study in Germany. He becomes radicalised by the revolutionary student movement and after hearing Lennon sing "Revolution" – the B-side to the Beatles' "Hey Jude" – decides his old friend needs his help. He returns to England and makes the pilgrimage to Kenwood, Lennon's mock-Tudor country house in Surrey. Here, he becomes lead player in his old mate's entourage of dealers, fixers, drinking buddies and hangers-on.

Sutcliffe likes to see himself as his friend's moral conscience. He cultivates Lennon's political reputation among London's freak scene, claiming that the Beatles front-man is more than a rock star – he is a man of the people, an enemy of the corrupt status quo, the champion of an alternative society. The level of hero worship is intense. Sutcliffe is inevitably setting himself up for disillusionment.

The second thing to say about this version of Lennon's life is that many of its chief details match those of the received history. Lennon did indeed appear to be a bit of a political radical. He backed the IRA in its guise as a national liberation movement and was sympathetic to Trotskyist ideals of autonomous revolutionary vanguardism, involving himself with both the International Marxist Group and the Workers Revolutionary Party. He supported the squatting activities of Sid Rawle's Hyde Park Diggers and when they ran into trouble with the authorities invited them to move to the uninhabited island of Dorinish, which he had bought on a whim. Rawle's aim was noble. He wanted to establish a self-sufficient commune without landlords, private property or wage labour. In this, he was inspired by the example of Gerard Winstanley's famous Digger commune of the post-Civil War period, which was much in vogue at the time.

Winstanley is a hidden thread in the authorised version of Lennon's life. Kenwood had been built on Surrey's St George's Hill in Surrey, the very site of Winstanley's original commune. Lennon must have known this, because he part-financed Kevin Brownlow's film about Winstanley, in which Rawle had a bit part. Winstanley's vision of a commonwealth where the distinction between landlord and tenant had disappeared was also the theme of Lennon's greatest hit "Imagine", which he wrote in 1971. "Imagine all the people sharing all the world." Again, a noble aim.

In *Life #9*, the Winstanley theme is brought out. Sutcliffe gets hold of Winstanleys's 1649 pamphlet, "The New Law of RIGHTEOUSNESS", and reads out portions aloud to Lennon in the upstairs recording studio at Kenwood. He says that Winstanley had argued that the royalist lands confiscated by the New Model Army during the Civil War should be added to the estates seized at the Dissolution of the Monasteries and the whole lot turned over to the people. Lennon nods at the idea. It never happened, says Sutcliffe. Instead, the land was parcelled out among themselves by the aristocrats of the Restoration and Winstanley's commune was forcibly dispersed. Sutcliffe is furious. Lennon, he says, has an opportunity to correct this historical injustice. He should use his social position to advance the cause of land reform. And what better way to do so than by setting a personal example? Lennon should open the gates of Kenwood to all the freaks and squatters of the world.

In *Life #9*, just like in real life, Lennon was none too keen on living in a hippie commune. He preferred to have servants. In December 1968, he sold Kenwood and moved with Yoko to the Dakota, a private apartment block renowned for its exclusivity. In *Life #9*, a disappointed Sutcliffe joins Rawle in the Republic of Dorinish. The experiment in utopian living is short-lived. The angry storms blowing in from the Atlantic prove too much for the little tented settlement, and Sutcliffe follows Rawle back to England, where the pair involve themselves in the free festival movement, first at Windsor Great Park and then at Stonehenge. Sutcliffe has lost none of his fire. He becomes an advocate for the English land reform movement which Lennon had abandoned.

The climax of *Life #9* sees Sutcliffe flying to New York just after Lennon and Yoko have released *Double Fantasy*, their collection of soft rock songs about the ups and downs of domestic life. He books a room in the Sheraton Hotel, procures a gun from a hustler in Times Square, and lies in the bath listening to

"Watching the Wheels" on repeat play. He is upset. Lennon has returned to public life after a long period of self-imposed exile and it appears he has changed. He is on record as being a supporter of President Reagan, who had turned out the National Guard to crack down on student demonstrators when he was Governor of California. He has said that the revolutionary politics of the late '60s and early '70s were "insane" and that his involvement with them was a "mistake". He claims that "Imagine" was no political manifesto, but "just a bloody song". All this, of course, actually happened. What *Life #9* does is turn it into an experience of political betrayal that provides the motive for murder.

The day before he shoots Lennon, Sutcliffe calls up 77WABC. He denounces his old Beatles band-mate on air as a hypocrite. He says that Lennon has always been a phoney, more committed to his portfolio of multimillion dollar property investments than to the revolutionary ideals of the 1960s. He calls him a *poseur*, a Blanquist, a traitor. He says that come the revolution, he deserves to be put up against a wall. At that point, Sutcliffe is cut off by his radio host.

When Sutcliffe doorsteps Lennon outside the Dakota the next evening, his old friend greets him warmly. Sutcliffe smiles and shoots him in the face. The .38 hollow-point kills the rock star instantly. Sutcliffe pins a copy of Winstanley's pamphlet to Lennon's bloodied jacket. His statement. Then he sits down to wait for the police.

The clatter of market traders packing up for the night reached me from down below. I had come to the end of *Life of Lennon #9*. My beer was long gone.

I still have my copy of *Cyber-Fatwa*, even though it's a long time since I had a computer capable of playing a CD-ROM. I wonder how many versions of Lennon's life could have been generated by now if Eddie had run his software on the Goldman biography repeatedly since he created it in 1996. Enough, I should think, to cancel the memory of Lennon if they were published in a season of fake news and disinformation. Enough to kill Lennon's ghost for good.

One last thing to note is that the fatwah against Salman Rushdie never went away. In 2022, the man was attacked on-stage by a crazed Lebanese-American fanatic and lost the sight of one eye. I couldn't help thinking of the vicious piety of Eddie's brother Sajid when I read that. May he be visited by the salaams of his God.